Rose of Sharon

AND OTHER STORIES

GARY A. BRAUNBECK

Rose of Sharon and Other Stories
By Gary A. Braunbeck

Published by Creative Guy Publishing
Victoria Canada
December 2013

Ebook edition
ISBN 978-1894953-924
This work is also available in ebook formats.

Cover artwork, "Nostalgia #7"
©2013 Kristin Elizabeth Fuller Photography,
www.kristinfuller.com
Used under contract and with great thanks.

Many of the stories in this collection have been previously published elsewhere, see "Publishing History."

Rose of Sharon
AND OTHER STORIES

GARY A. BRAUNBECK

creative guy publishing
victoria | canada

"I don't believe that the meek will inherit the earth: the meek get ignored and trampled. They decompose in the bloody soil of war, of business, of art, and they rot into the warm ground under the spring rains. It is the bold, the loud-mouthed, the cruel, the vital, the revolutionaries, the might in arms and will, who march over the soft patient flesh that lies beneath their cleated boots."

–Sylvia Plath

"I can hear you saying what a dreamer, what a fool to life
Isn't it a pity that he won't come back to earth?
Haven't you imagination, and is it not available
How you can be sooner or later than your thinking?
Haven't you imagination, and is it so impossible
That you ask of everything so your eyes can see clearly?"

–Jon Anderson, "Song of Seven"

"That is where it all has to start:
With the simplest things. More kindness will do nothing less
    Than save every sleeping one
      And night-walking one
            Of us.
            My life belongs to the world. I will do what I can."

–James Dickey, "The Strength of Fields"

"It all looks fine to the naked eye
But it don't really happen that way at all …."

–The Who, "Naked Eye

CONTENTS

DEDICATION

For Brian Shoopman

The friend every person wishes they had, and the reader every writer dreams about having.

You can no longer say you've never had a book dedicated to you. Now get over it. Seriously.

Seriously ... I know where you live, dude. Think about it.

I also want to extend my thanks to: Pete Allen and CGP for taking a chance with this somewhat eclectic assemblage of works; Cee C. Moriarty for invaluable last-minute input; Gale Moss for reminding me that true friends never leave one's heart; and, of course, my wife, Lucy A. Snyder, who, after nearly a decade of marriage, surprisingly, has yet to smother me in my sleep.

In Memoria illorum Quisnam Nunquam Erant: A Misdirected Beatitude

THE MOST BEAUTIFUL songs I have ever heard were never sung; the most beautiful paintings I've ever seen were never committed to canvas; the most beautiful rooms I have ever found myself in have all been empty; the most beautiful faces I have ever seen are those blurs in photographs where the person turned their head the moment the photograph was snapped, leaving a smudge atop the shoulders, something with no features, no expression, their identity forever a frozen ghost of possibilities that most of us will never recognize; the most beautiful movies I've ever seen were never filmed; the most beautiful stories I have ever read were on blank pages; the most beautiful thing I have ever experienced I have yet to experience — that moment when all the memories and desires of those most beautiful things that never were shall be lifted from my eyes as my mind is emptied and the death-rattle escapes my throat and all concerns and sadnesses and regrets be cast away, replaced by the possibility of encountering all of those never-were most beautiful things and recognizing them as old friends.

MAN WITH A CANVAS BAG

WHEN I WAS A little boy there lived on our street—
four houses down from my family, to be exact—a man
who killed his five-year-old daughter. I can't say "accidentally
killed" because for all the years my family knew Earl and
Patricia Spencer, Earl spoke of the event (when he spoke at
all) as if Cathy's death was a premeditated act on his part, the
culmination of some grand evil scheme, meticulously planned
and skillfully executed. He spun the narrative of his crime
with such deep conviction that anyone listening would almost
believe he *had* deliberately taken her life. Earl needed to believe
that we thought him guilty, so we pretended that we did, and
that our forgiveness was implicit. It made the truth easier to
live with when never a word of it was spoken. It was simpler
for Earl to blame himself for Cathy's death than it was for
him to accept the probability that we live in a charnel-house
universe where everything was, is, and always will be a random
fuck-up, including the formation of certain dissymmetrical
protein molecules that arbitrarily gave way to the double helix
and—*voila!*—humankind doing its endless happy dance across
the face of this planet.

I was nine years old on the morning Cathy Spencer was
killed. American troops were still in Vietnam. Richard Nixon
was still president. It was the twenty-ninth of October and
every house on either side of North Tenth Street had two things
in common: Halloween Jack-o'-lanterns, and autumn leaves
raked into neat piles at the curb, or at the foot of driveways,
or the base of trees. The air was rich with the after-scents
of neighbors having burned leaves the night before (you were
still allowed to burn leaves back then, and, God, how I miss

that smell being part of the world). The Kid-Countdown-to-Beggars'-Night clock was ticking so loudly it was all anyone under the age of twelve could hear or wanted to think about.

I was raking leaves in our front yard. I loved raking leaves into a great big pile because then I could take a good running jump into that pile, watch the explosion of autumn colors, and hear that unmistakable dry scratching whisper that only autumn leaves can make as the wind pushes them across a cold sidewalk. Sometimes I'd hide in the pile when I saw one of my friends approaching, and then jump out with a monster scream just as they reached our driveway. One of the greatest joys of childhood is that ear-splitting shriek of terror made by your friends when you've successfully scared the living shit out of them.

"Hey, *Tommy*," shouted Cathy Spencer, jumping up and down and waving her arms like she was trying to signal an airplane. She was dressed in her Wilhemina W. Witchiepoo costume, her favorite character from the *H.R. Pufnstuf* television show. I was an Orson Vulture fan, myself, but only my parents and Cathy knew that.

I waved back at her. "You aren't wearing your nose."

She giggled and rolled her eyes. "Dummy."

"Well, you *aren't* wearing it. But, hey, it looks real good, anyway."

Cathy smiled at me and pointed to my ever-growing leaf pile, then to the one at the foot of her parents' driveway. "Lotsa leaves, huh?"

"Uh-huh."

"I still go trick-treating with you?" Her eyes got really wide when she asked this, like I was going to say no. I'd taken her trick-or-treating for the last three years. She was fun to be with on Halloween.

"I don't know," I said. "You *did* forget to put on your nose."

She stuck out her tongue and giggled.

"We'll have the best costumes, you and me."

"Uh-huh. Thank you, Tommy."

"You're welcome."

"There's lotsa leaves." She scooped up a handful and buried her face in them, taking a deep smell. "Pretty." She dropped the leaves, smiled again, then waved as she made her way back toward her front porch. I turned my attention back to the project at hand and doubled my raking speed. I couldn't stop smiling. Cathy had that effect on you. She was sweet, courteous, a little sneaky when she put her mind to it, and everyone's friend. Cathy was also retarded. Back then, it wasn't called "Down's Syndrome," a person wasn't "developmentally disabled," and the term "special needs," as it's known in its current context, didn't even exist. A person like Cathy was retarded, period. It wasn't a contemptuous term—no, for that, you pulled out that old chestnut "mongoloid," a word no one in the neighborhood ever used or *allowed* anyone to use. Though she was five—almost six, she'd remind you when given the opportunity—Cathy would always be three years old. And like any three-year-old, Cathy could be, as my mom put it, "…a little stinker."

When I looked back, Earl Spencer was trotting out the front door, lunch pail in one hand, keys to the bus in the other. Earl's "bus" was actually an extra large passenger van that held a maximum of twelve people. He drove a route that took him from one end of Granville Street to the other, then into downtown Cedar Hill where he made a circle around the square before heading back. The Cedar Hill City Council contracted with Earl and three other drivers (all of whom owned his own "bus") to cover the entire city, and while there was decent enough business to keep all four drivers busy year-round, the last two-and-a-half months of every year were a particularly busy time – lots of people doing early Thanksgiving shopping, early Christmas shopping, or making last-minute Halloween candy and decoration runs.

Earl gave me a quick wave as he rounded the front of the bus and climbed in, firing up the engine. Looking at my trusty Superman watch, I realized that he was running about fifteen minutes late. He put the bus in gear, honked his horn as he waved good-bye to Patricia, and backed out of the driveway. Then the pile of leaves at the foot of the Spencer's driveway moved.

Lotsa leaves.

To this day I can't tell you how I knew it was Cathy and not the autumn wind.

"…a little stinker."

I just *knew*, period.

I threw down the rake and ran toward the bus as fast as I could, screaming for Mr. Spencer to stop, Stop *Stop, STOP!* but he either didn't hear me or didn't realize what had happened until he looked in the rear-view mirror and saw me standing in the middle of the street, my pants soaked in Cathy's blood because I'd slipped in the heavy wet streaks left by the tires.

I remember the loud *pop!* as the bus backed over the leaves and into the street (he'd run over her head right away, but I didn't know that yet). I remember seeing the great, wide splash of bright red spit up from inside the leaves and spatter the back side of the suddenly too-white bus (and running over her head first, that was a blessing in disguise, wasn't it?). I remember looking down and seeing one of Cathy's arms shudder (involuntary muscle reaction, but at the time I thought she was still alive). I remember looking up and seeing her other arm being dragged by the rear bumper (that proved she was still alive, because she'd grabbed the bumper as if she really were Wilhemina W. Witchiepoo and could stop the bus just by touching it). I slipped in the blood, scrambled to my feet, screamed at Mr. Spencer again—"She's hurt real bad! She's hurt *real bad!*"—and then spun around, dropped to my knees, and began pulling Cathy from the now-soaked and half-crushed pile of leaves.

I was later told that it took three people to get my arms loose of her body. I was later told that I tried to put her head back together using the bits of skull and pieces of brain that I could find, and then clumps of bloody leaves and small broken twigs when there was no more skull or brains to be found. I was later told that Earl Spencer stood frozen at the back of his van, howling like a wounded animal. I was told all of these things by my parents, and so never questioned whether or not they were true.

Since I was the sole witness to what happened, the police talked to me first. I remember that Mom knelt beside me the entire time, holding my hand in hers. I told the police everything that I'd seen, up to the moment I started digging Cathy out of the leaves; from there, I had no concrete memory of events.

"He's in shock," said one of the officers. "We'd better get him to the hospital."

I pointed to the middle of the street. "What's he doing?"

Both Mom and the officer looked, and saw nothing.

"But he's *right there*," I said. "See? That man with the bag?"

Mom shook her head and put her arm around my shoulder. "Hon, there's no man with a bag in the street."

"Okay," said the officer. "He's seeing things. We take him to the hospital *now*."

I turned around, feeling dizzy, and bumped into the gurney carrying the slick black bag that held what was left of Cathy's body. My elbow bumped into it as I stumbled back, and something inside the bag made a thick, wet, slopping sound; it moved just like the pile of leaves. I imagined Cathy's hand inside, trying to find the zipper and open the bag before she drowned in the leakage from her own broken pieces. I watched as her remains were loaded into the coroner's wagon—what all of us kids used to call "the meat wagon," a term that suddenly made me sick—and for some reason, I waved at her and whispered, "Good-bye, Witchiepoo."

I waited for her hand to come out of the bag and wave back.

I still go trick-treating with you?

I guess she was all gone by then.

They gave me some kind of a shot at the hospital that made me feel all sleepy, so I don't remember the drive home or Dad carrying me upstairs and putting me to bed. I came wide awake sometime around four in the morning and for a few moments wasn't sure where I was, then I saw my shelf full of Aurora monster models and let out the breath I didn't realize I'd been holding.

I got up, dressed, and put on my shoes. I saw that Mom had put a glass of water on my bedside table, which was good because I was really thirsty. Mom always thought of those things.

I finished the water and walked over to my bedroom window. My bedroom was at the front of the house, so I could see the street. I wanted to see the spot where Cathy had died, and I was going to sneak out if I had to. The street seemed a lot brighter than it usually did at night. I pulled back the curtain and saw the man with the canvas bag walking down the middle of the street. At every house he'd stop and kick through the leaf-piles, looking for...I don't what.

But when he got to Cathy's house, he put down his bag—that now glowed this bright kind of silver from deep inside—and began to sort through the leaf pile where Cathy had been hiding. I was surprised that one of our neighbors hadn't gotten rid of that pile yet. I couldn't imagine anyone thinking that Earl and Pat would want to look at it again, not after this morning.

Then I realized that the leaf pile *was* gone; what the man with the canvas bag was sorting through were…well…*the ghosts* of the leaves, and they gave off a bright silver light. When he got to the inside of the pile, to where Cathy's body had been, there was this soft blue light that was kind of shaped like a human body…only one that had been crushed and broken apart and killed.

I must have been really quiet when I went downstairs and unlocked the front door, because Mom, she was a really light sleeper, *anything* woke her up, but I got out of the house without waking her or Dad.

The closer I got to the man with a canvas bag, I saw that even Cathy's blood left a kind-of ghost behind; where the street had been slick and dark, there was now a smear of the same light blue that marked the spot where Cathy's body had been. The man with the canvas bag was picking out very small things from the ghost blood, as well as from the gutters across the street. I looked closer, and I could see that there were these little blue pieces—and some that weren't so little—scattered all over the street, even past the point where Mr. Spencer had stopped the bus.

"They never close off the areas for long enough," said the man, still gathering ghost pieces. "They forget that the other cars that come through here afterward might catch the smallest bits in their tires and carry them—ah, here it is!" He held up something that looked like a jagged section of glass, and it was only as I walked closer that I saw it was a piece of skull, only blue.

"Yes," he said to the question I hadn't even asked yet, "even your blood and bones leave ghosts behind."

"Is that what you're doing? Finding the missing pieces?"

He stopped, grinned at me (his grin was kind of sad and scary), and said: "You catch on fast. I knew you were going to be trouble when you spotted me this morning."

I began backing away. "I...I won't tell anybody, I swear. *I swear!* P-please don't hurt me."

"*Hurt you?*" he said. "Why would I want to hurt the first person to see me in a while, let alone come over to talk to me?" He found another ghost piece but I didn't want to see what it was.

"Just so you know," he said to me as continued about his task, "Cathy didn't feel much pain. I won't lie to you, Tommy, she *did* have one moment of pain and pressure—kind of like when you've got a really bad stuffed-up nose and there's a sneeze coming on and you feel the burst of pain rushing toward the front of your face and for a second or two that pressure is all you can think about. You ever have that feeling?"

I nodded. "When I had the flu last year. It hurt."

"But was it a terrible hurt?"

I though about it. "No, I guess not. Kinda like what you said."

"That's all the more pain Cathy felt, just that and nothing more. Everything went bright and she was pulled away before the worst of it happened." He stopped his task and looked at me. "She didn't suffer, is what I'm saying. Do you understand?"

I could feel my throat getting all tight and the snot building up in my nose and my eyes starting to burn. I didn't want to cry. "Yessir," I said. "That's good. She was really sweet. She was gonna go trick-or-treating with me. She was going to go as—" And that was all I got out before the tears and shakes overtook me. I felt so alone, so sad, so helpless and... *responsible.* I almost always watched to make sure Cathy went inside but I was too busy raking leaves this morning to bother.

Maybe if I had, I would have seen her climb into the pile and cover herself up. Maybe if I had—

"*Please* don't do that, Tommy," said the man with a canvas bag. "I mean, go on and cry for the loss of your friend, of course, absolutely, I'd be surprised if you didn't – but don't you *dare* try and blame yourself for what happened."

"...b-b-but if I'd've...if I'd've..."

"If you'd have what? Watched her climb into the pile, then you could have warned Mr. Spencer and none of it would have happened? What if you'd had to go to the bathroom before she got into the pile? Would you blame yourself because you were inside doing a Number One instead of out here keeping an eye on her? What if your mom had called you inside for some reason? You'll ruin what's left of your childhood with What If...? Yes, I can tell some of what you're thinking, not *all* of it, but the loudest parts. And right now your thoughts are pretty damned loud."

I looked up at him and pulled in a deep breath. "I miss her so much already."

"You should. She was a great little girl. Nothing wrong with missing someone you love."

I started to say something in protest, but realized he was right. I'd loved her like she was my own little sister.

"And she knew that, Tommy. She knew that."

I wiped my nose on my shirt sleeve, then wiped my eyes with my hands. "So, is there anything I can do to help?"

"Yes," he said, walking toward me and opening his canvas bag. The silver light was really bright, and I wondered why it wasn't causing people to wake up.

"Only people who can see me can see the ghostlights," he said. "Stop worrying so much."

I looked at the opened bag. "Do you want me to help you gather up more pieces? Or maybe take something out of there?"

He shook his head. "No. But isn't there something you'd like to put in here?"

I stared at him. "I don't have anything."

"Yes, you do. And if you don't put it in here, I can't reassemble Cathy's ghost, and if I can't reassemble her ghost, well…no one will remember that she was ever here. Oh, sure, I mean you, your folks, her parents, people in this neighborhood, you'll remember her for a while. But as the years go by and all of you grow older, the memories of her will start to dim, becoming less specific, less important, less necessary, until, at the last, everyone who was alive on this street on this day will die, and forget to pass Cathy along to those left behind who never had a chance to see her smile, hear that goofy damn giggle, or catch her being sneaky around Christmas or her birthday.

"That may seem like an awful long time to you right now, Tommy, but trust me—it's the blink of an eye. Part of my job is reassembling broken ghosts, but I also have to…I have to find the *glue* to use when putting them back together."

"Like with my monster models?"

He considered this for a moment. "Not a bad simile, not bad at all. Yes, like with your monster models."

"I could run back to the house and get my glue and put in here. It's real good glue, but you gotta watch out if you get it on your fingers, because then it dries kinda fast, and it's smelly and sticky, and…and you don't mean *that* kinda glue, do you?"

He grinned again. "You do not fail to surprise, I'll give you that."

I was sore, and thirsty, and tired, and I knew I was going to start crying again. I had no idea what he was talking about, only what he *wasn't* talking about. I walked over to the pile of ghost leaves and looked down at the smoky-blue form that now lay where Cathy's body had been. For a moment I was tempted to kneel down and touch it, only what if my hand went through? Or what if I lost my balance and fell in? Where would I be?

"Do you want to know why it is that my bag is so full and shines so brightly?"

"Yessir."

He knelt beside me, both of us looking into the smoky-blue emptiness inside the ghost leaves.

"I have one of the hardest jobs of all the...well, I guess you'd call us janitors. It's my job to gather up the missing pieces of the broken ghosts of children who died too soon. Cancer, starvation, abuse, neglect, terrible, *terrible* accidents like this morning. All of them always leave missing pieces behind. Sometimes—like with Cathy—there are more pieces than usual, but there's always *something* missing. And I have to find it, and then put everything back together so that these children will not be forgotten. That's what ghosts really are, Tommy—our forgotten memories given eternal life outside of our minds and hearts. Do you understand?"

"I think so."

He pulled the bag closer to us. "The reason my bag is so full, Tommy, the reason it shines so very brightly, is because it is filled with the broken ghosts of children that I could not put back together. There are broken ghosts in here of children who died hundreds, even *thousands* of years ago. And I can never fix them, so they've been forgotten by everyone except me. Care to guess why I couldn't fix them?"

The tears started coming again, but I was ready, and managed to keep most of them back. "Because the people you asked for...for 'glue,' they said no?"

"That's exactly right. And when they awoke the next morning, I was nothing more to them than some errant wisp of a dream that was forgotten before their feet even hit the floor. And the little ones whose broken ghosts were in my bag, they're trapped in there forever. They don't even have the comfort of knowing that they're not alone. All any of them are aware of is their own isolation, their own loneliness, their own sadness. And each of them remembers the moment of their death in terrible, awful detail. Oh, I can relieve a little of their loneliness from time to time. I can open the bag and pick one and talk to them briefly, but it's not enough. What they suffered during the last moments of their lives follows them even past death. And that *stinks*, Tommy. It stinks on ice.

"Is that what you want for Cathy?"

"Oh, God—*no*. I don't want her to feel all lonely and forgotten. I don't want her to feel like nobody loved her."

"Then give me what I need—or, rather, give me the thing you need to put in here."

"I don't understand. I'm real sorry, but I *don't*."

He looked into my eyes and did not blink. "If you could do it, would you die to bring her back? Did you love your friend that much? That you would give your life to have her back in the world?"

"I don't wanna *die! Please?*"

"Most people don't want to die, Tommy. I'm not asking you to die. I'm asking you if it were possible to bring her back by giving your own life, would you do it?"

"I—"

He held up a finger to silence me. "Before you answer, there's something else you need to know. If you say yes, and you give me that, if you give me that willingness to offer up your life to have Cathy back in the world, you can never make that offer again. Believe it or not, Tommy, there comes a moment in everyone's life when they get the chance to make that offer *once*, and have it accepted, without dying themselves. If you say yes and give me that so that I can put Cathy's ghost back together, you can never make this deal again. Ten, twenty, thirty years from now, you might have a wife, or a child of your own, who is very sick and on the brink of death, and you won't be able to save them because you will have used your one 'Get Out of Jail FREE' card. This is no small thing I'm asking of you."

"Is this why so many people said no to you and left the broken ghosts in your bag?"

He nodded.

I looked at the smoky-blue form left in place of Cathy's body. "Can I ask you something before I decide?"

"Of course."

"Why does stuff like this have to happen? I mean, what you said, kids who get killed, who die of cancer or starve to death? How come anyone has to be hurt or sad or sick and lonely like that?"

"Look at me, Thomas Franklin Ireland."

I did.

"I'm going to tell you something that I've told maybe, *maybe* four other people in all the thousands of years that I've been on the job. Listen carefully.

"There *is* a reason for all of this. We are heading toward something so…so incredible, so beautiful, so indescribably wonderful, that when it at last happens, everyone will look back at all of the savagery, all of the starvation, all of the brutality and disease and suffering and loneliness and fear and misery, and as one they will say: 'It was worth it. To get *here* to achieve this wondrous thing…all of the pain and anguish suffered by every living thing since the beginning of time was *worth it*.'

"I can't tell you what that thing is, Tommy, because I don't know. I didn't get that particular memo. I'm just the janitor."

I wiped my eyes and inhaled a bunch of snot. "She was a really great little girl."

"Yes, yes she was."

I stood up. "Yes."

For a moment, he looked confused. "Do you mean…?"

"Yes. I would give my life to have her back."

He held the bag toward me. "Then, please, drop it inside."

I looked down and saw that both of my hands were clasped around something that looked like a bluish-silver leaf. I carefully moved my hands until they were over the bag, and then let it go. It drifted down as if caught in a gentle breeze, back and forth, back and forth, back and forth, and I felt—though I didn't have the emotional vocabulary to articulate it at the time—I felt something of sadness lifted from my eyes.

"I'll remember her," I said. "I'll make sure everyone will."

"I know that," said the man, pulling on a rope laced through the top of the bag, drawing it closed. "Cathy won't be trapped in here with the others now. You did that. You did a great thing, Tommy. It's too bad you won't ever be able to tell anyone about it."

"Why not?"

That grin one last time. "Do you think they'd *believe* you?"

I shrugged. "Probably not."

"You're quite the kid, Tommy. Maybe we'll meet up again sometime."

"That would be nice."

He pointed back toward my house. "Your dad is going to get up in about five minutes to take a leak, and he's going to look in on you afterward. It would be best if you were in your room when he does."

I turned and looked at my house, then turned back to him. "I'll be real quiet. I was quiet when I left. My mom's a light—"

But he was gone.

I lost my mother to emphysema. I could do nothing to save her.

I lost my father to cancer. I could do nothing to save him.

They both suffered so horribly, and for so long.

I married. We had a little girl. She was born with hydrocephaly, and died when the shunt operation didn't work. She was six days old, and left this world without even a name. I could do nothing to save her, could offer nothing in exchange for her life.

I lost my wife to suicide five months later. I'd suspected it was coming, but could strike no bargain to keep her with me.

I see the man with a canvas bag often; in news footage of a traffic accident, in pictures taken of villages in starving countries, in crime scene photos where a child or several children were killed or tortured or beaten or died of neglect. He's always in the background, waiting for everyone to leave so he can begin the process of putting those broken ghosts back together. I never ask anyone else if they see him there, because I know they can't. Once, during a breaking news report about a local man who'd shaken his four-month-old son to death, I actually saw him wave at the camera and mouth the words, "Cathy says hi."

My mother. My father. My daughter. My wife. Any one of them I could have saved had I not...

But I could ruin what's left of my life with Had I not or What If...?

On those nights when it gets bad, when I hate myself for having been an impulsive child, or think that maybe he'd always *known* what was coming my way and just conned me because *he* couldn't bear the thought of another child's broken ghost being forever trapped in a state of perpetual loneliness within his canvas bag, when there's nothing more I'd like to do than find him again and wrap my hands around his throat and just *squeeze*...it's then I remember what he told me: *We are heading toward something so…so incredible, so beautiful, so indescribably wonderful, that when it at last happens, everyone will look back at all the savagery, all the starvation, all the disease and suffering and loneliness and fear and misery, and as one will say: 'It was worth it. To get* here *to achieve this wondrous thing… all of the pain and anguish suffered by every living thing since the beginning of time was* worth it.'

I remember. And wonder if I'll be around to see it happen. I know I won't be, that I'll be long gone and forgotten by then, but on those nights when it gets bad, I remember his words, I remember Cathy's smile, and for a little while, I can forgive myself—at least until morning comes—and I can hope.

Sometimes it helps. Not much, but some.

And I fall asleep with the echoes of thousands of broken ghosts calling out from the bottom of a canvas bag.

Cocteau Prayers

THE SNOW HAD BEGUN falling again, lightly, but seemed heavier because of the sharp, steady wind blowing in from the east. The cemetery looked fresh, almost pristine; a newly completed ice sculpture. The mourners clustered together near the head of the grave, their backs to the wind. Looking at them with their hair and coats flowing forward, Anne couldn't shake the feeling that all of them were fighting against some force, unseen and unknown, was trying to suck them into the ground. She walked quickly around the grave and the eight or nine floral arrangements positioned at the head, noticing as she did that someone (not her) had thought to send irises—Kate's favorite flower. She took a place next to her brother who, like most of the people assembled here, had his hands shoved deep into his coat pockets and was staring at the ground—not into the open grave but somewhere just to the right where a bit of soil could still be seen through the snow. A few people folded their arms across their chests and watched the sour sky, blinking against the new snowflakes that fluttered down and clung stubbornly to their eyelashes. Everyone stood in postures that seemed more distracted than grieving. Anne looked around at the faces, none of whom would meet her gaze. It didn't surprise her that Kate's mother hadn't shown up; she was either stoked on tranqs or bouncing off the walls, deep in the grip of a manic phase. Just as well; she and Anne had never much gotten along and had only been courteous to each other out of respect for Kate's feelings, even though her mother took every available opportunity to remind the two of them that she did not approve of their lifestyle. It suddenly occurred to Anne that everyone looked drugged, and she didn't know what to make of it. Had they already wrung dry their grief? God. She felt as if she'd stepped into the fifth reel of some impenetrably enigmatic art film, one of those profoundly ponderous black & white meditation pieces where no one speaks for minutes on end, then some minor character no one has given a second thought to steps into camera range and starts paraphrasing Camus or Borges while the trees melt behind them: A head-on collision between Cocteau and Dali. Even the minister looked surreal, his face something that was hastily painted on a nesting doll ("*Matryoshka* doll," Kate always corrected), his gourd-shaped body standing at the head of the grave with a Bible clutched in one shaking blue-cold hand, squinting as he read the passage committing Kate's mortal remains to the earth. Completing the requisite benediction, he signaled the men from the funeral home to lower the coffin into the ground. It hissed hydraulically into the cold, dark, open maw of the grave. Anne had to fight the urge to turn away. She didn't want it to end like this, with distracted *matryoshka* mourners and surreal Cocteau prayers and sour snow on an ice-knife wind. Even her own hand looked like some fuzzy image on a screen as it scooped up the symbolic handful of frozen death-dirt and tossed it down onto the lid of the coffin. The gourd-shaped minister stalked over, misting some words of comfort, then grimly wobbled away. Anne looked at her brother, who nodded his head, understanding, and she walked toward the ice- and snow-sheened northern plat of the cemetery, then down a small incline that led her to a stone sculpture of an angel standing at the less-accessible north entrance. She was glad she'd walked away; she needed a few moments alone before saying her final good-bye to her lover, her friend, her companion of some fifteen years. She wiped a few stray tears from her eyes and looked up at the face of the angel. If ever a sculptor had captured an expression of grief so purely, she'd not seen it. In its face was everything from anguish and rage to acceptance and peace. She saw in that face the way all mourners were meant to be; diminished, yes; broken-hearted and scared, certainly; but if you looked at the face long enough you saw a certain, enviable measure of tranquility which hinted at actualization, a look suggesting that all the conflicting emotions associated with death eventually coalesced to warm a sorrowing heart with the knowledge that, though it seemed to take forever, life was over in a second but that was all right, because there would be someone waiting for you at the end to make Act IV a little easier. And though Anne had often laughed at that sort of psychobabbling sentimentality, she found herself hoping now that some of it might be true, even though all her years as a biology teacher had taught her otherwise. Death wasn't instantaneous, the cells went down one by one; it took a while before everything was finished. If a person wanted to, they could snatch a bunch cells hours after somebody'd checked out and grow them in cultures. Death was a fundamental function; its mechanisms operated with the same attention to detail, the same conditions for the advantage of organisms, the same genetic information for guidance through the stages that most people equated with the physical act of living. Now, standing in front of this angel of perfect grief, Anne couldn't help but wonder: If it's such an intricate, integrated physiological process—at least in the primary, local stages—then how did you explain the permanent vanishing of consciousness? What happened to it? Did it just screech to a halt, become lost in humus, what? Nature *did not* work that way; it tended to find perpetual uses for its more elaborate systems. Maybe all that crap from the 70s about "All of us, together, make up God" was true; maybe human consciousness was somehow severed at the filaments of its attachment and then absorbed back into the membrane of its origin. Maybe that's all reincarnation was: the severed consciousness of a single cell that did not die bur rather vanished totally into its own progeny. Maybe it was more than that—and maybe she was full of shit and needed to get some sleep but how was she supposed to do that? The bed was so small, suddenly, a child's crib, barely enough room to roll over, and knowing that Kate would no longer be there to hold her in the night, Anne couldn't face it. She could sleep on the couch again, or go over to her brother's place. It didn't matter. Sleep would never be the same again. She looked up once more at the angel of perfect grief and felt her heart skip a beat; it seemed to be half-smiling, half-snarling at her, as if she'd accidentally hit on something human beings were never meant to realize. "Thanks," she said to the statue; then, looking up at the sky: "And fuck you, too." Words that came easily, because none of this was real; they were all only images on a screen, somewhere, blurry and disjointed. Even now she thought that if she looked hard enough, she could see the scrim hidden out there in the distance, maybe even catch a glimpse of the audience out there in the theater, sitting in their seats, watching, watching, watching as the cells went down, one by one…

Later that night, she got up from the couch and shambled into the kitchen, opening the refrigerator door and removing two small Petri dishes that she held in her hands while whispering, "Oh my love, my love, my love…"

YELLOW SLEEVES

The world is a stone, soldier,
It holds no thought of long brown girls, dead gulls,
vanishing town.
The great clock with its golden face, face-down;
Beneath these cloud-ribbed skies where stars would rot if
stars were men.

No alien gods remain along the boulevards.
In this bleak land Civic ghosts dissemble.
The street lamps stand, delinquent angels weeping in the
rain.

There are greener worlds, soldier, and other skies;
Music in the square, women under flowered trees,
And summer slides into soft decay, leaf unto leaf.

There are always tomorrows, soldier, and other battles
done;
This music in the square, these women under flowered
trees,
As summer slides into soft decay, leaf unto leaf;

As larks into falcons rise
From the yellow sleeves of eternal day.

MAIL-ORDER ANNIE

H E WAS BEING FOLLOWED.
John Nitzinger wasn't sure by whom—or possibly what (his aunt had often written to him before her illness with stories about the wildcats that came down out of the mountains when winter began)—but for the last hour his horse had been skittish as hell and the hairs on the back of his own neck had been standing on end from something more than the freezing night wind and skirling clouds of snow.

And so John Nitzinger, age thirty-seven, a man who'd been alone on the plains for most of his life riding fences for a succession of ranchers, a man now with no one to call family, who felt the chill of the winter slowly making itself a part of his soul, rode on with weary deliberation through the December night in the year 1888, his eyes looking from one side of the darkness to the other while his right hand rested on the stock of his Spencer rifle.

It was so cold that his breath turned to iron in his throat, the hairs in his nostrils webbed into instant ice, and his eyes watered and stung. In the faint starlight and bluish luminescence of the snow everything beyond a few yards of his gaze swam deceptive and without depth, glimmering with things half seen or imagined. He listened beneath the low, mournful call of the wind and there could detect no sounds save for those made by himself or his horse. Everything else in the world might have died out there in the cold.

"Sometimes you are one damned cheerful fellow," he muttered to himself.

His horse chuffed its agreement, its metal shoes making lonely sounds as they struck against the cold-hardened ground and occasionally smashed through patches of silver ice. Even in this God-forsaken temperature the horse stank of frozen sweat and manure. Nitzinger figured that after these last three days of riding he probably didn't smell much better.

He was going to be right pleased to see the lights of Cedar Hill in a few hours, even if it was just another town full of strangers.

I will warn you, Johnny, his aunt had written in her last letter, *that you might assume this town to be just another shabby little place where miners and outriders lay down their burdens for a few days before venturing back out to their labors, leaving the wives and children to fend as best they can on what meager earnings the men bring back with them, but this is not a sad place at all. You will find the people are quite friendly after they get used to you, and in many ways become outright protective of you once they realize you are here to stay. I hope you will stay on here, Johnny. Your mama would have wanted for you to have a home. I know that I do.*

His reverie was broken at the same instant as the chill night silence.

Something in the frozen landscape nearby released a long, loud, unearthly yowl that rose above Nitzinger's head and spooked his horse.

He tried to pull the Spencer from its case but had it only halfway out before his horse reared back, cried out, and threw him from the saddle. He landed with an unflattering thud on a sizeable snowdrift and felt the wind ripped from his lungs.

Whatever had made the sound made it again and started out of the shadows for him.

Nitzinger scrambled to his feet, slipped on a patch of ice, and fell face-first into the snow.

The unearthly yowling was closer now, and Nitzinger silently cursed his foolhardiness at deciding to travel on during this night, for now he was about to perish—none too neatly, he imagined—at the claws and teeth of a cougar before he could get to Cedar Hill and claim the generous inheritance his late aunt had bequeathed him.

Not with my face in the snow, he decided.

If he was going to die, he'd do so facing his enemy.

Nitzinger took a deep breath and pushed himself up onto his knees, ready to die like a man.

Five feet away from him, sitting on its backside as if watching a mouse struggle in a trap, a dirty-gold tomcat no bigger than a man's forearm stared at Nitzinger's actions then slowly, with what looked to be great pity, shook its head, rose, and sauntered away.

A boisterous laugh exploded from Nitzinger's chest with such force it knocked back down into the snow.

A stray cat.

Good thing he hadn't muttered a prayer for his immortal soul before throwing himself into battle; the Good Lord probably wouldn't take too kindly to a man who was feared of a pet. No room for them nervous types in Heaven.

He laughed again at the thought of the cat's reaction (and at the odd notion that something about it seemed familiar to him), shaking his own head. His horse stood a few yards away, staring at him and leaning forward.

"Like to thank you for your bravery," Nitzinger said through his laughter.

"Hello?" came the echo of a female voice. "Hello? Is anyone there?"

Nitzinger got to his feet and mounted his horse, making sure the Spencer was secure, and rode to the top of the rise.

She stood at the edge of the passenger platform above the train tracks. A single lantern hung over a bench behind her, giving off very little light. She was small, thin, and looked to Nitzinger from this distance to be a bit blanched. Her coat wasn't near heavy enough to keep a body warm on a night like this, and as he started down the rise toward her, Nitzinger hoped that she hadn't been waiting out here too long.

She leaned forward, peering into the darkness, then stepped back quickly when she finally caught sight of him.

"I know I must be a frightful sight, miss, but I ain't gonna bother you or nothin' like that."

"Are you all right, sir?" she asked. "I heard the most terrible ruckus a few moments ago."

"That'd been me engaging in a life-or-death struggle with a tomcat."

"Oh," said the young woman, trying to suppress her grin. "I wondered why the poor thing seemed so rattled."

Nitzinger looked behind the young woman and saw the dirty-gold cat perched comfortably on an old sea-trunk.

"That yours? The cat, I mean?"

"No sir. I saw it for the first time just a few moments ago. After your…encounter with it."

"Encounter," said Nitzinger, dismounting his horse and tying its reins to the station's post. "Mighty nice way to put it."

"To have put it any other way would risk insulting your pride, sir, and I gather that's been wounded enough for tonight."

Smiling to himself at her unusual directness, Nitzinger brushed the snow from his person as best he could and started up the steps. Mounted on the wall at the top was a badly-tarnished brass plaque declaring that this station had been one of the monitor stops for the great "Tom Thumb" race in 1829 on the Baltimore and Ohio.

And though this place can't lay claim to much history, his aunt had written, *it is selfishly proud of what history it can call its own.*

Nitzinger silently wondered why, if they were that proud of their history, the plaque was so badly in need of polishing.

He nodded a greeting to the cat then removed his hat, pulled back the scarf he'd been using to cover his ears, and extended a gloved hand. "John Nitzinger, Miss."

"Amanda Jakes," she replied, shaking his hand.

Even through his heavy woolen gloves, Nitzinger felt how cold her own gloved hands were. He blinked to clear his eyes, and saw then that her face wasn't blanched at all, as he'd mistakenly thought, but flushed from the cold. Her ears looked ready to fall right off from freezing and she was having a time of it keeping her nose from running all over her lip and chin.

"You mind, miss, if I ask exactly how long it is you've been waiting here?"

"Do you have the time?"

Nitzinger dug into one of the pockets of his duster and fished out the silver turnip watch his aunt had given him for his thirty-fifth birthday. Popping the cover, he turned into the dim lantern light and said, "Looks to be about five-forty."

"Then I have been here six hours."

"Six hours!" He snapped closed the watch immediately removed his scarf. "Hell's bells, miss—pardon my language—but it's a wonder you ain't froze to death. Here, you take this and wrap it around your neck and ears—"

"—there's no need for you to—"

"—not in a state of mind for arguin' with anyone, miss. Can't believe the station-master'd go off and leave a body out here in this weather."

"There was no station-master on duty when the train arrived. There weren't even any porters. I was the only passenger who disembarked at the stop."

"Still," Nitzinger mumbled as he tried the station's sole door. "They ought to have left the waiting room open if they knew a train was comin'."

The door was locked.

He brushed a circle of snow and ice from one of the glass panes and looked inside. A padded bench, a pot-bellied iron stove, and three dark lanterns.

He bent his arm at the elbow and smashed in one of the panes, then snaked his hand through the opening and fumbled around until he found the latch and unlocked the door.

"Let's get you inside, out of this wind."

Amanda Jakes—appearing not in the least offended by his actions—nodded her thanks, picked up a small carpetbag and cardboard box, then went inside.

The dirty-gold cat followed, immediately curling up next to the iron stove, then yowling its displeasure at finding no heat waiting there.

"Sit yourself down right over there," said Nitzinger, striking a match taken from his pocket and setting flame to a lantern wick. "I gotta get some stuff from my horse, then I'll be right back."

He took from his horse his own bedroll and well-used pillow (hand-sewn, another gift from his aunt), a rusty coffee pot and sack of coffee beans, a dented cup and plate, a small satchel containing dried beef, a small slab of bacon, his last two eggs, a griddle and, as an afterthought, his spare Navy Colt pistol. He thought about taking her something to read, but all he had were a couple of old and well-thumbed copies of *New York Detective Monthly* and didn't think a lady would find that proper material.

He made sure to cover his horse with its blanket. "Rest up for a bit, then we'll be on our way."

Back inside, he emptied the small satchel and used it to cover the spot where he'd smashed in the glass pane, then found the station's water closet (which to his surprise had a working gravity toilet) and cleaned himself, then started a fire in the stove with some of the coal from a bucket near the ticket counter door (that made the cat very content), and set about making Amanda comfortable while he fixed her up something hot.

While he tried his best to make the food look halfway edible, she began humming a soft tune to herself.

"Pretty song," he said over his shoulder. "What's it called?"

"'Waltzing With You.' I'm afraid I don't know the words. To be honest, John, I'm not even sure where I heard it. It just suddenly popped into my head."

"That's all right. Some things is pretty enough they don't need words." He checked the pot on the stove. "Afraid my coffee ain't as tasty as the restaurant-bought kind, but it's hot."

"Then it will be some the best I've ever had," she replied.

Realizing he'd forgotten to bring in a fork and knife, Nitzinger was getting ready to go back out to his horse when Amanda removed the lid from her cardboard box and produced the items.

"I didn't have enough money to afford but one meal aboard the train," she explained. "So I packed myself enough makings for two additional meals, thinking, naturally, that three meals would be all I'd need."

Nitzinger piled the eggs and bacon onto the plate, poured the steaming coffee into the cup, and set everything on the bench next to Amanda.

"Looks delicious," she said, and then took a sip of the coffee, made a nasty choking sound, and started coughing.

Nitzinger ran a hand through his hair, embarrassed. "Guess it's a bit strong."

"It's…it's fine, really," Amanda croaked, her eyes tearing.

The eggs and bacon went over much more successfully.

As she was finishing the last of her meal, Nitzinger cleared his throat and said, "Not that it's any of my business, Miss—"

"Call me Amanda," she said. "Any man who cooks for me has my permission to be on a first-name basis."

He smiled at her and she smiled in return and for a minute they just sat like that smiling at each other and making Nitzinger feel like a love-struck schoolboy.

Finally he said, "I was just wondering' who it was that was supposed to meet you."

"The man I'm to wed."

He tried to tell himself that the pit that opened in his chest at that moment was just his being tired and nothing more. "Oh. He got a name?"

"Yes, it's...uh, well..." She shrugged, then reached into her carpet bag and removed a bundle of papers. "I'm not a stupid woman, John—may I call you John?—it's just that I'm exhausted from the trip and the weather and that my marriage is, well...an arranged one."

Nitzinger shrugged. "Arranged?"

Amanda found the paper she'd been looking for. "Yes. For the sum of five hundred dollars and the deed to some land in Oklahoma, Mr. Cletus Walters of Cedar Hill has bought himself the right to my hand."

Nitzinger looked at the cat; he could have sworn the thing hissed at the mention of Walters' name.

Amanda offered the paper to him. "When I turned twenty-seven it finally occurred to my father that he was going to have a spinster on his hands if he didn't do something about it."

Nitzinger looked over the paper, reading slowly, and without being aware of it muttered, "A Mail-Order Annie."

"I beg your pardon?"

"I'm sorry, Miss—uh, Amanda. I said 'Mail-Order Annie.' That's what my aunt always called ladies in your position."

She cautiously sipped more of his coffee and said, "I don't whether to be offended by that or not."

Panicked, Nitzinger spoke rapidly. "I meant no offense, really, it's just what my aunt always called mail-order brides on account of, well, my mother was one herself and her name was Annabelle. She was one of the women who sailed on *The Angelique* to California with Eliza Farnham in 1849. She married my father there. He was a miner. Mama always used to complain in her letters to her sister that the life of a mining-camp wife was lonely in the extreme and my aunt, she used to write back that that's what my mother deserved for becoming a 'Mail-Order Annie.' There weren't no harshness in the words, understand; my aunt, she had herself a pretty sharp sense of humor. She raised me after my mother died. Summer of '57, a cholera epidemic took out half the mining camp where we was living. Mama, she sent me here to Ohio right when the first case was reported. Said she didn't want to take no chances with her boy. I was only six then, and I didn't know it was gonna be the last time I saw her or my daddy. Anyway, my folks, they both died that summer and my aunt kept me on. Whenever she used to talk about my mother, she always called her 'Mail-Order Annie,' and I guess that just sort of stuck in my mind. I really didn't mean for you to think I was lookin' down my nose at you or anything."

"Do you remember her, your mother?"

"Some. I remember her laugh and how dark her hair was." He looked down at his hands. "Years go by, though, I keep less and less of her in my memory. Not from lack of trying, you understand?"

"I do," said Amanda, petting the dirty-gold cat that had crawled up into her lap. "And I take no offense, Mr. John Nitzinger. I don't think it's in you to purposefully offend a lady."

"Thank you."

She smiled at him again. "You're most welcome. So—are you here to visit your aunt?"

"In a way. She owns a boarding house and restaurant in Cedar Hill. I ain't seen her in I'll bet ten years."

"You must be very excited."

"She died a couple weeks ago. I got a...a letter from her lawyer tellin' me that I was her sole beneficiary and she'd left the place to me."

Amanda took in a sharp breath, placed a hand over her mouth, then reached out with the same hand and took hold of Nitzinger's. He could still feel the warm traces of her breath between their skin.

"I am so very sorry, John."

He nodded his head. "She was one great lady. I miss her already." He looked into Amanda's soft grey eyes. "But don't you...don't you fret none about that. We stayed real close, wrote to each other all the time, so I got no hard regrets about things. Besides, we got to figure out what we're gonna do about your situation and that rude Cletus Walters."

"Now that I'm warm and fed," Amanda whispered, not removing her hand from his, "I think I can survive until morning in here. My guess is that the road from town must be fairly high with snow. A man couldn't very well get a wagon through on a night like this."

"It wasn't night when you got here, and a man who's takin' on a new wife ought to have enough damned sense to bring a shovel along in his wagon during winter. You ask me, this Mr. Walters has better have himself one powerful excuse for treating you this way."

There was something more in her smile and her eyes than there had been before as she said, "I suppose it's not the most promising start to a marriage, is it? But you know what they say, 'A spinster can't complain.'"

"Don't you be saying that, Amanda—hell, if you was coming here for me I'd swim across a damn river to make sure I was waiting to greet you when you stepped off that train."

"Thank you."

"No need to thank me," he said, rising and gathering up his coat, hat, and gloves. "I'll ride on into Cedar Hill and find your Mr. Walters. Now, there's still some bacon left in the bag, and some dried beef, and my awful coffee. You're welcome to use my pillow and bedroll if you can stand the smell. There's plenty of matches and coal for the stove, so you won't freeze. Lock the door behind me and—oh, yeah, almost forgot." He handed her his spare Navy Colt. "You know how to use a gun, Amanda?"

"I do. My father taught me how to shoot all manner of firearms."

"This is just in case any animals come wandering down from the mountains."

She gestured over her shoulder. "Like our bloodthirsty friend here?"

Nitzinger grinned and blushed, looking down at his feet. "Don't remind me."

Just then, another loud yowl echoed in from the coldness, and the dirty-gold cat jumped off the bench and clawed at the station door until Nitzinger let it out.

It bounded off the platform and across the snow to where another cat, this one much darker, sat waiting. Instead of circling one another like most cats did, each animal regarded the other as if it were a long-lost friend, someone they'd known all their lives. They stared at one another for a moment, then set off, side-by-side, in the direction of town.

With a greatness of purpose Nitzinger didn't usually associate with such creatures.

"My father was a road engineer," said Amanda beside him. "After my mother passed on and my three younger sisters all married, I traveled with him to many exotic countries. That autumn when the British were in Egypt, when President Arthur was raising dust about the tariffs, Father was advising the British on some construction. A woman who did the cooking told me a story about cats, that many people regarded them with great awe and respect because they were the form our loved ones who'd passed over took when they returned to this life to watch over and protect us. I always used to think that there were certain cats that just automatically took to you for no good reason—like that cat did to me."

Nitzinger stared after the cats. "I swear to you that thing's been following me for the last few hours."

"Maybe it has. They are very mysterious animals." She poked his arm and Nitzinger turned to look at her. "Maybe that cat was your aunt, come back to make sure you found your way safely."

"A night like this," he replied, "I wouldn't dismiss anything." He finished readying himself for the ride into town—a good hour-and-quarter, at least—and was starting out the door when Amanda removed his hat from his head and wound the scarf he'd given to her around his head to cover his ears.

"I'll hear no arguments from you, John. It's cold out there." She put his hat back on his head, thanked him again for all his kindnesses, then gave him a quick, warm, polite kiss on the cheek.

When she pulled away, though, she didn't let go of his hands—nor did he wish for her to do so.

John Nitzinger figured he'd probably relive this evening over and over in his mind for the rest of his days, and would find it as wondrous then as he did right now.

"A man would be right proud to have a woman like you for his wife."

"A woman would be a fool to think she could do better than you, John."

They regarded each other tenderly in the warm silence of the station, their eyes betraying all that words would have only diminished.

Then Nitzinger went outside, mounted his horse, and began his journey toward Cedar Hill.

"John!" Amanda called from the doorway.

He turned back and waved.

"Remind me sometime," she called to him, "and I'll tell you the story of my life!" Then she laughed. It was music in his ears.

"If I can't find your Mr. Walters, I'll rent a wagon from the livery and come back here to get you."

And, with great purpose, he snapped the reins and his horse broke into a trot.

Covered candles gave Cedar Hill's main street a soft glow. The little church at the end of the street was aglow with yellow light and the sound of a choir rehearsing Christmas carols. The people who walked past on the boarded sidewalk between the one- and two-story frame false-fronts seemed pleasant enough; several of them even offered a small wave or a tip of their hat to the stranger who was riding into town.

Nitzinger figured that maybe the Christmas season softened their suspicion of strangers a bit. It was easy to see why his aunt had liked living here so much.

His flattering first impression of the town was dampened considerably by the reception he got from the livery manager, a cantankerous old man who made no attempt to hide his displeasure at having his dinner interrupted in order to take in Nitzinger's horse; his manner became downright cool when Nitzinger made an inquiry about Cletus Walters' whereabouts.

After that, what he found waiting for him at his aunt's establishment was a blessed relief.

The first thing that hit him when he came through the doors was the smell of the food from the kitchen; roasted chicken and buttery potatoes and fresh peach pie. His mouth watered at once.

He approached the lobby desk slowly, wanting to take in the sights; the ribbons and green pine garlands that decorated the stairway, the cluster of mistletoe that hung over the entrance to the dining room, the splendid way the restaurant patrons were dressed; the men in three-piece suits, the women in dresses of silk and organdy. Low-hung Rochester lamps cast a homey glow down onto the tables while a tall, gallant-looking Negro man in pressed-whites glided from table to table with a frosty pitcher of ice-water to refill patrons' glasses. At the far end of the dining room another Negro man sat at a piano—a baby grand, not an upright—while his graceful hands played sweet Christmas music.

Nitzinger had always imagined the place would be like this but had never dared hope.

Most times, riding the fences, you found that dreaming about things made it all that much easier to be disappointed by their reality.

He turned away from the dining room and approached the short, stoutly attractive woman who was checking a ledger behind the desk. He removed his hat and stood there for a moment, not wanting to interrupt her.

After a moment she sniffed at the air, made a face, then looked up. "Something I can help you with, mister?"

"I hope so. My name's John Nitzinger, I'm—"

"Ethel's boy!" the woman cried out, then slammed shut her ledger and came gliding around to the front of the desk. Before Nitzinger knew what hit him she had him in hug that would have made a bear cry out for mercy or death.

"We was all wondering when you were gonna get here," said the woman, releasing him and stepping back to get a good look.

Nitzinger pulled air into his lungs and felt to make sure she hadn't broken any ribs.

Little lady's stronger than she looks, he thought. Hell, she's stronger than *I* look.

"Ma'am?" he said to her.

"Oh, no. You'll not be 'ma'am'-ing me. I'm Sarah Cobb. I manage this establishment for your aunt." She took hold of Nitzinger's hand and squeezed it.

He wasn't surprised that her grip hurt.

"Ethel spoke of you all the time," said Sarah. "She used to read your letters to me—Lordy, was she happy whenever something from you came in the post!" Then the woman's eyes filled with tears. "Ain't no one sorrier than me that she passed—except maybe for you."

Nitzinger could feel the eyes of the restaurant patrons on his back. "Um, I'm sorry to be coming in during dinner like this."

Sarah playfully smacked his forearm. "Don't you be apologizing, Johnny. This place is yours now. You can come and go as you please."

"Uh, about that…" He dug around in his saddle-bag and produced the envelope he needed. "I'm supposed to meet with a Mr. Daniel St. James?"

"Danny's out of town, up in New York on some business or other. We expect him back at the end of the week. You are planning on staying here, ain't you?"

"For a little while."

Sarah's face wrinkled with concern at his words, but she brushed it away with a wave of her hand. "Well, come on, let's you and me go back into the office and have ourselves a talk."

Before Nitzinger could say anything, she had him by the arm and was pulling him behind the desk and through the doorway just beyond. She then put him in a terribly comfortable padded leather chair and thrust a cup of hot cocoa into his hand.

"I want you to know right now, Johnny, that your aunt was a fine, fine woman—a splendid woman. Everybody here in Cedar Hill just thought the world of her."

"She always said real nice things about this place and the folks here."

Sarah smiled at him. "I also want to put your mind to rest on another matter right now: I was with Ethel when she passed, and a more peaceful leaving you couldn't have asked for. Benjamin was down here on the piano, playing her favorite song so's she could hum along, and it was a pleasant night with stars out in abundance, and her room was warm, and Reverend Maddingly was present with his Bible, and all manner of friends stopped in to say their good-byes. She had your last letter in her hand and a picture of you and her sister on her bedside table. Her heart problems had been troubling her something fierce the last few years. The doctor said that most of the muscles surrounding it was shot. And with her coming down with pneumonia on top of that…well, it was for the best. But she died as happy as a person can, on that you have my word."

John was surprised to find tears in his own eyes. "That's good to know, Sarah. I don't mind telling you, on the ride here I often wondered about how…well, you know, if she had any regrets."

Sarah started crying. "No regrets, Johnny. None at all."

"Well, now…ain't that just fine?"

This time, Nitzinger was ready for Sarah's rib-cracking embrace.

And didn't mind it in the least.

Dear Johnny,

If you are reading this then you made it here all right and for that I am most grateful to our Good Lord.

I imagine that Sarah has made herself known to you by now. Don't mind her going on about things like she does, it is just her way. Believe me when I tell you that you will not find a more dependable or loyal friend than she. I have made some last minute arrangements with Mr. St. James to bequeath Sarah either a small sum of money or a share of the business. The choice will be yours. Please keep her, Johnny. She knows more about running this place than I ever did.

In the small box accompanying this letter you will find what few worldly possessions I truly treasured, a photograph of your mama and you as a child among them. The silver frame was made from materials your daddy mined with his own hands. I'm sorry I don't have a picture of your daddy for you. He wasn't much to look at, truth be told, except when he smiled. Then a more handsome man didn't walk the earth. Until you, that is.

I would strongly advise you to make yourself known to folks around here before they decide to make themselves known to you. I'm afraid you have inherited more than a business establishment, Johnny. You have inherited a town filled with friends who have heard countless stories about you as a boy and a man. I apologize if I told them of anything that you might find embarrassing. I have always thought of you as my boy, and will not be held accountable for boasting of a child as a mother should.

This is your home now, if you want it. I sincerely hope you will. You have been alone for far too long, and in the end a life lived in loneliness is no life at all.

I will stop with my lecturing now. Always remember me fondly. I have loved you as my own and am certain to continue doing so once I am by our Lord's side. You never forgot to write to me and I treasured your letters. Don't go getting all disagreeable with yourself about not being here when I left. You have always been a part of me and so were here with me at the time.

I should mention that you will find all the books in order. That is Sarah's doing. There are no outstanding debts for you to worry about and a goodly sum of money in the bank.

I have had as fine a life as a woman who never married can expect. Finer, in some ways.

Bless you, my boy.

With Love,

Ethel

Damn if this wasn't the second time in as many hours that Nitzinger felt tears in his eyes.

He looked down at the sparse contents of the box that contained the letter. There was the photograph of himself and his mother in its silver frame, several ribbon-bound bundles of the letters he'd written to his aunt over the years, a few pieces of jewelry (he thought Sarah might fancy a particular broach), a piece of old rolled-up sheet music, and a wedding ring.

His mother's wedding ring, sent to his aunt a few weeks after his parents had died only an hour apart.

He held it up to the light and reveled in its simplicity: A single stone set into a gold circle.

"Ah, well—shit," he whispered, letting go of the tears at last.

A life lived in loneliness is no life at all.

And so, for the first time in his life, John Nitzinger admitted to himself that he was lonely, and had been for a goodly while. His aunt had left behind a legacy that would survive through generations of Cedar Hill children—stories about her and her kindness, the way she could host a ladies' tea in the afternoon and drink any man in town under the table at night and still retain the respect of both groups, countless other tales and memories people would keep alive—and what would he leave behind? Miles and miles of repaired fences that would surely crumble to dust and be forgotten long before he himself was dead, and once he was gone who would remember him or what he did? Was there ever a man he worked alongside of who could recall his face, the sound of his voice, or any conversation they'd had?

This place was his home, if he wanted one.

A life lived in loneliness is no life at all.

And he wanted it. He wanted nothing more to live out the rest of his days in a place where neighbors greeted you by name each day and inquired after your health if they didn't see you out and about. He wanted to marry himself a fine woman and raise a family while there was still time to do so.

Amanda Jakes' smile blossomed in his memory, and he felt that pit in his chest open again. He was going to find Mr. Cletus Walters and punch the man right square in the mouth if he didn't have himself a good excuse for abandoning that fine lady out there in the cold.

Without realizing he'd done it, Nitzinger had unrolled the sheet music and suddenly found himself looking at the title of the song.

Waltzing With You.

Before the chill snaked down his back, he remembered what Sarah had said: Benjamin was down here on the piano, playing her favorite song so's she could hum along.

What brought the chill to him were Amanda's words: I'm afraid I don't know the words. To be honest, John, I'm not even sure where I heard it. It just suddenly popped into my head...

A movement to his left caught his eye and he turned toward the window of his aunt's bedroom.

On the outside sill he saw the dirty-gold cat sitting, its black-and-white friend at its side, and a couple of other, smaller cats.

Watching him.

He knew then, somehow, that he'd been right: The dirty-gold cat had been following him.

But why? Cats weren't supposed to behave like that, were they? Sure, maybe they were good trackers, had inherited that from their ancestors, but weren't they supposed to track by smell? This thing had to have been tracking him by sight.

It didn't make sense.

"John Nitzinger?" came a gravelly voice from the doorway.

He turned, quickly wiping his eyes. "Yes?"

A short, stocky man with reddish-grey hair stepped into the room, removing his hat. "My name's Jack Baines. I'm the sheriff here."

Nitzinger rose and shook Baines' hand. "Can I help you with something, Sheriff? I hope I ain't done nothing wrong, broken a town ordinance or something like with my horse or—"

"No, hell no," said Baines, waving his hand. "Nothing like that. I wanted to introduce myself and welcome you. Your Aunt, she was a good friend of me and my family. My wife, well, she's been feeling right poorly ever since Ethel left us. You see, every year about this time, her and your aunt, they'd start in with baking the Christmas goodies, cookies and candies and such. Me and the kids, we couldn't get within five feet of the kitchen until after New Year's. The two of them practically set up armed guards to keep us out of the way." He ran a hand through his hair. "Yessir, the two of them was a holy terror this time of year." He shrugged. "My wife, she ain't so much as whipped up a batch of cakes in two weeks."

"I'm sorry to hear that."

Baines nodded his head. "Yeah, well, I reckon that once she gets wind that Ethel's boy has come to town, she'll perk right up. Probably lay down the kitchen law again and insist you come over for dinner every other night. Needless to say, you'll be having Christmas dinner with us. I'm just warning you ahead of time, you understand?"

"I stand warned."

"Okay, then. What I come here about was—" Baines' words died in his throat when he caught sight of the cats outside the window. "Christ on the cross," he whispered. Then, to Nitzinger: "How long them things been out there?"

"A while, I guess. That dirty-gold one there in the middle, I think it followed me from at least the train station."

Baines said nothing, only stared at the cats.

Something in the sheriff's manner betrayed his anxiety; the man seemed downright spooked by the cats.

Composing himself, Baines turned back to Nitzinger and said, "Reason I come is that Raymond from over at the livery came to see me a while ago. Told me about this here fellah that was askin' about the likes of Cletus Walters."

"That was me. At the train I met—"

"Did you know Cletus Walters?"

"Uh, no. Like I was sayin', out at the train station there's— wait a minute. How come you said it like that? Did I know Cletus Walters?"

"On account of the son-of-a-bitch is dead."

Nitzinger felt a sudden rush of deep sympathy for Amanda Jakes. "Oh, Lord. Are you certain that he's—?"

"I killed him myself not ten days ago out at his cabin. Two barrels right in his chest and he still kept coming at me." He saw the way Nitzinger blanched, glanced nervously at the cats outside, and said in a low tone, "I think you and I need to go over to my office and have ourselves a chat."

The first thing Nitzinger noticed in the sheriff's office was the hand-carved chess set, evidently abandoned in mid-game.

"You play any?" said Baines, nodding toward the board.

"Whenever I can."

"You and me'll have to have ourselves a game sometime. You gotta be more of a player than my deputy. Man keeps using checkers strategy even though I keep trying to explain they're two different games. Them pieces're in the same positions they was in a week ago when the idiot came down with a case of the gout. I keep telling the man that if his diet didn't consist solely of bacon, beer, and tobacco his body might not up and attack him so much, but there's just some people you can't pound any sense into."

Baines poured them both some fresh coffee that was far and away superior to the sludge Nitzinger had damn near killed Amanda Jakes with, and the two men sat across from each other over the chess board.

"What happened with Cletus Walters?" asked Nitzinger.

Baines leaned over, examining the chessboard. "First thing, Mr. Nitz—ah, hell, can I call you John? I heard so much about you from your aunt I feel like I know you."

"John's fine."

"Your aunt—now there was a chess player. Woman beat the pants off me more times than I care to admit."

"I'm finding out all sorts of things about her. I hope she knew how many friends she had."

"She did, indeed." Baines began to move his knight to Queen's-Pawn 7, thought better of it, and continued to stare at the board. "First thing you need to know, John, is that there's only a handful of folks around here who know the whole story about Walters—Raymond at the livery is one of 'em, and only because I needed extra horses and a wagon after it was over… anyway, only a few know about what happened, and I'd like to keep it that way, so what is said here in this room tonight stays here in this room, understand?"

"Understood."

Baines rubbed his eyes, took another sip of his coffee, then pulled a store-bought cheroot from his pocket. "You mind?"

"Got an extra one?" asked Nitzinger.

Baines did, and the two men lit up.

"It started with the cats," said Baines. "Two of them—that dark one, and a smaller reddish-brown one. That dirty-gold cat's a new one. Anyway, when Walters moved here from Oregon a couple years ago, him and his wife bought the old Myers place outside of town and started up their farming. Nice enough folks but they didn't much socialize with the rest of us. His wife in particular seemed stand-offish, but it weren't like she was stuck-up or nothing; she struck me as one of them terribly-shy types.

"People who'd go out by their place on the road to Granville always commented on the amount of cats they saw hanging around the property. At first it was just them two cats I mentioned, but as time went on other cats started showing up. Last count, they had something like eight of them. Now, what always struck folks about the cats was the way they behaved. Weren't cat-like at all, you ask me. They went everywhere together, real orderly. And whenever they'd stop to sit or sleep for a spell, they always did it together, real close in a circle, like they was resting in some kind of protection formation.

"Okay, so the Walters had a thing for cats. Fine by me. The animals was clean enough, never got into any of the chickens or such on other farms. Long as a pet ain't any problem, I don't bother with it.

"Long about eight, nine months ago, Walters comes into town and hires himself a little Wyandot Indian gal to come out and care for his wife who took sick. Didn't seem odd to anybody around here. Them Wyandots, they got a way with sick folk. So off they go back to the farm, and that's the last anybody hears for a few weeks.

"Wyandot gal came into town all by herself one day to pick up some supplies for Walters, only instead of going into the general store she heads over to your aunt's place, all nervous and scared-acting. Come to find out later that she told your aunt this wild story about how the cats was talking to her and Mrs. Walters. I don't mean opening their mouths and talking like you and are doing, but inside their heads, right? Told your aunt that the reason Mrs. Walters got all sick was because the cats was warning her to get out before it was too late. So this Wyandot gal, she goes into a dream-trance or some-such nonsense and she asks the cats how come Mrs. Walters has to get out. And you know what she told your aunt them cats said to her? Said they told her that they was the spirits of 'his victims' and was trying to save Mrs. Walters.

"So your aunt, she tells me all this after the Wyandot gal goes back to the Walters' place. Me, I laugh it off, but Ethel, she don't think it's so funny. 'Don't you be making light of others' ways just because they're so different from yours,' she snapped at me. 'Now maybe that Wyandot gal has a few boards missing from her upper floor, but she didn't get any ideas in her head that Mrs. Walters didn't put there in the first place.'

"I decide that maybe old Cletus isn't treating his wife like a God-fearing Christian man ought, so I decide to go pay a visit just to see how things are. I get out to his place and there're all them cats, lined up straight as you please on the hitching post outside Mrs. Walters' bedroom window. I go to the front and raise my hand to knock on the door, and Cletus, he's got it open before my knuckle touches wood.

"Man looked like he'd seen a ghost. He was all shaky and pale and wild-eyed, telling me that I'd best be on my way and mind my own business, they're all down with a fever and best be left alone. If it hadn't been for something I caught out of the corner of my eye, I probably would have believed him. But over in the corner I see this little Wyandot gal, right, sitting there with one of Mrs. Walters' fancier dresses in her lap, mending it. And there's dried blood on the dress. Now, you tell me—why in hell would someone bother mending a dress that's got a set bloodstain on it? Wouldn't you try to get the stain out first, then mend the thing?

"I ain't a suspicious man by nature, but something about all this gets me thinking. This is a nice, boring little town, and we like it like that. I don't tell anyone about this except for Ethel, and she says to me, 'Didn't he say he moved here from Eugene?' 'Yeah,' I says. 'Then why don't you send a wire down to see if the sheriff there has anything you might need to know?'

"That's exactly what I did. Six days later I get woke up at three in the morning by a couple of Pinkerton boys who look ready to spit nails and eat the hammer. They tell me to get dressed and come with them out to the Walters' place. Along the way, they fill me in on a couple of things that about turned my blood to ice.

"'Cletus Walters' wasn't his real name. The Pinkertons had no idea what his real name was, but they had a nice little list of names they thought he'd been using. When he'd been in Eugene, he took advantage of the Land Act—you know, that a married man was entitled to twice the acreage of a single fellah. Him and his wife, they farmed that land for about a year or so, then he just up and sold it for a nice profit and moved on without telling anyone where he was going. The folks who bought the place from him started complaining after a couple of weeks about two things. Guess what one of them was?"

"Cats?" said Nitzinger.

"You got that right. Cats...and the smell. So this fellah who bought the place, he eventually runs the cats off and starts digging around the property to find the smell. Well, he found it, all right. Walters had murdered his wife and buried her in her wedding dress under the water closet. When they was finally able to track down the paperwork on her, they found out that she married Walters—he used the name 'Simpkins' then—because of an arrangement he made with her father."

"She was a mail-order wife?"

"Yessir, that she was. According to the work the Pinkertons had been doing, their best guess was that Walters had done this at least three times before, maybe as many as seven or eight. He'd marry himself a mail-order bride on account of there wouldn't be no family of hers nearby, he'd use his marital status to snag himself twice the property he was entitled to, then, after him and his wife got the place into shape, he'd sell off the property at a decent profit, murder and bury his wife—he always buried them in their wedding dresses—then change his name and move to another county or state and do it all over again. The man was either damned stupid or damned arrogant. To this day I can't figure if he wanted to get caught or thought that the men on his trail weren't smart enough to catch him.

"It was while the Pinkertons was telling me about this that I realized the Wyandot gal had been mending what could very well have been a wedding dress, and I tell 'em this, and they slapped leather to the horses to get to the farm double-quick.

"You never heard such noise as what greeted us that night. There must have been a good half-dozen or more cats all around the outside of the cabin, howling up a storm. I could see a light was on inside the house and heard what sounded like a woman screaming. So we jump out of the wagon, the Pinkertons splitting up on either side of the house and leaving me in front with my old double-barrel. I go up near the porch and call for Cletus and all the cats just went quiet—" he snapped his fingers, "—like that. Scared me right down to the ground. I call Cletus's name again and the door flies open and this little Wyandot gal comes running out, all beat-up and bleeding and screaming something in Indian at me that I don't understand, and next thing I know here comes Cletus looking like the Devil his own self, and he's yelling something at the cats about how they should just go back to their graves and leave him alone, then he opens fire on me with a set of pistols he's got and hits that poor little Wyandot gal right smack in the back of the head with one of the shots, and she goes down at my feet and I empty both barrels into his chest and he still kept coming. The Pinkertons finished him off, and both of them had to empty six shots each to bring him down.

"He was in the process of burying his wife when we got there. She'd been dead a couple of days at least…it was fairly grim. The Pinkertons tore the place up, and they found plenty. Crazy bastard'd kept every marriage certificate. Eight of them. He even kept wedding photographs of himself with each of his brides. And the money. They found something like sixty thousand dollars he'd stashed away from selling off all that land. I did some checking after it was all over, and found out that Walters had been making some inquiries over in Delaware County about land over there for himself and his 'new wife.'"

Nitzinger's blood turned to ice in his veins at the thought of what might have happened to Amanda at the hands of a demon like Walters.

"Sheriff, I don't mean to seem rude, but there's something I gotta take care of as soon as possible."

"Anything I can help with?"

Nitzinger told Baines about Amanda Jakes.

"Christ on the cross," whispered the sheriff. "I wonder if that gal will ever know how lucky she is."

"You think Raymond would give me too much trouble about renting a wagon and couple of fresh horses?"

"Not if I'm with you, he won't."

Nitzinger rose. "I need to get a few things from over at my aunt's place."

"Your place now," said Baines. "That is, if you plan on staying put for a while."

"I do," replied Nitzinger. "This is my home. Now."

❁

He brought a shovel, and cleared the snowdrifts from the road so that the wagon would have easy passage. As he rode along he sang softly to himself "Waltzing With You." Words and all.

She was asleep when he got there, and so for a few moments, after quietly letting himself into the station, he stood there staring at her soft sleeping face and hoping she'd smile at him when she finally awoke.

She at last wakened when the dirty-gold cat and the rest of its friends began yowling outside; only this time there was nothing mournful or eerie in the sound. To Nitzinger's ears, it almost sounded like they were singing.

It then occurred to him why the dirty-gold cat had seemed familiar to him.

Its fur was the same color as his aunt's hair.

Rubbing the sleep from her eyes, Amanda sat up, saw Nitzinger, and smiled at him with a sleep-blushed face that was, for him, the most beautiful thing he'd ever seen.

"John…hello."

"Hello, Amanda."

"What time is it?"

"Almost midnight. I would have been here sooner but I—"

"Oh, stop apologizing," she said. "If you apologize to me one more time about anything tonight, I'm going to charge you five dollars each time you say 'I'm sorry.'"

"I got a wagon out front. Road into town's cleared."

"Wonderful. Except that I seem to have been left standing at the altar in a way." She looked him straight in the eyes. "I have been left, haven't I?" There was quiet kind of desperate sadness under her words.

"Yes, you have."

And that was all he ever intended to tell her about it.

"Would you really have married him? A man you never met and didn't know?"

She nodded her head. "Look at the likes of me, John. I'm not as pretty as most men would like, and I am spinster-age. Besides, my father would be very angry if I backed out on a business deal he made."

"I think you're very pretty," said Nitzinger. "I just wish I was more of a Fancy-Dan."

"John," she said softly. "I think you're just fine as you are."

"Good. That'll make this a lot easier."

"Make what easier?"

Nitzinger didn't say anything. He looked out at the cats and gave them a wink, then took off his hat, removed his mother's wedding ring from his pocket, and slowly, with great dignity and purpose, took Amanda's left hand in his and got down on one knee.

" ... He Didn't Even Leave a Note ... "

IT HAS BEEN A long day and the hour is late and you are impatient to get home. You stayed at the office a bit later than usual, tidying up some last-minute paperwork before leaving for the weekend, but as a result you missed your bus and so find yourself walking. Which isn't really so bad, after all, is it? No, not in the least. It's been ages since last you walked home from work, and at least the weather is nice.

It has been a long day and the hour is late and you are impatient to get home, despite the lovely weather. You wonder if any of your friends are going to bother calling you to see what plans you have for the weekend. "You work too damned much," they say; "We never see you anymore," they say; "It's not good for you to spend so much time by yourself," they say, all the while knowing that your job takes a lot out of you—how else could you have secured the recent promotion, had not you put your career first? "And what's wrong," you say to them, "with wanting to spend my time away from work watching movies or reading or listening to music?"

"Those are *solitary* activities," they reply, "and too much of that can alienate you from the people in your life." You love them all the more for their concern, but wish they'd get it through their heads that there are some people who don't need the constant companionship of other human beings in order to feel that their life has meaning. It doesn't mean you don't care for them, but for some reason they don't understand that. You are involved with them. You are involved with life.

Still, it has been a long day and the hour is late and you are impatient to get home, but there is a man in the distance running toward you. He is a feeble and ragged creature, a depressing sight. There is another man chasing at his heels, screaming. You step aside to let the first man pass. Perhaps the two are running for their own amusement, a good-natured race; maybe they are both in pursuit of a third man you didn't notice; it could even be that the second man wishes to harm or even murder the first and any involvement on your part would make you an unwitting accessory. Regardless of the circumstances, you remain standing off to the side, impatient for the whole incident to play itself out so you can get on home, pour a glass of whiskey, and relax to some music, forgetting about the pressures of the week.

The second man nears you and you see that he, must, indeed, have murder in his heart because he's holding a long and very sharp knife; the early moonlight glints off the blade with an eerie kind of beauty.

The second man runs smack into you, thrusts the blade deep into your belly, and twists.

The pain begins. You grasp the murderer by his shoulders and whisper: "Why?"

He glances in the direction of the running, ragged man, and smiles sadly. "If you hadn't stayed to tidy up the paperwork, you would not have missed the bus; if you had not missed the bus, you would have been home in time for Beverly's phone call; if you had been in time for Beverly's phone call, you would have known that she still loves you and wants to try again."

The first man stops running, turns, and shouts back: "You probably haven't even thought of her in months, have you?"

Then, with a last twist of the blade, the second man pulls the knife from your belly and runs back the way he came.

You can no longer see the first man but, still, you call out to whomever may hear: "Don't I have the right to be tired?" You crumple to the ground and watch your life ooze from your belly, staining the sidewalk. "I didn't want to get involved. It was none of my affair. I only wanted to get home."

Then you die.

Everyone calls it suicide.

THE QUEEN OF TALLEY'S CORNER

"Here lies a most beautiful lady,
   Light of step and heart was she…"

–Walter de la Mare, "An Epitaph"

THEY CAN SAY WHATEVER they want, but they weren't there, were they?

They weren't there on Talley's Corner on those Saturday nights when the East End of Cedar Hill was still the place to be, before the big fire in '69 reduced it to a place where those at the end of their ropes crawl into the shadow of poverty to fade away in slow, lonely, miserable degrees—but we're not talking about the way it is now, no; we're talking about the glory days, the grand days, the days of music and laughter and the lovely ladies whose ebony, amber, coffee, and tan skin shone under the lights like fine gemstones—onyx, topaz, coral; we're talking about the days when Talley's Hideaway always had lines of people waiting to get in so they could listen to the entertainers play Ellington and Armstrong and Calloway and Ethel Waters just like it was the real honest-to-God Cotton Club, the Saturday nights when you could always find Mousey, Stringbean, and Jackpot harmonizing and scatting and snapping their fingers over an ashcan fire, waiting for a glimpse of Miss Hattie and her elusive, mysterious man, Mr. Granger, the music rising up from the open speakeasy windows and swirling with the street-dust dancing in the glow of the lights that always shone brighter whenever Miss Hattie and her Mr. Granger would pull up in their elegant Minerva and she'd step out in the grandest of style.

See her then.

A stone marten fur around her shoulders, glistening from the smoke and the glow of the ashcan's flames, the golden silk tassel caught between the spring of its jaws, her coat of sable, a string of pearls around her neck that can't begin to outshine her smile or overshadow her laugh that the Ashcan Boys waited all week to hear, back there in the glory days, the grand days, down at Talley's Corner where the crystal clink of glasses filled with gin echoed down to the street along with the music of the singers and the smoky piano and the big bands giving life to the jazz and the blues and the good old honky-tonk.

See Miss Hattie.

—*Sing for us, Miss Hattie*, they would say.

—*No, boys, I can't, not tonight. I got me some dancing and drinking and loving to do.*

Then she would glide up to her man, her Mr. Granger who looked like a king on these Saturday nights, and she'd slip a white-gloved hand through his fine strong arm, blow the Ashcan Boys a kiss, and the two of them would float up the stairs to Talley's Hideaway, leaving Mousey and Stringbean and Jackpot by their fire to shake their heads and wonder why they could never find a woman as fine as that to love them the way Miss Hattie did her Mr. Granger.

Sing to me now, boys; sing to me a song about Miss Hattie and those glory-day Saturday nights, waiting to hear her laugh. Sing to me and see her now.

See Miss Hattie now.

Emma looked up from the butcher's block when she heard the humming from the top of the stairs. Her sister, Rose, came into the kitchen, saw the look on Emma's face, and said: "Don't start."

"So long as you don't tell me Hattie's getting her dress out again."

Rose shrugged. "Okay. I maybe won't tell you, but that won't change anything."

Emma threw down the mound of fresh bread dough and untied her apron. "Not today, Rose. I can't take her craziness today. I like her just as much as you do, but every once in a while…"

Rose walked over and took her by the arm. "You stop it, Emma. The woman's *old* and it's hardly her fault that she ain't…*all there* anymore. Just leave her be, she's not hurting anybody."

"I just wish the nursing home had told us about the way she gets before I told 'em it was okay for her to take our last room. I know she was a friend of Mom and Daddy, but she gives everybody the willies—ever notice how no one else comes down to eat with her except for you?"

"At least they thought to give us a call, instead of someplace like The Maples or one of them other places downtown."

"You mean in one of the *nicer* areas, don't you?"

"For pity's sake, Emma! Nobody lives in the East End unless they have to. And you just keep in mind that Hattie's money at the end of the month comes in real handy since Daddy died and left us this place."

"That's just it," said Emma. "We *know* that Daddy's gone, just as well as she knows her Granger is dead and has been for almost as long as you and me been alive. The difference is we don't make believe any different. Why do you insist on letting her go on pretending like she does? Putting on that dress and acting like Granger's coming by to take her out dancing and all that? I don't think—"

"How do I look?" came a voice from the doorway. Rose and Emma turned toward Hattie.

See her now, boys.

Her threadbare elegance and thinning, grey hair that now grows in patches. Sing to me a song of age, boys; snap those fingers and scat for Hattie, the Queen of Talley's corner, come 'round to grow old and frail, there in the shabby relic of her Saturday-night dress, smiling in the doorway to the kitchen of Emma and Rose Long's Rooming House.

Hattie crossed to the table and seated herself almost daintily, taking care not to smudge or stain the silk white gloves that now bulged halfway up her sagging arms where once they glided elegantly nearly to her shoulders. The chair creaked when she sat, but no one said anything. No one ever said anything.

"Gonna be a grand Saturday night," said Hattie.

"You going out on the town again?" asked Rose, giving her sister a you'd-better-stay-quiet glance.

"That's what Saturday nights were made for, hon."

Rose smiled. "Got yourself a new beau we don't know about?"

Hattie laughed; despite the sandpaper rasp of too many years of too many cigarettes, something in it still chimed. "There is no man but my Granger, Rose—and you keep them young hands off him, hear me?" She winked.

"Oh, I don't know, Hattie. He's a looker, your Granger is."

"*Rose!*" snapped Emma. For a moment the two sisters glared at one another, and then Emma turned away and continued preparations for dinner, still three hours away.

Hattie reached for the cup of afternoon tea that Rose set in front of her. Her hands shook and the cup rattled against the saucer. She smiled to herself for a moment, took a small sip, then set it back on the table, releasing a soft, weary sigh. "Did I ever tell you that Granger used to read poems to me?"

Rose smiled. "No, you never did."

Hattie removed a small cloth-bound book from the tattered sequined purse that hung from her arm. "Granger, he said that a lot of the poems in this book made him think of me. Isn't that sweet? The poems, a lot of 'em are real pretty."

"Can I hear one?" asked Rose.

"You most certainly can…just give me a minute." She rummaged through the sparse contents of the purse until she found her bifocals. Putting them on, she gave Rose a smile, turned to a dog-eared page, and read:

"If in the twilight of memory we should
    meet once more, we shall speak again together
    and you shall sing to me a deeper song.
And if our hands should meet in another
    Dream, we shall build another tower in the sky."

"That is one of the loveliest things I've ever heard," said Rose. "Wasn't that lovely, Emma?"

Emma grunted, pounding a fist into the bread dough.

"Who wrote that, Hattie?"

Hattie squinted at the faded name on the worn cover. "Can't rightly make it out. I think it says here the fellah's name was 'Carl' or something like that, but spelled different."

Rose took the book from Hattie and looked for herself.

But you know the name, don't you, Hattie? Remember the way you joked about it? You always insisted on saying it wrong because your eyes were never that good—or so you tried to convince Granger. Mostly it was because it always made him laugh, wasn't that it? You knew the name was Kahlil Gibran and that Granger always read him—it was the only book he owned. Saying his name wrong, calling him 'Carl Gibbons', that was your grand joke, yours and Granger's, shared on soft, cool autumn nights as the two of you lay between warm sheets in one another's arms, inhaling the sweet aroma of the lovemaking still on your skin.

"If in the twilight of memory…" Remember how you said that was your favorite line, how it sounded like something from a dream?

But it's not a dream anymore, is it, Hattie? You're the only one who knows he still comes back for you on Saturday nights, that he can still take you back there to Talley's Corner when the music was hot and the gin was cold. Even now you hear his voice, don't you? And you love it so over there, because over there you're your old self, you're the Queen, the loveliest of all the lovely ladies in their fineries, not some used-up little bit of a thing who's traded the best of herself in for sadness and nursing homes and snickers behind your back as you pass by, never being able to tell anyone how scared you are, how lonely this place is, the way it is now; you can't tell them about his visits because they'd never believe you, they'd think you were just some crazy old lady, you've heard them call you that when they think you can't hear them, and maybe part of you started to believe it, so you chose to play the part, didn't you? But now you sometimes wonder if maybe, just maybe, you aren't really crazy, after all, because how could your Granger love you enough to come back from the world of honky-tonks and speakeasies to take you dancing and drinking and loving while Mousey and Stringbean and Jackpot wait by their ashcan fire for just a glimpse of your smile? Slim and beautiful and the envy of all who see you on these Saturday nights, that's you. Listen: your ears fill with their compliments, your spirits soar with the looks in their eyes as they watch you, the evening vibrates with your laugh.

Hattie reached over and took the book from Rose. "Some of the boys, they used to say they never saw a lady as light of heart and step as me."

"Oh, I've seen pictures of what you looked like back in the day," said Rose. "You were a heartbreaker. Put you next to Dorothy Dandridge and no man'd give her a second glance."

Hattie reached over and squeezed Rose's hand. "You are so sweet, hon. Thank you."

"I speak nothing but the truth. You were gorgeous. You still are."

"That's what Granger always said to me. But he was *never* the jealous type, nosiree, not him, not my man." She once again lifted her cup and drank her tea, this time with little shaking.

"That was delicious as always, Rose, and I thank you." She then excused herself and, humming some long-forgotten gospel hymn, made her way out the back door for her afternoon walk.

"*That* is one sad woman, you ask me," said Emma.

"Even if I didn't ask, you'd tell me anyway," said Rose. She watched Hattie walk down the path to the sidewalk before turning left and strolling away. Rose picked up the saucer and teacup. "Still, you've got to wonder why she can't…hey, can I ask you something?"

"Seein' as how I couldn't stop you if I wanted, you might as well."

"How did Granger die?"

Emma stopped pummeling the bread dough and stared at the wall. "Oh, my. It, uh…" She wiped her hands on her apron and sat down, gesturing for her sister to join her. "You sure you want to hear this?"

"Is it that bad?"

"Yes, it is. 'Bout as bad as it gets."

Rose sat down opposite Emma and gave a slight nod.

"Granger did bootlegging for old Bill Talley. Talley, he got most of his hooch from Kentucky, and Granger was always the one who drove down to make the payoffs and the pickups. Well, one night he ran into some Prohibition boys who didn't take too kindly to his 'uppity' attitude—that's what one of them called him, 'uppity.' That's all the excuse they needed to pull out their pistols and start firing. Some uppity nigger in a Minerva full of booze gave them good target practice. But Granger, he was strong and he was big and he was fast. Made them Prohibition agents chase him all over hell's half acre before they shot out his tires and he had to take it on foot. You know what those bastards did? They shot him in the backs of both his knees and he dropped like a sack of wet cement. But that wasn't enough, not for them and not back then, oh, no. *Then* they turned their dogs loose on him. After that, they tied him to the back of their car and dragged him all the way to the downtown square where they strung what was left of him up by the neck so the birds could have a little snack. Papers back then, they said he was still alive when they hanged him. He stayed there for damn near two days before some folks from Talley's come to cut him down. Daddy was one of the men who helped do it. Him and another fellow, they were the ones who went to fetch Hattie and take her down to identify Granger's body."

Rose exhaled and covered her mouth. "Dear God."

"You know how Hattie knew it was Granger? By feeling his hands. Daddy said she held his hands up against her cheek and knew it was him. Wasn't enough of his face left for her to—"

"Jesus, Emma, *stop*."

"You asked. Now, it's not that I don't have any sympathy for the woman, you understand that, right?"

Rose looked out the back door. "Poor Hattie."

"The whole damn world's got problems and heartaches, Rose. Everybody feels lonely and miserable because somebody they loved isn't here anymore and, yes, maybe some of them didn't die very nice, but what can be done about it now? I know her Granger's gone and that she misses him something terrible, but so is Mom and Daddy, and you sure as hell don't see *me* going around setting two extra plates at the dinner table, do you?"

"Not anymore."

"Oh—why don't you go sweep off the porch or mop the bathrooms or something?"

Rose smiled to herself. "You raise your voice like you're ready to throw a skillet at my head, but you love me, Emma. Admit it."

Emma began kneading the dough once again. "Everybody needs a hobby. Some people put off doing the housework—me, I love my sister. Besides, I wouldn't damage a perfectly good skillet that way." She looked at Rose. "I'm sorry I've been so bitchy today, but Hattie kept me awake half the night pretending that she was talking to Granger. Half the time I swear she was talking back to herself in his voice. Gave me the shivers."

"It's a sad world some days, Emma."

"Isn't it, though?" She smiled. "But I'm glad I got you. You're real good company. So's Hattie, except when…"

Rose walked over and gave Emma a hug. "You're a good person with a good heart, Emma. You just hide it from us more than I wish you did."

Emma returned the embrace, and then said, "Are you still here?"

Hattie stands before the wall that is all which remains of Talley's Hideaway. When the Beaumont Casket factory burned to the ground in '69 it took over a dozen other buildings with it, including Talley's. The city decided that its money would be better spent making improvements elsewhere, and so Old Towne East—the East End—came to be known as "Coffin County." Hattie hates that nickname; it reminds her that too soon she's going to be under the ground in the cold, cold darkness.

Now the wall draws the ruined and the crazy to its shade. Today, it's a young man who's muttering about needing something cut from his face, but Hattie sees nothing wrong with the young man's face; it is, in fact, quite handsome. She smiles at him and gives him a dollar so maybe he'll go and get himself a cold drink of soda. The young man says something about this fish and staggers off, just another crazy who calls the shade of Talley's wall sanctuary.

She's thinking of Granger right now. For as much as she loves him, there are times when she wishes that he would just leave her be. At first the Saturdays weren't every week, were they, Hattie? At first they came only every few years, then once a year, then once a month, and now it's every week. You stand before the wall and worry that Granger's going to come and try to bring you all the way back, don't you? You worry because you like this here world you're living in, even if it means living without him. Somehow living without him makes your time here even more important; you want to honor his memory in the twilight of your days and turn your life into a tower in the sky.

But Granger, he doesn't like it over there without you, and you know that. But what's a soul to do?

It's up to Granger, Hattie knows this. Her Granger, her good, loyal, loving man. He's there behind everyone's smiles, in everyone's gaze, in the sounds of their voices as they pass by; near her always, somewhere just behind, or around the corner, gaining on her, calling for her to slow down, to give a body a chance to catch its breath.

You were so young, Hattie, barely twenty years old, and you'd never had a man treat you the way Granger did, never had a man buy you things, beautiful, sparkling, expensive things, things that cost more money than you'd ever dreamed of having, but those things, as splendid as they were, didn't mean half as much to you as the touch of his fingertips against your cheek in the middle of the night. Oh, and his *words*, his glorious words and stories whispered in your ear when sleep wouldn't come: stories of tailors and poets and bootleggers and thieves, of heroes and peddlers and songmen and train chasers; tales of healers and gamblers and summer nights on the run and they just made you *sing* inside, made you wish for a full and rich life by this adventurer's side so one day you could tell your friends and children and grandchildren about all the crazy, wild, dangerous, wonderful times you had in your youth.

Standing before the wall now, Hattie closes her eyes and holds out her hand.

You comin' now Granger? Look—I got on my best dress and my good gloves and those pearls you always said made you crazy for me. I think I want you to come, darlin', but please do it quick before I change my mind and get all nervous and start to shake like I do. I can't stand it here without you, but it scares me something fierce to think about the place you want to take me. There I'm the way I used to be, but it's always only for a while, and if you take me back there permanent, I might be the way I am now…and I don't think you'd be too crazy over me now. I'm old and fat and tired and I got nothing in my life except these Saturday nights. But I still love you, I still try to make you proud to have a woman like me. You made me a queen, darlin', you made me special, something I never was before and haven't been since. So I'm holding out my hand, Granger, and I hope you take it and never let go. You comin' now, Granger? Please don't make me wait. Please don't leave me here. Please come before I change my mind.

Hattie waits, holding her breath. She stands that way, a crazy old lady with her eyes closed, for almost half an hour before she thinks about giving up, but just as she begins to lower her arm, to let it all go, to admit that it's all been in her head for all these years, she feels familiar fingers take hold of her own, and close tightly, and whisper to her of twilight memories and singing a deeper song as something in her chest pulls tight for only a moment, and then lets go…

See her now, boys.

See Miss Hattie, back with us at last.

Snap those fingers and raise those voices and harmonize those songs, Ashcan Boys; sing to the smoke and the lights and the scent of sweet gin from Talley's Hideaway; make room for night, boys, for those grand Saturday nights, and sing it proud.

The Queen of Talley's Corner done come home, and only we understand, don't we? Only us, and not the others she left behind. They never understood. They never would have.

But they weren't there, were they?

For Sharon Cullars

DANAÏD NIGHT

HE WATCHED HER from a distance, stunned and frightened and tongue-tied as a schoolboy, hidden in the shadows between the azure of the horizon and the cracked, desiccated grey of the earth. For as long as he could remember he'd waited here, hoping for a glimpse of a consanguine spirit, but each day brought with it only lengthening shadows, chill nightwinds, and tears that could not be shed, no matter how hard he closed his eyes and tried to force them out.

This had been his home, and his only companions the songs, the figures, the stories and pictures he created in his mind to pass the time. He knew every detail of these pictures, every nuance of these stories, every curve and fold in the figures' flesh, and every subtle chord-change in each song. This, he knew, was important, for someday one would come along with whom he could share these things, these creations birthed in loneliness and blue-hued isolation, and when this someone came he wanted to be her wizard, her lover, her weaver of fables, teller-of-tales, her singer of songs that, once heard, would fill her heart near to bursting from the volume of the joy and wonder.

And now here she was.

He knew it was her; without so much as hearing her voice, or her laugh; without so much as feeling the warmth of her breath against his cheek or the touch of her fingertips against his palm (his *sweaty* palm, dammit; why did he always perspire so when the promise of happiness loomed so close?), he knew it was her.

She carried herself like a dancer, lithe and graceful and, perhaps, with just a little sadness underfoot.

She carried with her an exquisite jar, covered in ancient words and pictures of dancers who encircled the base. She stood for a moment, still as a statue in the deepening twilight, then turned and began pouring water onto the dry ground. She moved as if riding waves of ether, first straight up, then side to side, pausing here and there to scatter a few select droplets before moving on a few yards and beginning the dance all over again.

He moved toward her under the tail of a night shadow. She was drawing something in the dead soil, and he wanted to see what it was before the night took it away forever.

Trees.

From her exquisite jar of water and wonder she was drawing the shadows of trees that once might have stood here, before the world turned on and on and time brushed its uncaring hand in another direction and left this place just another ruined, forgotten corner of nowhere-in-particular, one of those spots you pass by on your way to someplace better, someplace brighter, someplace where you didn't have to think about places like this—but places like this were all he'd had for so very long. They'd sent him here—but with kind words, so as to ease their own consciences at night. *You're a bit too high-strung. You make people nervous. We really have no idea what it is you're talking about half the time, perhaps it would be best if you found a place of your own. We know such a place. It's quiet. It's very quiet. And very far away from us.*

He rubbed something from his eye and blinked.

She had now drawn the shadow of a third tree, and with this third shadow, she stopped, set down her jar, and said: "You can come out now. I know you've been watching me."

Hesitantly, he moved out from under the shadows and stepped into the waning light.

"Hello," he said, the word crawling out of his throat as if afraid of the air.

She was even more beautiful than he'd dared imagine. Pale, creamy skin flowing over a face chiseled from crystal, and gold-flecked eyes of brown so soft and pure he could taste their gaze.

"Why have you drawn the shadows of trees?"

She smiled at him, only for him; he could have swum a thousand raging rivers on its memory alone. "Because I miss them. I miss their smell, their shade, the feel of their bark against my skin as I sit back to rest against them. Can you understand that? Can you understand what it's like to miss something so terribly that you'll accept even the shadow of its memory to keep your heart from withering away?"

"How did you come to be here?" he asked, feeling the perspiration covering his face. What an inept, bumbling, ineffectual fool he must look.

"My sisters abandoned me," she said. "Our duty was to fill our jars with water from a well and then fill a river whose name I've long since forgotten…but my sisters, they lied to me. They sent me off on an errand, knowing I would lose my way. But I don't care, not now. They can have their eternity of lonely labor. I shall have the shadows of my remembered trees. Do you like them?"

He examined the shadows closely, admiring the details of the bending branches, the drooping leaves, the slow, tired, summer-afternoon-nap feel the shadows conveyed.

"They're wonderful," he said. "But why did you make only three?"

"The first," she said, dancing backward, "is for me. It is the tree under which I will sit and dream of one who will be my wizard, my lover, my teller-of-tales and singer-of-songs. The second—" And now she danced closer to him, her body spinning, not touching the earth, not part of the earth but something Up There, something Wondrous. "—this tree is for my muse, my lover, he who shall dream the tales to tell, compose the songs to sing, and in the earth draw pictures of places that never were but ought to have been. And this last tree—" Up There, she was Up There again, spinning, laughing, pirouetting, a dream of fallen angels to make their time on earth less cheerless. "—*this* is the tree under which we shall meet in the evening and share with one another the secrets and wonders and mysteries of the day. He shall sit here, and I next to him with my head against his chest. He will hold my hand in his and I will breathe to the beating of his heart. 'Tell me a story,' I'll say, 'and make it as happy a tale as you dare.' And he will tell me the story of his life, and when he reaches the end, I'll say, 'Start again.' And this time, when he tells it, it will be the story of *our* life."

"He would be a fool to offer any less."

A glint in her eyes, a soft glistening of moonlight from her smile. "Would you know of any such person, sir?"

He thought of pictures, stories, figures, and songs; he took a full inventory of his heart and spirit and imagination and, seeing the way he looked reflected in her eyes, found them and himself to be sadly lacking. No, it could not be him, as much as he might long for it, desire it, wish for and weep over it, he did not deserve one so exquisite and mysterious as she.

"I know of no such man," he said.

"I hoped you would say that." And suddenly she was by his side, taking his hand and guiding him through the shadowed trees. "The muse I seek, the lover I crave, would not see himself to be as unique as he is. That's why I knew you at first sight."

And I you, he wanted to reply, but it sounded too corny, so he simply shrugged and said: "I don't know how to dance."

"You don't have to. I'll dance for you. And later, under our tree, hidden in the shadows from a world that no longer knows how to look up and wonder, you'll tell me a story about a dancer."

"A dancer who one day found herself alone with a jar of water in the middle of a ruined place?"

She kissed him. Every window in his soul opened wide.

"That sounds like a wonderful beginning," she said, pulling him down beside her under their tree. "Tell me more…"

AISLE OF PLENTY

> "If we lived long enough to see the result of our actions
> it may be that those who call themselves good would
> be sickened with a dull remorse, and those whom the
> world calls evil stirred by a noble joy."
> —Oscar Wilde, The Critic as Artist

SPORTING GOODS, you have a call on Line One;
Sporting Goods, Line One."

"Jewelry, Line Two, please."

"Gifts, Lines Three and Four, please."

Shoppers swarmed idly by, bumping into one another, trying
to avoid carts haphazardly abandoned in the middle of aisles
that were already far too narrow; people cursed and laughed and
complained, some left items lying on shelves dozens of yards
from the department where they had originally been picked
up, a few were busy eluding security cameras in an effort to
switch price tags on items they felt were too expensive, spastic
unattended children were playing hide-and-seek among the
clearance racks, and occasionally there would come the sound
of something high-priced and too-fragile smashing to the floor.
The check-out girls droned the required pleasantries to each
person who passed through their long lines—"Thank you for
shopping at Carol's, Cedar Hill's oldest and best department
store…"—and, all in all, it was business as usual, no real
surprises, no serious screw-ups, no moments that were funny,
unique, or irritating enough to be remembered.

Only two people noticed the strange little man in the turban
enter the store and head towards the stairway that led down to
Sporting Goods.

The first was Wendy Tyler, who today found herself stuck across from the main doors at Checkout #2, the register that everybody seemed to be going through, she supposed, because they could just grab up their bags and make a beeline from the register to the doors without having to step around anyone or anything or—God forbid—take a few extra steps from any of the other registers closer to the service desk: what was it today, a contest or something to see how fast you could get out of here? She wouldn't even have to be here today if Suze hadn't gone out partying last night—did the girl know nothing but how to get falling-down drunk? If Wendy had known that Suze was going to be such a bust as a roomie, she'd have found someone else to share expenses with, but they both worked here, and Suze's family had the bucks if they ever came up short, and Wendy was damned if she'd ever go to her family for help. She'd get through her nursing classes on her own, thank you very much. But if she had to keep covering Suze's shifts here at the store, well, that was going get hairy. Too bad nothing really interesting would happen today, something to make Suze feel bad or disappointed that she wasn't here. But everybody was too tense today, what with it being the Anniversary and everything, a year after those creeps drove those planes into those buildings in New York and killed all those people. The manager had even told everyone to keep an eye out for anyone suspicious-looking, and what the hell did that mean, anyway? It wasn't like some terrorist was just going—

—and then she saw the man in the turban.

Wow, she thought. He just, like, walked in.

The second person to notice the odd little man was Mitchell Perry, the security guard, who at the moment was rubbing his eyes against the overhead fluorescent lights because he was still slightly hung-over from his medication last night; goddamn cluster headaches had been wailing on his ass ever since his days at the TOC in Truong Son—and this was after managing to walk away upright from ambushes in Ia Drang Valley, Dak To, and the Mang Yang Pass: come out of all that shit with gunshots and powder burns and all the rest of that shit courtesy of Uncle Sam and the North Vietnamese, and what permanent damage do you wind up carrying with you? Tinnitus, fer chrissakes! The ringing in Mitchell's ears eventually gave way to severe cluster headaches, and though standard treatments over the years had managed to get the problem under control, there were times—last night, for instance—when nothing but a shot of the Big Bad D (Demerol) would do the trick , so he'd haul himself out of bed, call his doctor's emergency number, and drive himself over to the ER. That got dicey on the drive back—he almost passed out behind the wheel before he got home—but at least the pain was gone. But the hang-over… Jesus. The last thing he needed was for the manager to start giving him the once-over—guy already thought Mitchell was weird, and a call to the security company complaining that he looked like he'd been drinking would only cement the love in their relationship. Mitchell couldn't afford another transfer—the company'd moved him three times already this year because he made people "nervous." And today would not be a good day to antagonize anyone. It was, after all, the Anniversary, and the manager had been adamant that today, of all days, Mitchell be on his toes for any suspicious-looking people. Right. Like a terrorist was going to walk into this store because Cedar Hill was Ground Zero for the next attack that would lead to the downfall of all capitalistic society as we knew it. Christ, if only these lights weren't so bright today. So Mitchell sighed, promised himself he'd be on his best behavior today, and looked outside where the light wasn't so harsh—

—and saw the man in the turban.

Holy shit, he thought. You got guts, walking in here looking like that today, pal. Maybe I should make sure no one gives you any trouble.

As for the man in the turban, he walked with a nervous shuffle, rubbing his hands together to avoid the temptation of hiding them in his pockets. A man with his hands in his pockets aroused suspicion among the soldiers…and he stopped for just a moment to remind himself that he no longer needed to worry about the soldiers. Not anymore. Not here.

His beard was moist from the heat of the summer outside, making the contrast between the coal black and grey only more pronounced. His brow was drawn and ruffled like blinds against the bright season, and his eyes were fixed sternly on his small feet. The aisles of Plenty were like a maze from some drunken fantasy story—everything here and no one to tell you how much you could have for yourself. The Plenty seemed to laugh at him in his awkwardness—and he still felt awkward, probably always would. It didn't matter that he'd been an American citizen for three years, he still felt as if he were a tourist. After what happened in New York last year, he'd have given anything not to come out today, but the boys had been promised something special from their grandfather, and their grandfather was not about to let them down.

He'd seen too many children who'd been let down. On the streets of Peshawar and Qunduz, grubby, thin, traumatized, begging for coins or stooping to gather cardboard that could be recycled for a few rupees, carrying their long-handled cups for passing strangers to drop change into. He'd once asked a young boy how much money he collected in the course of a day, and the boy proudly proclaimed that, on a good day he went back to his tent with 25 rupees—roughly forty-two cents. There was an entire generation of ruined children coming to age in his former country, a destroyed generation, and he promised himself long ago that, if he ever lived long enough to make it to America, he would make sure than his children and his children's children would never know the kind of grubby, tragic pride he'd seen in the eyes of that boy in Peshawar that day.

He stopped in front of the magazine stand. A woman bumped him in the side with a shopping cart. It hurt his hip—quite a bit—but he smiled at her anyway.

"I beg your pardon," he said softly, hoping that he'd used the right phrase.

"Do you mind?" snapped the woman. "I've got things to do."

He bowed his head and moved out of her way. She paid him so little regard as she passed that one of the wheels of her shopping cart ran over his toe. He shook his foot in an effort to subdue the pain, which it did, somewhat, but not to his total satisfaction.

The woman made her way over to the makeup counter. The man in the turban watched her, fascinated. It still amused him that here women worried about whether or not their shoes clashed with their outfits, for that was a matter of embarrassment. In Qunduz women worried about whether or not their hard-soled shoes would click against the floor, causing them to be severely beaten for drawing attention to themselves.

He picked up a copy of Cosmo and flipped through its pages, marveling at the way the women presented themselves. He read a portion of an interview with one of the models where the discussion focused on her "defiant" style. He laughed as he placed the magazine back on the rack. The women he'd known back in his old country could teach the Cosmo models something about defiance: because their faces must be covered at all times, many of them had taken to painting their toenails, even though discovery of that would mean one of their toes would be cut off; others wore lipstick behind the cotton screens that must cover their faces, even though they could be disfigured if unmasked.

Two teenaged boys pushed roughly past him, one of them muttering, "Fuckin' towel-head!" and the other, "Outta the way, Mohammad!" as they went by. The man in the turban closed his eyes, took a deep breath, and reminded himself that today, of all days, he mustn't get angry or upset. It made no difference to them who was the oppressor and who was the escaping oppressed; they saw only the way he looked, the hue of his skin, his headdress. He looked like one of them, one of the killers, and he knew it. Knew it and hated it. I am Afghani, not Iraqi—you may not want to understand this, but there is a difference. And by the way—I hate flying. But this was not the day or time to try and point that out, especially to two young thugs who, he guessed, were just looking for an excuse to start trouble. He wondered how they would have reacted if he'd said to them, "How did you know my name was Mohammad?" Probably wouldn't have gone over well.

He opened his eyes and touched the breast pocket of his light jacket; the papers were still there. Good. He thought it was one hell of a thing, to be a citizen and yet feel the need to carry your citizenship papers with you in order to prove it. But today…today he had a feeling. Just a feeling. He turned and saw the security guard staring at him.

He remembered, briefly, the one time he'd been interrogated by a group of Taliban soldiers, how they'd made him lie flat on the floor while they hoisted up his bare feet with rope and then beat his soles with their clubs. He'd had to crawl home through the streets, and couldn't walk for two weeks after. Because he'd picked up a turnip and handed it back to the woman who'd dropped it.

There are no soldiers here, he reminded himself. You're safe. And they don't sell turnips here.

Not a great joke, but he smiled at it, nonetheless.

Shoppers swarmed idly by, bumping into one another, running into carts haphazardly abandoned in the middle of aisles...

"Electronics, Line Six, please; Electronics..."

Wendy watched the turban guy look at some magazines and then stand there smiling to himself. Guy looked like he wanted to perv on someone, all sweaty and quiet like that. And who the hell would want to wear any kind of a jacket on a day like this? Sure, it was a really light jacket the dude had on, but, still...

It made her nervous. Maybe he had, like, a gun or something hidden under there. Or a knife. Or something.

Man, wouldn't that be something, to have some political shit go down today, right here? Break up the monotony, that was for sure—and it'd give her something to tease Suze with tonight. You are gonna flip when you hear what happened!

Guy was probably a nobody, but, man, wouldn't it be cool...?

Still, the manager had said anyone suspicious, so she reached over to pick up her handset when Mitch tapped her on the shoulder.

"Saw him too, didn't you?" he asked.

"I know. Isn't he weird-looking?"

"Definitely not from around here. Were you getting ready to call Fearless Leader?" "Fearless Leader" was Mitch's nickname for Toby Armstrong, the manager of Carol's. No one liked Toby; he was here because his father was on the board and thought his law-school dropout son needed to find himself some direction in the world. Armstrong thought this store and everyone who worked in it—excepting himself, natch—was beneath him, and took any chance he got to remind them of it. Wendy thought it was cool that Mitch called Armstrong

"Fearless leader" to his face. In fact, she thought a lot of things about Mitch were cool. Sure, he was kinda old, fifty-two, but he looked good, really sexy in a rugged way. Suze had once said she wouldn't kick Mitch out of bed for eating crackers; Wendy supposed she wouldn't, either.

Wendy shrugged as she replaced the receiver. "Yeah, I was gonna say something, why?"

Mitch shrugged. "I don't know for sure. Seems to me the guy needs watching over more than watched."

"Huh?"

"Looking like he does, he has to know that he's gonna attract some trouble. You tell Fearless Leader about this and he'll want to get Dirty Harry and the boys in here, stir up some excitement so he can look good for the old man."

"Sounds like something Toby'd do."

Mitch seemed to consider this for a moment, sucking on his lower lip. Wendy wondered what it would be like if he made that sound while sucking on her lower lip.

"Wait a few minutes," Mitch finally said. "I'm gonna follow him and make sure no one hassles him."

"Okay, but if anything happens and Toby wants to know why I didn't—"

"—tell him I said not to. All he can do is call my supervisor and complain."

"Your funeral."

Mitch chuckled. "Not at his hands, it isn't." Then, with a wink, he headed toward the stairs as a woman with a cart full of clearance items threw a knotted pile of bras onto the conveyer. "These don't have tags," she said, and Wendy rolled her eyes as she began helping the woman sort them out. Too bad—she would've like to have watched Mitch walk away. For an older dude, he had a dynamite ass.

Once downstairs, Mohammad looked around at more of the Plenty. In front of him stood a long glass counter filled with things of special wonder. He looked up to see a very pleasant-faced young man talking into a telephone. The young man looked tired from a long day's work. Mohammad smiled at the young man as he looked up. The young man returned the smile, though it was a cold one from weariness.

"Thank you for calling, ma'am," said the young man into the telephone. "We'll hold that for you until tonight. Good-bye." He turned his attention to the customer in front of him now. "May I help you, sir?"

"Yes," replied Mohammad. "I have come to ask about, oh, what do you call them…?" Now he had to draw a blank? That's great—not only do you have to dress this way, now you have to sound like you don't have even a rudimentary grasp of the language. "Ah, yes— basketball goals? Bank-boards?" Dammit! He hated the way that word came out: baz-keet-ball. The evening English classes were a tremendous help, but he was still having trouble with his sibilants, and as a result sounded, to his ears, like a moron.

"Well, sir," said the young man, "we carry a variety of boards and goals. Was there any particular brand you were interested in?"

"I don't know brands very well. All I know is that I have two grandsons who are in dire need of a bank-board and I promised them the best one I could find." Thee bezt one.

"The best one, you say? Yeah, you'd want a good one, one that was worth the money." The young man's smile quickly became warm.

Mohammad returned the smile. "Yes, that would be nice—" his eyes drifted to the young man's name-tag, "—Greg. Fine."

Greg was busy watching a well-built blonde in shorts and a halter try to reach the top shelf for a cooler. "I'll help you, miss," he shouted, and pushed his way passed Mohammad, who watched as Greg graciously climbed up to get the cooler for the young lady. Afterwards, she smiled at Greg for a long time as they talked. Their eyes sparkled at each other's words and Greg found a pen and paper and wrote something down. A number of some sort.

As the young woman started up the stairs, Greg called to her: "Seven be all right?"

"That'll be great," she called over her shoulder, then giggled. Greg smiled to himself, released a held breath, then returned his attention to Mohammad. "If you'll come with me, sir, I'll show you what we have in stock."

He followed Greg down endless aisles of the Plenty, talking to his new host as they walked, unaware that his every move for the last few minutes had been carefully watched.

Mitch nearly jumped when he felt the hand on his shoulder. Turning, he saw Toby Armstrong standing next to him with one of those "I'm-here-to-make-your-life-miserable" expressions on his face.

"Mitchell," he said.

"Toby."

"Something going on I need to know about?"

Mitch glanced up and saw the security camera that was usually trained toward the jewelry counter was now directly on him. Little bastard had been watching all along.

"You know, Toby, there are two types of ways to ask a question. One of them is in that sincere way which tells you that the person asking really needs some help, and the other way tells you that the person asking the question already knows the answer and is just making you jump through hoops because they can. Now, I wonder which of these you just employed." Way to not antagonize anyone today, Mitch. Have to open that charm school real soon.

"I understand you're not feeling well today, Mitchell, but please, could we not be adversarial with one another?"

"Then how about you ask me a direct question instead of some namby-pamby word-loop designed to test whether or not I'll lie to you? You've been watching on the cameras, so you saw the guy as well as I did, so you know that I've been following him."

They stood on the landing, in a small open area that gave them a clear view of all the aisles down here. It was impossible to miss the guy in the turban from here.

"Do you think there's any reason for concern?" asked Armstrong.

"If you mean do I think he's going to activate some small nuclear device and take the fishing tackle department hostage, no; if, on the other hand, you mean do I think someone might take offense because of the way he looks and want to spread a little 'God Bless America' all over his face and unmentionable parts then, yeah, I think there might be reason for some concern."

"Have you seen anything that—"

"—a couple of punks earlier went out of their way to bump shoulders with him. I couldn't make out what they said to him, but they looked the type." He smiled at Armstrong. "You wouldn't know the type, though, would you, Toby?"

"I thought we agreed not to be—"

"I wasn't being. Sincerely. I'm just guessing that you never had to deal with guys like that."

"Bullies? You're standing very close to me, Mitch. On my best day, when I am overflowing with charm and good will toward my fellow man, you'd like to punch my lights out."

"True."

"And you have to ask me if I've ever had to deal with bullies?"

Mitchell almost laughed. Fearless Leader was displaying something akin to wit.

"Please keep a close eye on him, Mitchell."

"Don't worry, Fearless Leader."

"I really hate being called that, you know."

"I'm a bully. Calling things like that's in my job description."

"It doesn't do to alienate the management, Mitchell."

He looked directly at Armstrong. "Do you know what the difference is between an ass-kisser and a brown-noser?"

"No."

"Depth perception, Toby."

"Is that supposed to be funny?"

"Yes."

"Oh."

Mitch scanned the aisles again and saw the two punks from earlier over by the bow-and-arrow display. The guy with the turban was several aisles over and up from them. Okay, this was okay. So far.

"Do you mind if I ask you a personal question, Mitchell?"

"I guess we'll see, won't we?"

"Why do you dislike me?"

That almost caught Mitch by surprise. "It's not that I dislike you, Toby; it's just that I think you're a spoiled, petulant little toad who thinks that washing your hands at the end of a day's work is something to be ashamed of."

"Please don't sugar-coat it, by the way."

The punks were staying put. The guy in the turban was down there with Greg by the basketball crap. So long as everyone stayed where they were, things would be peachy.

"Mitchell?"

"Yeah?"

"Are you sure there's not going to be any trouble?"

"No, but you can trust me when I say that I'll put a fast stop to it if there is. And I don't dislike you, Toby. You just seem to me to be a very lonely guy who feels like he has to prove something to the whole fucking world so you can go home nights feeling like you're worth what your old man thinks you should be worth. And don't get pissed with me—you asked."

"That I did."

"I want to give them something nice, you see," said Mohammad to Greg. "They made it possible for me to come here, to your country, and live. My son, he worked hard to bring me over. I studied and I learned for my trip, because I wanted to be with them here for the rest of my life. Their home is here." He reached into his pocket and removed the papers, unfolding them. He didn't know why he was blabbering on like this, but he was suddenly very anxious. "My son flew us all to Washington so I could take the oath—here, see? I remember: 'I will perform work of national importance under civilian direction when required by the law; and that I take this obligation freely without any mental reservation or purpose of evasion; so help me God.'" He stopped for a moment to admire the certificate and show it to his host, but when he looked up Greg was at the end of the aisles talking to a well-dressed older gentleman. Mohammad let his eyes drop to his feet again, and he folded the photocopied copy of the certificate back up (he would never fold the actual certificate, no; that was already in a lovely frame hanging over his bed) and slipped it into his pocket. He was very proud to have it, maybe he didn't have to tell people. He'd just suddenly felt the need to tell someone that he was an American, just like them.

He reached up and wiped some perspiration from the back of his neck. He remembered the Taliban soldiers, how he'd felt their gazes on his back as they followed him after he'd picked up the turnip. There had been a small wave of tingling sensations, as if a hundred tiny needles had been shot into him at once, and then the sweat, so much heavier than it usually was…like now.

He wiped his neck as dry as he could, then pulled a handkerchief from his pocket and properly finished the job, drying his hands after.

Still, the feeling persisted.

Shoppers swarmed idly by, bumping one another, cussing and complaining…

"They're right here, sir," called Greg to his customer.

"They look very nice, all of these. Are they good ones?"

"You'll get what you pay for, I assure you sir." Greg smiled, but then his eyes moved toward something on one of the higher shelves.

A row of opened golf-ball boxes.

"Son-of-a— I'm sorry sir, I just hate it when people open up boxes and leave them. It hurts business. People don't want to buy used shit, they want everything new just for them. That's why they pay so much for what they want."

"You must pay for things you want," one of the soldiers had said to him as they drew back to strike at the soles of his feet, "and if you wish to demean yourself by stooping at a woman's feet—"

—no, no soldiers. Never again.

He squinted against the sweat in his eyes, unable to see what the young man was holding. "What are those?"

"These," said Greg, holding out a box of golf balls with a broken seal, "are useless, that's what they are, useless. No wonder the economy's so frigging screwed up. Damn people. And all of the suppliers have been giving us grief about filling orders because everything's still messed up from when the planes crashed into—" Greg looked at him and snapped closed his mouth. "I'm, I'm sorry, sir, I didn't mean anything by—sorry, I'll be right back. We're not allowed to just tape it up and put it back on the shelf, no; once it's been opened and left like this, we gotta report it, mark it on the inventory as 'slightly damaged,' get a manager to sign off on it, then we can tape it back up and sell it at half off in the discount bin. Isn't that terrible? All someone has to do is pop the seal, and a sixteen dollar box of golf balls is worth about seven bucks. It'd be better if they just stole the damn things—at least we have insurance to cover the loss, then." He abruptly turned and left.

Mohammad looked the already-opened box containing the backboard. The rest of the Plenty no longer interested or entranced him. This was the one he would buy, it didn't matter if the box were already open. All he had to do was make sure everything was still there.

He began to pull the massive backboard out of the box and examine it when he felt the needling sensation across the back of his neck again.

He was being watched. He could feel it.

"We need to step over here now," said Mitch, gently taking Armstrong's elbow and moving them toward the far side of the landing.

"Why—what the—?"

"He was about to spot me."

"Who?"

"The guy in the turban. He was about to look right at me. He knows he's being watched." They took their place beside one of the neo-Roman pillars whose like supported every ceiling on every floor in the building. The architect had been from the Richardsonian school of design, only the one who'd designed Carol's evidently couldn't decide whether he was aiming for classical or Hammer Horror Movie Gothic; still, they were concealed from the guy's gaze, and Mitch could still see the punks over by the bow-and-arrow display.

Armstrong pulled his arm from Mitch's grasp—no easy feat—then straightened his jacket and tie. "How the hell could you know he was about to spot you?"

"I just know, that's all."

"Maybe he was just looking around for something else to buy."

Mitch shook his head. "No. His body language was all wrong."

Armstrong laughed. "'Body language'? You sound like some B-movie detective."

Mitch put his hand on the holster of his .44. "Toby, have you ever wondered why it is, of the five security guards from our company who work here, I'm the only one who's permitted to carry a firearm in addition to the Taser and stun-gun?"

"I can't say I really gave it much thought, but now that you mention it…yes, why is that?"

"Because I'm the only one who's ever killed another man with a firearm."

Armstrong blanched. "You mean, in Vietnam?"

"Damn right I mean in Vietnam. You know what I did there, Toby? I was a sniper. I'd be out in the bush for weeks, sometimes months, at a time. That's how it worked—they sent you out, and you didn't come back in until you had your seven kills. Then you'd get some R&R at Vung Tau or someplace, get your head back in one piece, then they'd send you out again. You had to get seven confirmed kills, Toby. And when you spend that long being that still and watching for your target, you get to understand body language, my friend. You can tell when someone knows he's being watched—and our buddy in the headdress down there knows he's being watched."

It took Armstrong a few moments to find his voice. "How… how many times were you sent out?"

"Five. Five times out, five times back. Do the math. I'm the only guard who carries a firearm because I'm the only one who's ever looked another human being in the face and then shot them. I know when not to remove it from its holster, Toby. That's why I carry it and not one of your Grenada or Desert Storm post-graduates who want to be Bruce Willis when they grow up. Ever notice the way Rick touches that Taser of his every chance he gets? Mark my words, that idiot's going to pull that thing on someone someday and get us all in a lot of trouble."

"I had no idea," said Armstrong.

"Yeah, well, I don't tell too many people about it. It's not something they enjoying hearing about."

"Explains why you always seem so tense."

Mitch kept looking back and forth between the man in the turban and the Arrow Punks, as he now thought of them. "I know you're also wondering whether or not I'm hung-over, Toby, and I'll tell you the truth, I am a little—but I haven't been drinking. I had to go to the hospital last night because of my…you know, my ears and headaches."

"How did that happen, anyway?"

Mitch shook his head. "Are we—what? Bonding here, having a moment? It might explain this odd feeling in the pit of my stomach."

"No, we're not having a moment. You're just bullying a petulant little toad who thinks he has to prove something to the world."

"Oh."

The Arrow Punks, having grown bored with the display, now moved over to the skateboard aisle. Still over and down enough from the guy in the turban not to cross paths. Mitch moved forward a little, glancing over his shoulder. The guy in the turban was no longer turning in this direction.

"Mitch?"

"Yeah?"

"How did you get hurt in Vietnam?"

"Hey, roomie."

Wendy looked up to see Suze smiling at her, looking about as hung-over as a nun after Sunday mass.

"Well, don't we look all rested and happy?"

Suze shook her head. "Look, I know I was a real bitch this morning, guilting you into coming in and taking my shift. I wasn't feeling all that bad, to tell you the truth, but the thing is, well…Jim spent the night. I didn't want to leave him there, all alone, you know?"

Wendy nodded. "You needed a morning lay?"

"Exactly! And oh, God was it worth it!"

"Spare me."

Suze laughed and smacked Wendy's hand playfully. "Look, you, I feel bad about your being here instead of me, so after you get done in—what?—an hour, I'm taking you out to dinner and a movie and maybe some shopping."

"I think I've about had my fill of shopping today—shoppers, at least."

Suze looked around. "Anything interesting going on? Anyone try to crash a plane into the lingerie department?"

"No, there's—oh, wait. There's this weird-looking guy in a turban wandering the store. Mitch is following him around."

"Mr. Yummy is on duty today? Damn, and I missed him."

"'Mr. Yummy' has Fearless Leader gunning for him, I think. He and Toby don't like each other very much, I think."

"Toby just needs to eat crackers in the right bed. Then we'd all be better off."

"Have you ever met a man you didn't want to screw?"

Suze laughed. "Of course I have. Odds are I screwed him anyway, but I probably hated myself for it in the morning."

This was a joke. Suze was not easy, did not sleep around, but she and Wendy had seen and loved *American Beauty* and decided they needed to finesse their own Thora Birch/Mena Suvari routine. Suze felt it gave them a "mystique"; Wendy thought it made them look like a couple of closet lezzies but liked the way it made guys give her a second look: is she or isn't she? Maybe she just needs the right guy to help her decide.

"Mitch is following him around now. Wanna stick around and see if anything interesting happens?"

"Nah. I wanna go pick up a new pair of boots. I hear we're having a sale."

"That's very funny. You're working my shift Saturday, by the way."

"I figured as much. I'll leave you to your good labors, peasant."

Wendy checked through the next few customers, all the while marveling at Suze. Yeah, she could be a bit of a flake, but she was such fun. It didn't matter where they were or who they were with, Suze could break the ice with anyone. That's probably why she was so popular. She had a line or a story for any situation. Wendy didn't. Just once she wished something really interesting or exciting would happen to her so she'd have a great story to tell. Just one, that's all. She could milk a good story. It would be nice to walk into a room with Suze and have something in her own arsenal of wit. But what the hell ever happened around here to make a good story? "I watched Mitch's great ass all day," wasn't exactly, "It was the best of times, it was the worst of times."

Sighing, she smiled at the next customer and began scanning through their items.

It was very nice looking, the backboard, and seemed to have all its necessary parts for assembly. Mohammad thought it would look nice hanging in the back yard. His grandchildren would play and laugh and he would spend the remaining years of his life watching them grow and laugh and play, and he would take those moments with him when he left.

He allowed his thoughts to drift back to his wife, a fine woman. He longed to tell people of her, of her kindness and warmth, but he was afraid here in his new home. People were very busy here, they hadn't the time to listen, not right now. (Busy people would call the soldiers if you were bothering them.) Maybe later. (No soldiers.) Maybe. (Not here.) Maybe later he could arrange for his son to have his mother's body brought here and buried near her family, not across an ocean so vast and forbidding leading to a shore where the soldiers patrolled in their tanks and armored cars. Maybe then she would feel a part of it all, also.

He glanced down the aisles to find them empty, excepting, of course, for the Plenty. There would always be the Plenty for those who didn't care if it was always there. He slid the backboard back into its box and carried it back to the counter. Greg was no longer there, but there was a pretty young lady who was talking into the phone.

"May I help you, sir?"

It was her eyes. They were so cold, so distant.

"'I cannot find the young man who was helping me. I want to buy this, it is a gift for my son and his children, my grandchildren, you see…his mother is gone now and we are all we have, and I am a an American and I wanted to…to thank them somehow…"

He could not have felt any more nervous had the soldiers been coming for him.

"You can pay upstairs," the young lady said to him, her eyes fixed on a handsome young man looking at the fishing gear. She left Mohammad standing there with his gift, his solace, his sleeping stories of another place, across a vast and indifferent aisle.

Shoppers swarmed by, cussing and complaining, the check-out girls droning the required pleasantries to the customers in their all-too-long lines, "Thank you for shopping at Carol's..."

Mohammad gathered up the bulky box and began making his way upstairs to the checkout lines.

Mitch watched as the guy in the turban pulled the backboard out of the already-open box and examined it, then sifted around inside to make sure everything else was there.

"It happened at a TOC—"

"TOC?" asked Armstrong.

"Tactical Operations Center. That's where the chopper dumped me after I hitched a ride from Two Corps in Pleiku. Pissed me off—I managed to survive three different ambushes, and still they keep sending me out because a sniper's got to have seven kills per mission, right? So this last time, I've been in the bush for something like eight weeks, and I got my seven kills, got 'em clean, and I was due for R&R. I thought that's where the chopper was taking me, but instead the fucker dumps at this little piss-hole communications outpost. Nobody there bothers to explain a damn thing to me, just tell me that I have to go back out again and there's no way, you hear? But the lieutenant there, he's one of them by-the-book kiss-asses—you remind of him sometimes, and I say that with nothing but love in my heart— and this little twerp threatens me with a court-martial if I don't go back out, so—

"The chopper dumps me at this TOC center near Truong Son. Nothing much there, a few abandoned Montagnard villages, no companies or divisions, no roads, just jungle and NVA. Even support from 175-millimeter guns at Firebase

Mary Lou ten miles away couldn't save their asses if the NVA decided to attack in full force—and you bet your ass that's just what they did—screw the threat of B-52 arclight strikes that usually kept the gooks hunkered down in Laos—these guys were gonna take out the center no matter what. They hit 'em not three minutes after I was on the ground. So I'm out in the jungle, up in a tree, and I see the whole thing. Jesus, they killed everyone. I mean, I managed to pick off a few without giving away my position, but there was just too many of 'em. I bet I sat up in that tree for a good thirty-six hours before coming down, and by then there's been so much air and ground fire all around me I can't even hear myself breathe. Turns out I caught a sliver of shrapnel in my left ear, but it'd be another three weeks before I saw a doctor to find that out, and by then the damage was done."

"Jesus, Mitch."

"Hang on a second." The guy in the turban had put everything back in the box and was lumbering through the aisle toward the Sporting Goods desk. Cyndi was there, which meant the guy would get no help at all—Cyndi was always on the phone with some personal crisis that couldn't wait. Mitch wondered if he should offer to go down there and help.

Then he saw the Arrow Punks walking toward the desk, as well. One of them was carrying a baseball bat, the other a skateboard.

"Mayday, mayday…"

"What?" said Armstrong.

"Might have a problem here, Toby."

He started down toward the man in the turban when Suze stepped down in front of him.

"Hey, Mitch, Mr. Armstrong."

"Suze," said Armstrong. "Glad to see you're feeling better."

"I am, and I'm sorry about today but I'm going to cover for Wendy on Saturday—"

"—excuse me, Suze," said Mitch, trying to get past, but she put a hand on is arm and dug in.

"Hey, Mitch, listen, I know it's maybe none of my business, but I think—" She looked at Armstrong, then leaned closer. "—I think Wendy's got a thing for you."

Mitch blinked and looked away from the man in the turban. "You what?"

"I think—"

"I heard what you said, Suze! Do I have to remind you that I've got at least twenty years on both of you?"

Suze shrugged. "Maybe she's got a Daddy complex, who knows?"

"Oh, that makes me feel better, thanks."

He turned and saw the man in the turban lumbering up the stairs with his box, the Arrow Punks in tow. He moved aside so the man could pass, then deliberately set himself between the steps and the punks who, seeing this, wandered to another aisle.

"I have to go upstairs, Suze."

"Look, she's my friend, okay, and she doesn't go out with anyone, and I know she thinks you're cute…"

Mitch rolled his eyes at Armstrong, whose face didn't crack in half when he smiled. The three of them went up to the main floor, following the man in the turban toward the checkouts.

None of them saw the Arrow Punks come up behind them a few seconds later and split up, each one taking an aisle off to the side so Mitch wouldn't spot them.

Wendy saw Mitch and Armstrong coming up front, only now Suze was with them and had her hand slipped through Mitch's arm.

You bitch, thought Wendy. You know I like him, so, what? You have to go and put the moves on him because your Thora

Birch can't get the guy while you're around? Isn't that taking this *American Beauty* thing a bit too far?

The music on the radio faded out, and, as scheduled, the President came on to address the nation. We must remember. We must not forgive our enemies. The heroes who gave up their lives, the heroes who served when needed.

His words may not have been the most well-chosen, but the sentiment behind them, for the most part, spoke to Wendy: These people did not deserve to die, and those who took their lives do not deserve to go unpunished.

The television sets in the electronics department displayed the broadcast address, complete with film footage of the attacks interspersed with the president's comments.

Everyone in the store, in their own way, took some form of notice.

And like Wendy, found themselves looking at the man in the turban.

Still, she couldn't get over Suze. Trying to make time with Mitch—like she even had a chance.

Except she does have a chance, Wendy told herself. More than you ever will, and you know it. The Suzes of this world always have a chance, because they're interesting. Things happen to them. They always have the right story for the right occasion.

Just once she'd like to have a story to tell. Just once.

The man in the turban continued making his way toward her checkout lane, clunking along with that big, clumsy box...

"Mitch, I'm telling you, the age thing won't be a problem with her."

"Could we talk about this later, please?" He removed her hand none too gently from his arm. "I want to make sure nothing happens up here."

Suze gave the man in the turban a perfunctory glance. "What—him? Looks harmless."

"Just—look, Suze, my break's in fifteen minutes, talk to me then."

"But—"

"You heard the man," said Armstrong, stopping her from following Mitch, then trailing after him himself.

"Hey, Mitch?"

"Yes?"

"I, uh…I'm not very good with people—"

"I'll alert the media."

"—but I was wondering…"

Mitch stopped, sighed, checked the guy in the turban once more, and turned toward Armstrong. "You were wondering…?"

"If you maybe wanted to, I don't know, get a drink or some food or something after work one night. Don't look at me like that, I'm not asking you for a date, you're not my type."

"But you are gay?"

"Yes. Not that I advertise or anything."

"I'm not."

"I'll alert the media. Look, I just…I'd like to be your friend. I'd like to have you for a friend. If you think you can stomach being around a petulant toad."

"Stranger things have happened. But no dancing. Beer and pizza, but no dancing."

"You're an evil man."

"I get a lot of complaints about that, Toby. Excuse me a second, okay?" Not waiting for a reply, Mitch made his way up toward Checkout #2, where the guy in the turban was getting into line—

—and where the Arrow Punks were sauntering in behind him.

Shit.

"Hey, Mohammad, how they hanging?"

"Would you believe me if I told you that 'Mohammad' is actually my name?

The kid's face went blank. "You're shitting me?"

Mohammad shook his head. "And I am no towel-head, either. That would require a camel to be completely racist."

The second kid—the one who'd said it in the first place—blushed slightly. "Sorry, dude. He bet me five bucks I wouldn't have the nerve to say it to you."

"Nothing personal, man," said the second kid.

"Well, actually, it is, but you did not know it."

"Where you from, anyway?"

"Peshawar. It's a city in Pakistan."

"Dude! Pakistan. Wow."

Overhead, the President's voice spoke of sacrifice and readiness.

"We ain't no racists," said the first kid. "We're just assholes."

"Amen to that," replied the second one.

Mohammad moved forward and found himself facing the checkout girl, who seemed to him to be on the verge of tears. What could be bothering her? Didn't she know how marvelous it was to live in a place like this? To work among the aisles of Plenty.

"Miss, is there—?"

"Thank you for shopping at Carol's, sir, Cedar Hill's oldest and best department store."

The item had been scanned through and the money exchanged so quickly that Mohammad felt slightly stunned.

Smiling at her, he made a mock salute to the two young men behind him in line, and began dragging his package toward the door.

This would make something happen, Wendy was sure of it. This would give her a story to tell— "He went through my line, yeah. I talked to him and everything."

Everybody in the store was listening to the President's address and looking at the perv in the turban—probably buying the backboard to set up in his yard and lure little boys with a game of basketball, isn't that how they do stuff like that?—so if anything happened around him, people would flip out. The President and the Governor and everyone else had been saying we should expect something to happen today, on the Anniversary, so why not? She and Mitch could talk about it later, not Suze and Mitch, huh-uh. They could go out for drinks or something and talk about What Happened.

And something was about to happen. Wendy knew this for a fact, because though she'd scanned the bar-code on the side of the box, she had not deactivated the plastic security tag on the top. As soon as he stepped between the security gates, the alarm would go off. And with everyone looking at him, and him looking that way, and everyone watching him, and what the president was saying…

It was going to be cool.

And it was going to be her story, no one else's.

By the following evening, the video tape from the wall-mounted security camera near Checkout #2 had played on all three Columbus television stations at noon, five-thirty, and eleven p.m. The running times varied as the tape was edited for each successive broadcast, but one common thread united them: the final image.

The scene unfolded like this:

A man in a turban who is dragging a large box toward the doors stops when he gets between the security gates. His head snaps up, his eyes wide with panic as he looks around at the sound of the loud alarm. He tries to move through the doors but the box has gotten wedged between the gates. He tugs at it, growing more and more agitated (witnesses described him as "panicked" or "terrified"; one store employees said she thought she heard him say something about "the soldiers," but she couldn't be certain).

The more he struggles with the package, the tighter-wedged it becomes. A security guard near the door walks toward the man in the turban, one hand held in front of him as if to stop the man from moving, the other hand on the Taser attached to his belt. The man in the turban begins to flail his arms, shouting something ("No soldiers, no soldiers, never again!" according to the guard). A young man with a skateboard who was in line behind the man in the turban moves into frame. He's trying to tell the guard something but the guard pushes him back. Skateboard becomes visibly agitated, pointing upward, obviously shouting about the noise of the alarms. The man in the turban is crying and shuddering as he flails and kicks at the box. The security guard pushes Skateboard back once again, and removes his Taser from his belt.

As soon as he does this another security guard—this one with a holstered firearm attached to his belt—jumps up onto one of the register conveyers and runs quickly down its length in a crouch, then jumps down on the floor, landing next to Skateboard. This guard is shouting something at the other guard ("Put that damn thing away before you hurt someone!" witnesses later confirmed). But the other guard isn't listening; he's now making a grab for the turban-man's arm. The man in the turban swats at the guard and continues looking around in panic (the alarms had not been silenced yet).

By now Skateboard has been joined by another young man from the line, this one carrying baseball bat. Baseball, too, begins shouting at the guards about the man in the turban ("They were trying to help," said one woman; "The poor guy was so scared he was going crazy."). Other customers in the store have begun clustering near the scene; many of them are shouting at the man in the turban or at the guards or pushing at either Skateboard or Baseball.

Then from somewhere in the crowd a bottle of perfume is thrown at the man in the turban. It hits the security gate and shatters, sending a shard of glass into his face. He screams and clutches near his eye. Blood dribbles out from between his fingers.

The guard with the Taser takes aim at the man's arm but Skateboard lurches forward, swings his namesake, and knocks the Taser from the guard's grip. The other security guard makes a grab for Skateboard but Baseball swings down at his shin with his namesake and connects solidly, sending the armed guard to his knees. The man in the turban is now beating on the top of the box, screaming in hysteria. Skateboard grabs one side of the box and tries to shove it the rest of the way through the security gates but the first guard jumps up onto his back and pushes him to the floor. The second guard rises unsteadily to his feet, unholstering his firearm ("I really think he only meant to fire a shot in the air," said another witness). He gets the gun out, raises it over his head, and then someone in the growing crowd throws the discarded skateboard at the man in the turban; they miss, hitting instead the armed guard, who spins sideways as the gun accidentally discharges.

That's when the cashier goes down, her shoulder bloodied and blown.

Several member of the crowd move in now, and within seconds the scene becomes so violent and chaotic it's impossible to keep track of any individual.

The broadcasts end by saying that of the nine people injured in the riot, only the cashier remains hospitalized, but is expected to be released soon as her injuries were not life-threatening. Charges against the two teenagers involved are still pending.

And then comes the final image: a grainy but clear-enough blowup of the turban man's face, eyes wide, expression frozen in stark horror as tears and blood streak his face.

If you see this man, please contact Cedar Hill police immediately. Though he is not considered armed, he is badly injured and so could be dangerous.

Shuddering, weeping, face on fire, stomach roiling with sick fear, you stumble through the alleys and down the badly-lighted back streets, searching for a way home, a way back to your son and your grandchildren for whom you have failed to keep your promise. And you were there, amidst the aisles of Plenty, and you had it for them, you did, but then the soldiers came again, as they always have and always will, even here, where even the Plenty is not enough to hide you, and this is a lesson you must pass on to your son and grandchildren because they need to know, and because you love them, and because you want to stay here in your new country, but first, please, God, first please let the way home be made clear, for the soldiers are out there, and they know your name, and they have seen your face, and they are looking for you …

THE OBSCENITY OF GLOVES

WITH THE INDEX FINGER of his right hand he traced the ball of his left thumb—what the palmists called the Mount of Venus. The first phalange symbolized will-power, the second, logic. He touched the Mount of Jupiter at the base of his index finger. That symbolized…what? Ah, he had it—arrogance, haughtiness, and pride. No wonder it was his strongest phalange. Then it was on to the Mount of Saturn, the *digitus infamis* of the Romans; fate and destiny, that one. The Mount of Apollo at the base of the third finger stood for music and art and was easily the weakest of his hand's characteristics; at least that was made up for with his Mount of Mercury, another strong one, symbolizing learning—so maybe there was some untapped potential there. *Have to take up the piano right away*, he thought.

He continued tracing patterns across the Mount of the Moon and the Mount of Mars, both of which were at the heel of the hand and symbolized violence and lightheartedness, respectively; both were equally strong. He wondered if he should worry about that. The line of the heel joined the line of life and ran parallel to the line of the heart. The line of fate—yes, that was right, wasn't it? Yes. The line of fate ran up the center of the palm, and parallel to that on the heel side of the hand was the line of fortune. They didn't intersect very well for him; fortune crossed over into violence and fate met with lightheartedness. And this meant what? That his destiny was to become a rich middleweight boxer who could tell a good joke and play a mean *Moonlight Sonata*? How fickle was the universe. He laughed softly to himself and moved his fingertip along the curved line that ran from below his little finger to the base of the first—the Girdle of Venus. In his case it'd be more of a truss but why get picky this late in life?

He looked up at the bartender and gestured for a refill, then said, "Did I ever tell you that my mom used to work summers at the state fair mitt camp?"

"The what?"

"Mitt camp. Carny talk. She was a palm reader, a fortune teller. Made decent money and never once cheated a soul. She had the most exquisite hands. Long, delicate fingers, smooth fingertips, and her skin, especially on her palms, was so thin and soft it felt like tissue paper. Don't go writing anything either overtly or covertly Freudian into this, but she used to tell me that a person's hands were the sexiest part of their body. And she was right." He leaned in, lowering the volume of his voice. "I know it sounds weird, like maybe there was some kind of Endymion/Luna thing going on, but her fascination with hands, with their power and their complexity, their dexterity and grace, gave me a...a *mystery*, I'd guess you'd call it, to carry with me for the rest of my life. A person needs one unsolvable mystery to carry with them to keep life interesting, don't you think? Consider the hand. It can touch, it can grasp, it can add dimension, it can kill with tenderness, it can save or end a life, and it's usually the first thing that comes into direct physical contact with another human being. I'm sorry, it's just that I—and please don't laugh at this or—"

"I won't laugh," said the bartender. "I promise."

"It's just that...I love the hand. Even the *idea* of the hand excites me. Look at it. The miracle of the whole thing. Your whole life is mapped out in the lines and curves and ridges and whorls, all the answers are *right there* but you'll never have the time to find all of them. So many sensations enter the body through the hands—a baby grasping your finger, that crackle of electricity when you first touch someone you hope will be important in your life, cupping them together to splash cold

water over your face when you come inside on a hot day…"
He shook his head, tossed some bills onto the bar, put on his coat, and started toward the door.

"Hey, buddy," called the bartender, picking up something from next to the man's half-empty glass. "You forgot your gloves."

"Keep 'em."

"You gotta be kidding? These things look expensive!"

"Call them a gift for your good service."

"*Was* quite a wake, wasn't it?"

"Yeah. She'd've like it a lot."

"C'mon, friend, you need these. Christ, it's twelve degrees outside."

"Keep 'em." The man looked out the window at the snow coming down. Post-Thanksgiving Christmas shoppers scurried to and fro, their breath misting into the evening air. "I hate winter. People wear gloves in winter. Gloves are an obscenity."

He pushed on the glass of the door and walked out into the chill winter night, leaving a perfect print of his left hand as a souvenir.

NEED

"One can go for years sometimes without living at all,
and then all life comes crowding into one single hour."

–Oscar Wilde, *Vera, or The Nihilists*

THE LETTER, written on official department stationary,
tumbles across the autumn sidewalk, skimming the
surface of a puddle (soaking only the middle of the page,
smearing certain portions of certain words) before the wind
propels it against the base of a lamp post where it flutters,
trapped, neither the wind nor the puddle nor the letter aware
of their part if this brief mosaic nature is forming to amuse
itself. A nearby rat, searching for nest material, sits up on its
hind legs and regards the paper, then slowly moves toward it.
The rat doesn't care about the needs of wind or paper; it is not
aware of its own determined part in this mosaic; it only cares
about its own need, for which this sheet of paper will do very
nicely...

"I've got a special dessert for you guys tonight."

The two children look at each other and smile. It's been a
long time since they've had a meal this good—hot beef tacos
and now Mom says she's got a "special" dessert.

When the children don't say anything, their mother shakes
her head and laughs. Now the children are very excited—
Mom hasn't laughed in a long, long time.

"Well," she says to her son and daughter. "Aren't you even
going to ask?"

"What're we having?" says the little girl.

Mom leans back in her chair and folds her arms across her chest, then looks at the ceiling. "Oh, Jeez, I don't know if I'm going to tell you or not, seeing as how you weren't interested enough to ask me in the first place."

The children give out with groans of disappointment and frustration—groans they both know Mom is expecting—and their mom laughs again.

"Okay," she says, leaning forward and gesturing for them to lean closer.

Mom whispers—like it's some kind of a big secret— "Chocolate mousse."

"*Chocolate mousse!*" they both shriek, delighted. This is their absolute, hands-down, no-question-about-it favorite dessert in the whole wide world.

"But only," adds Mom, "if you guys have another taco."

The children tell her how much they love her, grab up another tortilla, and spoon them full of the sliced beef for the tacos.

…now Charlie's going on and on about how no decent woman would whore herself out like that because that's what it amounted to and how that spineless scumbag was more concerned about his parents' money than he was about being a man and owning up to responsibilities so as far as he's concerned you don't talk about it with him, not ever, and Henrietta nods her head and smiles at him but not too widely, too wide a smile and he might think she's humoring him (which she is but mustn't let him know it) and get even angrier, and Charlie, you never have to do or say much to get him started on one of his rants, like today, all it took was Henrietta's letting slip with a mention of "the whore's" name (Charlie only calls her that, "the whore") and off he went, asking how could she still *talk* to that whore every week, and he was still going on, so Henrietta nods again and waits for him to storm over to the other side of the room (Charlie likes to cover a lot of ground while he's ranting), and when he does, when he heads toward the other side of the living room, Henrietta sits forward to look like she's really paying attention, like she's really interested, and as she does she slips one of her hands down into the space between the sofa cushions because just maybe Charlie or her lost some change down there, and it won't kill her, walking to the Bridge Club meetings instead of taking the bus for a week, she could use the exercise and at least the weather's been nice and as Charlie turns to make his way back her fingertips brush across the surface of something that might be a couple of quarters, so she continues smiling (but not too widely) and nodding her head because as long as Charlie makes eye contact he won't be paying any attention to her hand...

Inter-Office Memo
From: Paul Gallagher, Principal

Darlene:

I know you meant well, I really do, but several of the other teachers have expressed concern to me over your actions during 2nd Grade Class pictures last Tuesday. You did not have permission to take that girl off school grounds, let alone to the mall. We have a lot of children from poor and disadvantaged homes in this school, and anything that even remotely smacks of favoritism is frowned upon, not only by myself and the other teachers, but the School Board as well. Your actions—caring though they might have been—can be looked upon as "playing favorites". It is not our responsibility to make sure the poorer students have decent clothes to wear for their class pictures, and it is certainly not your responsibility to buy them (though I've seen the pictures, and the little girl looks like an angel).

In the future, please keep your more dramatic humanitarian impulses in check. You're new here, and I'm sure you'll learn how things are done in due time.

Albert Morse sits on the front porch of his house on Euclid Avenue. He's enjoying the warm weather and thinking that he needs to trim the hedges this weekend. Just because the house isn't in the best neighborhood is no excuse to let it all go to hell. The house is paid for, and Albert takes a lot of pride in that. He and Georgia have made themselves a nice home here, one that the kids and the grandchildren love visiting. At the end of the day, what more could a man ask for? Work your whole life away on the factory line, retire with a good pension and good insurance, own your own home, have the family over for dinner and holidays.

Why the city decided to build those goddamned government-subsidized apartments across the street was a mystery to him, and an even bigger pain in the ass some days. Not a day goes by when someone who lives on Welfare Row doesn't drag their business into the street.

Like now, for instance; that young girl at the row of mailboxes, screaming "*Fuck!*" over and over again because of something she just read in a letter. Can't take your drama inside, no; you've got to play it out here in front of God and everybody like your problems are so much bigger and more important and painful than everybody else's.

Albert watches as the young woman continues screaming "*Fuck!*" over and over, louder and louder, until finally she breaks down into violent, wracking sobs. She wipes her arms across her eyes, shakes some hair from her face, reads the letter again, and then just tosses it away before starting in with the

"*Fuck!*" and the sobbing again, right there in the middle of the damn sidewalk. She continues screaming and sobbing until a school bus stops at the corner; as soon as she sees this, she turns around, pulls some tissues from her pocket, wipes her face and nose, and turns around, puffy-eyed and smiling as a little boy and girl run from the bus to her side. She kneels down and hugs them, then holds their hands as they make their way back inside, behind closed doors, where any decent human being ought to damned well keep their troubles.

Georgia comes out and hands Albert a glass of fresh iced tea. "Just got off the phone with Cal. He and Rhonda are bringing the kids over for dinner Friday night. Cal says he wants to take us all out to see the new Disney movie."

"That sounds like fun," says Albert, taking the iced tea but staring at the letter the young woman had tossed away.

"What was all that racket a minute ago?" asks Georgia.

"Some gal over there," replies Albert, nodding toward Welfare Row. "I swear, honey, some of *trash* they allow to live there…"

"Don't get yourself worked up," says Georgia. "You don't need to go and get all upset about the way they act."

Albert shakes his head. "It just…it just makes this seem like such a rotten place to live, and it isn't, you know? Or it *shouldn't* be." He discovers that he can no longer see the letter; the wind must have blown it somewhere. "I swear, the *trash*…"

"I tried so *very hard*," says the drunk as he's escorted from the bar by Sheriff Ted Jackson, who's been through this routine enough to know that this particular drunk doesn't require handcuffs.

"I *tried*, I really did," says the drunk.

"I know you did," replies the sheriff, as he always does. He looks over his shoulder and sees Jack Walters, owner and proprietor of the Wagon Wheel Bar & Grille, standing in the doorway, shaking his head in pity. Jackson nods to him that everything is all right, just business as usual, and Walters gives the sheriff a mock salute before turning around and going back inside.

The drunk stumbles, almost falling, but catches himself on the trunk of Jackson's car. "It wasn't my fault. It wasn't." He reaches out and grabs Jackson's collar. "You know that, right, Sheriff? You know that it wasn't my fault."

Jackson removes the drunk's hand from his collar, and gently guides him into the back seat. "You need to sleep it off, Randall. We've got your usual bed ready, and in the morning, we'll get you fixed up with a nice, hot breakfast, okay?"

"Nobody calls me that," says the drunk. "I mean, she used to, once…like it was a pet name, you know? But nobody calls me 'Randall.' I always hated that name. I should have said something once I was goddamn old enough. Fuckin' sissy-assed name like that." He curls up into a fetal position on the back seat and begins sobbing. "I should've said something about that. I…I should've done a lot of things, you know? If I'd've stood up to my folks, then maybe…" He leans over the seat and vomits into the plastic bucket Jackson had put there earlier, in anticipation of the usual pattern. Once he finishes vomiting, he wipes his mouth, sits up, and hands the bucket to Jackson, who empties it in the gutter.

"I'm gonna quite wasting my time and get on with my life," says the drunk.

"I know you are," replies Jackson, as he always does, as he always has every few weeks for the last couple of years after Walters calls to say, "Same old song and dance, my friend."

Jackson closes the door, stuffs the bucket into a plastic trash bag, then, as always, tosses it into the trunk of the cruiser, thinking as he does that all the money in the world—and God knows that the drunk's got enough money, having inherited it from his parents—can't do a damn thing to make the nights less lonely.

From the back seat the drunk's sobbing grows louder and more violent; the spasms wracking his body shake the entire cruiser, and Jackson cannot help but feel a morbid kind of awe. While there is the usual excess of self-pity in this puking, slobbering booze hound, there's also a depth of genuine anguish that Jackson cannot ignore—which is, he supposes, why people put up with this sort of behavior from the drunk.

There is some grief you never recover from.

to inf-rm you that, up-n revie-, the Cedar Hill Dep–tment of –ealth and H-man

Having completed the required six weeks of training, this Wednesday is Daniel's first night working the Cedar Hill Crisis Center phone lines without backup. It is a little before eight p.m. when his phone rings for the first time. Taking a deep breath, he answers, and after identifying himself and telling the caller whom they have reached, listens as the voice on the other end says: "How can you go on living when all there is to look forward to is more yearning?"

The caller hangs up before Daniel can say anything.

He notes the time in his log, and in parentheses adds: *probable crank call.*

Still, the question finds him again, as it will continue to do over the course of the otherwise uneventful evening, as well as a few mornings later when he happens upon the article and photos on Page Two of *The Ally*; it comes back to him again and again as it will for the rest of his life, never leaving him, never losing him, no matter how much he tries to hide from it.

Detective Bill Emerson stares at the stack of mail on his desk, none of which is addressed to either him or anyone else at the Cedar Hill Police Department. There's the usual monthly detritus you expect to find in the mail—phone bill, gas bill, electric bill—only all of these envelopes are emblazoned with the words **Final Notice** stamped in bright red ink.

Emerson cracks his knuckles, then runs a hand through his thick gray hair, noting that he needs to get a trim. Between his bushy hair and equally bushy moustache, it's no wonder some of the other officers call him "Captain Kangaroo" when they think he can't hear them.

He rifles through the mail once again, tossing the bills to the left, the junk mail to the right, and everything else in the center. He's been doing this off and on for the last two days, his variation on walking a labyrinth for the purpose of meditating on a problem, and, as always, he comes back to the business-sized brown envelope that weighs more than all the rest and has way too much postage on it.

They should have used Priority, he thinks. *Four bucks and it's there in three to four days.*

He checks the postmark date against the report. Five days. Even with all the extra postage, it had taken this letter five days to reach its addressee. If they had used Priority, it would have only taken three to four, and that might have made all the difference in the world.

He drops the letter on top of the center stack, unconsciously wincing at the muffled *thump!* it makes when it lands, and stares at it.

He's still staring a few minutes later when his partner, Ben Littlejohn, comes in with dinner in the form of four cheeseburgers and two orders of fries from the Sparta. It smells great—The Sparta makes the best cheeseburgers in the free world, period—and Emerson looks up as Littlejohn sets the food on the corner of the desk.

"Still haven't opened it?" he asks Emerson.

"And your first clue was…?"

Littlejohn wags a single finger back and forth. "Ah-ah, save the snappy banter for the rookies, not me." Littlejohn looks at his partner for a long moment, then says, his voice softer: "You want me to do it?"

"No. I was first on the scene, I found it. It should be me."

Littlejohn parks his ass on the edge of Emerson's desk and starts removing the cheeseburgers from the bag. "So…*when* are you and Eunice going to take that vacation she's bugging you about?"

"To London? Don't start, I'm warning you. She has talked about nothing *but* going there since she saw that damn *Notting Hill* movie. I rue the day Julia Roberts and Hugh Grant were born, because it set into motion the events that would lead to the making of that movie. My life has been endless misery since. Did you know they serve their beer room temperature there? Can you imagine that? No wonder we broke from the Crown."

"Uh-huh. Open the goddamn thing already, will you?"

Emerson picks up the brown envelope, noting again its weight, then looks at his partner. "You're a radiantly compassionate fellow, you know that?"

"I'm an intensely *hungry* fellow who's not going to be able to enjoy his dinner until whatever's in that envelope is out of our lives, and since that isn't going to be anytime soon—seeing as how you've put off opening it for almost two full work days—I'll settle for our knowing its contents."

"You should have seen it," whispers Emerson.

Littlejohn leans forward, rapping his knuckles on the desk to break Emerson's morbid reverie. "I *did* see it, Bill. I was only two minutes behind you."

"I know that, I'm not completely dim." He taps the envelope against his hand in a soft, steady tattoo that after only a few seconds annoys even him, but he doesn't stop. "Have you ever heard of something called 'The Observer Effect'?"

"That's a physics term, right?"

Emerson nods his head. "If I understand it correctly—Einsteinian whiz-kid that I am—it says that a person can change an event just by being there to watch it. They don't have to take any kind of physical action or what we think of as active participation, just *being there* changes it."

Littlejohn's expression grows concerned, albeit cautiously. "Okay...?"

"It was *different* after you came in. When it was just me, there was a...I don't know...almost a *peacefulness* there for a few seconds. But then you came in, and I saw your face and you saw mine and when we looked at it again, it was just... ugly and pathetic and sad." Emerson feels that last word fall from his mouth and land at his feet like a dead bird dropping from the sky.

"Bill," says Littlejohn, "I'm asking you now as your friend, not your partner, okay? I'm asking you to please, for everyone's sake, open it."

Not taking his stare from the cheeseburger bag, Emerson picks up the letter opener, slips it under the flap of the envelope (Scotch-taped, three times), slashes open the top, and removes the two sheets of paper inside.

The first sheet is blank, a twenty-pound standard weight of recycled typing paper that has been used to make sure someone couldn't hold the envelope up to the light and discern its contents.

You used a brown *envelope; no one could have seen through this, anyway.*

Unfolding the second sheet, he watches as the bills tumble down on the desk: two twenties, a ten, a five, and three ones. He reaches down with his other hand and arranges the bills side by side.

He looks at the letter, reads what it says—words written in a slow, unsteady hand (*probably arthritis*, he thinks; *a lot of older folks have trouble with that and can't write as neatly or steadily as they used to*)—but it's not the words that cause his throat to tighten, though they are bad enough, no; it's the two quarters, three dimes, one nickel, and four pennies that are taped across the bottom of the page (three pieces of Scotch tape, just like the envelope).

He blinks, pulls in a breath that is heavier and thicker than it ought to be, and hands the sheet to his partner.

"Fifty-eight dollars and eighty-nine cents," he says. "Who the hell sends someone fifty-eight dollars and eighty-nine cents? *Eighty-nine cents?* Why not just make it sixty dollars even?"

Before Littlejohn has a chance to finish reading the letter or respond to the question, Emerson speaks again:

"I'll *tell* you who sends someone fifty-eight dollars and eighty-nine cents, someone who only *has* fifty-eight dollars and eighty-nine cents. Someone who has to go through their purse or wallet, and then the pockets of their coat—hell, they probably even pulled the cushions off the sofa to see if any loose change had fallen down there, just to make sure they could send every *penny* they possibly could. *Anybody* could send you sixty bucks, but only...only someone who *cared* enough to scrape together all the money they possibly could would send you fifty-eight dollars and eighty-nine cents."

He realizes that he is almost on the verge of tears but doesn't care. "*Eighty-nine cents!* I'll bet that old woman had to walk to the store instead of taking the bus to make sure she could get that eighty-nine cents in there. Jesus H. Christ, Ben—*why* didn't she use Priority? That might have made all the difference in the world!" Emerson presses the heels of his hands against his eyes, takes a deep breath, then releases it slowly before wiping his eyes and lowering his hands, which aren't shaking nearly as much as he feared they would be.

"That was very moving," says Littlejohn. "Look at me—I am visibly touched."

"I'm turning into an old woman, aren't I?"

"No, you're just maybe possibly arguably a little too you-should-pardon-the-expression human for this job sometimes."

"And my cheeseburgers are probably cold."

Littlejohn shook his head. "Nope. I had them wrap everything in heavy-duty aluminum foil, just in case we didn't get to the food right away."

"I really *am* predictable, aren't I?"

"Let's call it 'dependable' and remain friends, shall we?"

"You're too good to me."

"I get a lot of complaints about that."

Emerson unwraps the first cheeseburger, starts to bite into it, then pauses and says, "Why didn't she use Priority?"

It is a question that will find him again and again throughout the rest of his life, never losing him, even when he tries hiding from it.

Edna Warner stands in line at the grocery store and thinks to herself, *The damn meat's gonna start thawing if she takes any longer.*

The young woman in front of her is riffling through a small stack of food stamps. The cashier exchanges a quick, exasperated glance with Edna, one that says, *I'm really sorry, ma'am, but there's nothing I can do*. Edna smiles in understanding, though it's a forced smile. Why did it seem she *always* picked the slowest line in the store? Just her luck, getting stuck behind a welfare case who doesn't have the sense to have her food stamps out and ready.

She takes a tissue from her purse and blows her nose, quietly, as a courteous lady is supposed to do. *Why* she felt compelled to stick her head in the pet store earlier would probably always remain a mystery to her, but that puppy in the window had been so *cute*. It never occurred to her that the pet store would also have cats. Edna was severely allergic to cats, couldn't even be near someone who *owned* the terrible things because people who owned cats always had at least a *little* shed fur on their clothes, and that's all it took to make her allergies go crazy.

Luckily, that was a few hours ago, and she's had a chance to take some non-drowsy allergy medicine, so now she's feeling much better, for which she is grateful. The last thing she wants is to be all stopped-up and red-nosed when Joe gets home from work. He always says it's hard for him to eat at the same table with her when she's like that, eyes all puffy and nose running like it was trying to win some kind of race.

Sometimes, her Joe can be awfully high-maintenance.

Edna busies herself with looking over the headlines on the tabloids in the rack by the checkout lane; this star has gained weight, another one has entered Betty Ford, someone else is having an affair. It's actually quite funny, when you think about it, how these newspapers try to make stars' lives seem even more dramatic than the characters they play in the movies; as if by splattering all their troubles on the front page will make them seem like regular folks. *We have problems just like the rest of you*, these stars' faces seem to say.

Sighing, Edna checks her watch and sees that she's been standing here for almost five minutes. The young woman in front of her hears Edna's sighing, and smiles at her in apology.

Edna is at first embarrassed to have been found out, then struck by how sad the young woman's smile is and—*Lord!*—how tired she looks. There are dark crescents under the young woman's eyes that stand out against her pale skin and make her smile seem even more cheerless. For a moment, Edna almost feels bad for having drawn attention to the awkwardness of the situation—*the poor thing looks like she hasn't slept in days*—then thinks again of the pot roast in her cart and how she hopes it doesn't thaw too much before she can get it home and into the freezer. If it thaws too much, she'll have to make it tonight, and Joe wouldn't like that; it's only Thursday, and Joe likes to have pot roast on the weekend. Feed him a too-heavy meal during the week, and he complains about how it keeps him awake and feeling tired all the next day.

Still feeling the young woman's eyes on her, Edna busies herself with the contents of her vinyl coupon holder, making sure that all the ones she'll need are in front, ready to go so that the cashier can scan them without delay. When she's sure the young welfare woman is no longer looking at her, Edna sneaks a peek at what she is buying. Edna's father always used to say, *You can tell a lot about a person by the contents of their shopping cart*, and over the course of her fifty-six years, Edna has found a lot of truth in that observation.

So she looks.

There is a coloring book with a torn cover and a bottle of over-the-counter sleep aids (both of which the young woman pays for with a handful of singles and change from her pocket), six cans of cat food (sliced beef in gravy), a quart of milk, a box of instant pudding mix (chocolate mousse, actually), a packet of taco seasoning (mild), and some frozen tortillas (corn).

The first thing that crosses Edna's mind is that she's not sneezing.

The second thing that crosses Edna's mind as she stares at the items is a commercial from the nineteen-seventies with that old gal—what was her name? *Clara Peller, that's right!*—where three old ladies are looking at a hamburger that's mostly all bun and Clara Peller starts squawking, "*Where's* the beef?"

Edna doesn't know why that, of all things, crosses her mind at that moment, but Clara Peller's famous question will find her again, during dinner, as it will find her again and again, for the rest of her life, never losing her, even when Alzheimer's Disease begins fragmenting her mind in another seventeen years: to the attendants on the ward at the nursing home where she will die quietly in her sleep, Edna Warner will always be known as the Where's-the-Beef? Lady.

Serv-ces has, aft-r conside–tion of yo-r individ–l case (#AB765-L7) determi–d

In the basement of St. Francis Church on Granville Street, the Monday night Alcoholics Anonymous meeting is winding down, and Chet Beckman—twelve years sober, know to his friends as "No-Skid" because he's got the best record of any bus driver for the Central Ohio Transit Authority—is adding an extra spoonful of sugar to his coffee when one of the other fellows in the group says, "Where's that guy who was here last week? That fellow whose family...oh, what was his name?"

"Randy," says Chet, sitting back down and stirring the creamer until the coffee takes on that soft golden color that means it's just right. "And they weren't his family except in his head, and my guess is he's down at the Wagon Wheel getting stewed to the gills."

The fellow who'd asked the question seems genuinely disappointed. "How can you *know* that?"

Chet sips his coffee and smiles; it tastes perfect. "I can know this because Randy comes in here about—what?—every three or four weeks after he's gone on a real bad binge, and sits there and says 'I'm gonna stop wasting my time and get on with my life.'" Chet takes another sip of his coffee. "He's been doing that for damn near two years, and the pattern never changes, no matter how many sponsors we sic on him or how many quit or how many he fires. Hell, *I* was his sponsor for a while, when it looked like he might actually get past what happened."

"It sounded to me like it wasn't his fault, hear him tell it."

"That's what he keeps telling us when he bothers to show up. 'It wasn't my fault. It wasn't my fault.' You ask me, he keeps repeating that because he's hoping that if he says it enough, he'll start to believe it." Chet shrugs. "Hell, maybe that wouldn't be such a bad thing, you know? Him starting to believe it."

The fellow who'd asked about Randy leaned forward. "Sounds to me like maybe you don't agree it wasn't his fault."

Chet sits back in his chair and regards the other fellow carefully. It doesn't do to get tempers flaring at these meetings; a bad argument's all the excuse someone needs to fall off the wagon, and this other fellow, the one who asked about Randy, he's only been sober five weeks and has got that desperate, anxious way about him that says he can go either way in a heartbeat. The first six weeks are always the hardest, and that sixth week is always the killer. Half the people AA loses they lose during the sixth week of sobriety, so Chet considers his words very carefully as he replies.

"Did you see that news story the other night about that avalanche they had in Colorado? The one that killed them two skiers?"

The other fellow nods his head.

"See, here's the thing about assigning blame to anyone or anything," says Chet, taking another sip of his perfect, golden-hued coffee. "I kept wondering—I wonder about shit like this sometimes when I can't sleep—I kept wondering, what if the snow itself could think like we can? I mean, imagine that every snowflake in that avalanche was able to think. Do you suppose any one of them would feel responsible for those skiers' dying, or would they just tell themselves 'It wasn't my fault'?"

The other man thinks on this for a moment, then shrugs. "I don't guess I see your point."

"So what's responsible for that?" asks Chet. "Is there any one word that I just said that's responsible for your not understanding me, or was it *all* the words?"

The other man shakes his head. "You're fucking with me now, aren't you?"

Chet shrugs, deciding that he's had enough coffee for tonight.

that you no longer qualify –r ben—ts as outlin– under O-io Co-e — and

"Would you look at *this?*" shouts Steve over the roar of the garbage truck's compactor.

His partner, Marty, pulls the wax plug out of his left ear and shots back, "What?"

Steve points to the contents of one of the trash cans they're emptying along Welfare Row. "This one bag came open. Take a look at this."

Marty peers over the edge of the trash can, looks at Steve, then back down at the contents.

The compactor finishes chewing up the last batch of trash, and howls loudly as it moves back into place for the next load.

"Looks to me like somebody's got insomnia."

Steve shakes his head. "That's more than insomnia, bud. There must be—what?—forty empty bottles in here. Fuck, that's enough to knock out Godzilla for a week."

"Is there anything else in there? Anything that might be salvageable? A busted radio or something we could maybe hock?"

Steve rummages through the rest of the contents. "Nah, ain't got shit."

"I guess that DVD player yesterday was a fluke, huh?"

"We were in a better section of town."

"Oh."

They toss the contents into the back of the truck, toss the cans back to the curb, and run to grab the next ones.

all mon—and oth— —- of —— sha-l be immediately discontinued. If you h-ve

The rat finishes shredding the paper for its nest, not caring that a large section of it has been caught by the wind again as is tumbling its determined way toward another role in a different mosaic that nature will soon form because of the need to amuse itself. The rat carries away the last of the shreds, knowing now that its nest is complete, is warm, is safe.

"So...how was dessert?"

"It was really *good*" say the children.

"It was different than last time," says the little boy. "It was kinda..."

"...kinda *crunchy*," says the little girl.

"Yeah," says the little boy. "Like there was sand in there. It made it a lot thicker."

Their mother brushes some hair from their faces. "But it was good, wasn't it?"

"Oh, yeah!" they cry in unison. "It was yummy. And we ate it *all!*"

"We sure did," says their mother.

"And you made so much of it!" says the little girl, laughing and yawning at the same time. "You never eat dessert when we have. You're always saying…oh, what do you say?"

"That chocolate goes right to her hips," says the little boy, who's also laughing and yawning at the same time.

Their mother laughs, as well. "Well…tonight was special."

"…sure was," says the little girl, fighting to keep her eyes open.

"That was the best dinner yet," says the little boy.

She kisses them both on the forehead, then the cheek, then hugs them and tucks them in for the night. She turns off the lights and sits on the floor between their beds, her right hands stroking her daughter's cheek, her left hand touching her son's shoulder.

She remains like that until they are both asleep.

She lowers her head and pulls in a deep, wet breath, then listens to their breathing.

She sees the coloring book lying on the floor at the foot of her daughter's bed. The two of them had been coloring in the pictures. They hadn't finished the last one.

It looked very nice. They played well together. They were each other's bestest friend.

They had loved the coloring book.

She listens to their breathing as she studies the colors, how well both of them stayed within the lines.

Later, she goes into the bathroom and runs hot water into the tub, lights a candle, unfolds the plastic bag, and measure out the duct tape.

"Good-night," she whispers in the direction of her childrens' room. "Sleep tight. Don't let the bedbugs…"

She begins to undress, feeling groggy.

Sometimes, First Thing in the Morning or Very Late at Night

SHE RISES BEFORE anyone else and checks the thermostat because the house seems a little chilly to her; it won't do for her family to come downstairs to a cold kitchen.

She begins preparing breakfast, drawing the collar of her old housecoat tighter around her neck, annoyed that her hands are cramping up on her again; she doesn't feel old enough to be suffering from arthritis, she's only forty-four, for god's sake, but the doctor has told her that's what it is so, reluctantly, she takes a couple of the pills he prescribed for her, then finishes making the toast and bacon.

A sound from upstairs; the kids pulling themselves out of bed, arguing over who should get to use the bathroom first. Her husband gets up and puts an end to the argument by sneaking past their teenagers and closing the bathroom door behind him.

She prepares their lunches; ham and cheese sandwiches for the kids, a roast beef sandwich for her husband. Everyone gets an apple, and an oatmeal cookie. She sets the plates on the kitchen table; steam from the bacon and mounds of pancakes wafts into the air, dancing, making morning breakfast-shapes that she stares at for a moment before her reverie is interrupted by her son and daughter bursting into the kitchen, talking loudly, in the midst of some harmless argument about male manners versus female independence.

She smiles and says good morning to them, they say the same in return without looking at her.

Her husband comes down, already dressed for the day, and tells her he cannot stay for breakfast, there's a meeting at the office in half an hour. He grabs a dry pancake off the plate and wraps it around two slices of bacon, then takes the Styrofoam cup of coffee she has already prepared for him, taking care to have torn a little section from the edge of the plastic lid so he can drink it while driving and not have to worry about spilling it on himself. He gives her a quick kiss on the cheek as he fumbles, stumbles, and laughs his way out the door.

She stands in the doorway looking out at his retreating back, hoping that he will turn around and wave at her before getting to the garage; some days he's in such a hurry he forgets to even make eye contact with her, and this morning is no different. She waves at his back and silently wishes him a nice day.

Back in the kitchen, her son and daughter have finished their hasty breakfast—between the two of them they barely eat one-third of what she's prepared. Her daughter says something about cheerleader tryouts and not wanting to stuff herself, her son says nothing at all as he jumps up from the table and rushes off to gather his books.

She takes the remaining bacon and carefully wraps it in aluminum foil, then munches on a piece of dry toast. She can use the bacon for a sandwich for her own lunch, and what's left after that she'll use for their lunch sandwiches tomorrow.

She hands her children their lunches as they run out the door to catch the bus, knowing that the sandwiches will probably go uneaten—they always seem to prefer whatever the school cafeteria is offering, but at least they pay for it out of their own money. This way, though, they have an option.

Options are very important.

Neither of them looks at her, or kisses her cheek as she hopes they might, but at least they remember to say good-bye. Her daughter even manages to whip around and give a quick wave as she's getting on the bus.

She spends the next thirty minutes cleaning up after breakfast, then starts a load of laundry and sits down with a cup of coffee a few minutes later.

She stares at the floor, sips at her coffee, then looks at her dry hands, the skin cracking in places, and tries to remember when they were smooth, those days when her husband couldn't wait to feel them against his own skin.

She finishes her coffee, then goes upstairs to make the beds and straighten up the bathroom.

She thinks perhaps she might put on some music to listen to while she cleans this morning, but as she heads for the small upstairs stereo she can't think of anything she wants to hear, and so opts for the empty, quiet sounds of the house.

In the bedroom she shares with her husband, she crosses to her bureau and opens the second drawer, arranging her undergarments so there will be more room for the other things once the laundry is finished.

She pauses as her hand comes across something wrapped in silk.

Slowly, almost reverently, she pulls out the pair of old ballet slippers and looks at them. Stitched inside each of the slippers is her name—her maiden name—and the age she'd been at the time she'd bought them: 8.

She sits for a while on the bed, smiling at the slippers.

She looks down at her bare legs which protrude from under the hem of her housecoat. The texture of their skin seems thicker, like clotted cream turned the color of an unripe peach peeled too soon. A few varicose veins can be seen even without looking closely.

She flexes her hands, hearing the bones crack; the stiffness isn't so bad as it was a little while ago. The pills helped.

She pulls in a deep breath and holds it.

Sometimes, early in the morning or very late at night, she thinks about her dreams of youth and wonders: *What happened?*

The years, how they slip through your fingers.

The chances, how quickly they pass by.

The dreams, how they are compromised.

And how, sometimes, early in the morning or very late at night, you realize too late that you've settled in more ways than one.

She releases her breath and brushes some hair away from her face, noticing as she does so that there's a bit more gray in there than the last time she noticed. Time to go see her friend, Miss Clairol.

Enough of this, though; she has a house to keep in order.

A job well done is its own reward, after all.

She decides to just turn on the radio while she works. The station is playing a Beatles song, "When I'm Sixty-Four." She finds herself singing along with it.

At five-forty-five everyone gets home. All of them go at once to the kitchen where she has prepared a little snack for them. There are abrupt hugs, short kisses, nonstop chatter from the kids about their day, and then, one by one, her family begins wandering off to their own evening activities as she sets about the business of cleaning up and preparing dinner.

Only her son notices the small, silk-wrapped bundle that's mixed in with the trash in the kitchen receptacle, but he's not curious enough to see what it is or ask her about it.

She pauses while seasoning the fish fillets, and listens to her family making their at-home sounds. She catches a glimpse of herself reflected in the small window over the sink and wonders if she's still pretty.

But it does her no good to think this way.

Still, sometimes, first thing in the morning or very late at night...

Sometimes ...

Sometimes, first thing in the morning or late at night ...

God, sometimes ...

At the "Pay Here, Please" Table

WHEN HE WAS A CHILD of eight he was taken on a camping trip by three teenaged boys who were friends of the family; all three were either about to ship out to Vietnam or were preparing to go off to boot camp in preparation for Vietnam. He was the youngest and weakest of the five children they'd taken along that weekend, so naturally when the fellows got good and drunk and dared one another to prove that there was nothing they weren't prepared to do, he was the one they grabbed from his sleeping bag and dragged deeper into the woods where the others couldn't hear him scream. Each teenaged boy raped him at both ends, two of them going at him at a time while the third held him still and firmly upright so no one lost their balance; guys readying to ship off to fight the dinks had to learn teamwork, after all. They left him there for the night, naked and bleeding and vomiting on himself. When he was dropped off at his house the next day, it was with a warning that if he told on them, he would be killed. He told no one. In the weeks that followed, each of the three teenaged boys visited him at the house, usually when one or both of his parents were at work. They made him dress up in his mom's clothes and put on make-up and lots of lipstick. Sometimes he had to wear a wig. He did the things they demanded of him because he was too scared and small and weak to think he had a chance to defend himself. Afterward, he'd put his mom's clothes back just as they had been, sometimes ironing them because they'd gotten wrinkled. Sometimes he'd wrap himself in a particular dress so he could smell his mom's perfume in the material and feel protected and loved for a few minutes. The lipstick always tasted terrible; it took him days to get that taste – and other tastes – out of his mouth. He didn't eat much and lost weight but no one asked him why. Eventually the teenaged boys stopped coming around. They went off to Vietnam. One of them was killed there. The other two returned unharmed. The first became a petty criminal who wound up being sent to prison for forty years; the second became a mail carrier whose route, until he shot himself and three co-workers a few years back, included the boy's family home.

Sitting at the Pay Here, Please table outside the garage now, the man who was once a boy of eight looking forward to his first (and only) camping trip watches as various young girls and women impolitely grope every last item remaining from the detritus of his childhood. Twenty-five cents for blouses, fifty cents for shoes and wigs, fifty cents for the dime-store jewelry Mom thought was so exquisite because she never knew better, a dollar for jackets and dresses. An appealing woman of perhaps twenty-seven with luxurious red hair says hello to him as she makes her purchase. He recognizes the dress: it's the one he was most often made to wear and sometimes wrapped himself in afterward. He feels a pang of regret (because it can't be grief, can it?) as the appealing red-head buys it (along with some shoes, some books, a couple of LPs), slips everything into a shopping bag, and leaves for her home.

He wonders what her friends will say when they see her in it. Look, they'll say. Look at _____'s new dress. It's so retro-chic. Have you seen it yet? Have you seen _____'s new dress?

He asks his sister to take over at the table. Rising, he feels sick as he begins following _____. That dress was his favorite. He wonders if she'll look as good in it as he did. The boys always said he looked pretty when he wore it. He'll wait for her to put it on and see if she's prettier. Then he'll have her take it off. They can maybe go camping there in her house.

He hopes she'll understand afterward. She should have just left it on the table.

IN THE LOWLANDS

"Do you know how a hobo feels?
Life is a series of dirty deals
Except for a kind word, a cup of coffee
And the song of the wheels…"

—Anonymous message scrawled on boxcar wall, Kansas City, 1934

THERE'S AN OLD SUPERSTITION among hoboes—especially those whose camps are made near the switch yards—that a 'Bo's death is mourned by the whistles of two passing trains; the sounds meet overhead in the night and, though each might be a bit mournful when heard by itself, they combine to create a pleasant song of welcome for the 'Bo's soul as he takes himself that last, great freight to Heaven.

When you hear that sound, you're supposed to remove your hat (if you wear one), close your eyes, and wish that fellow's soul good travel to the Pearly Gates, then say a little prayer that the body he left behind finds its way to the Lowlands—that is, that some good soul will see fit to give it a proper burial and not just leave it where the fellow shuffled off the ol' mortal coil.

A second blast of the dual train whistles serves as a message to let you know that his soul found its way home and his remains have been properly sent to the Lowlands. That's about the best a 'Bo can hope for when he leaves this world.

Fry Pan Jack told me about that legend right before the TB finally overpowered his body and he passed on, leaving his cat, Billy, in my care. I heard the trains cry for him that night. And

I put his remains in the Lowlands myself, reading a passage from Jack's Bible after I finished tamping down the soil.

Now I've got to stand trial for my life before a jury of my peers.

All of this in the same week.

It happened like this:

It was as good a jungle as a 'Bo could hope for in that spring of 1933: On the sunny side of the hills, within walking distance of a fairly clean creek, and not too far from a couple of switch yards and coal bunkers; a thick patch of trees offered shelter from the chilly night winds, and the town dump was within spitting distance and ready for scavenging; add to that the friendly atmosphere that greeted a fellow upon his arrival—and sometimes just getting past the railroad bulls was cause for major celebration on the parts of all residents—and, well, you'd be crazy to think you could do better.

Billy and I had decked a rattler—that is to say, rode spread-eagle atop a passenger train—for about the last half-hour before we jumped. (I did the actual jumping; Billy just sort of curled himself up into a ball inside my pack and hung on for dear life.) My landing was nothing to write home about—in fact, I thought I might've twisted my ankle (not the case, I'm pleased to tell you)—but luckily we were far enough away from any yards or stations that I didn't have to worry about any bulls seeing me.

Not that I've got anything against railroad police, understand. Most of them are fairly good sorts but there's always a couple wherever you go who make sport of cracking open a 'Bo's skull. Seems those types can't tell the difference between a bum and a hobo—and believe you me, there's a difference. As Jack used to say: "Bums loaf and sit; Tramps loaf and walk; but a 'Bo moves and works and he's clean."

Even on the road there's a hierarchy—and I learned myself that word from a dictionary Jack gave to me. "Nothin'll catch folks off-guard quicker than a 'Bo with a good vocabulary, son; shows 'em you got brains and folks're more likely to give a decent meal to a man with some brains who's willing to work than a moron."

Add to that formula a hungry pet—like a cute cat—and you're hardly ever turned away.

I suppose that's one of the reasons Billy and me found ourselves so welcome at this particular jungle that evening.

There were a couple of fellows standing watch over a pot of Mulligan stew in the center of the camp; they were the first to spot me. They'd been talking up 'til then, but once they got sight of me their conversing stopped and they just stared at me.

One by one, the other men in the camp took notice of their silence and had to have themselves a look at what was going on.

Every man there was staring at me as I walked toward the fire and the pot.

"Evenin'," I said, tipping my hat.

"Where you coming from, stranger?" asked one of the Mulligan Stew Boys.

"Michigan way. Found a couple days' work helping to unload coal at the River Rouge auto plant."

"Was they still needin' workers when you left?"

"That they were."

He considered this for a moment.

I knew what was going through their minds: Is he on the level or is he a damned yegg?

A yegg was any one of a number of disreputable fellows who posed as a 'Bo but didn't want to be bothered with actually earning his keep, and so made his way by robbing an honest traveling laborer. A yegg wouldn't think twice about beating up or even killing a 'Bo for whatever the man had on him.

I set down my pack and untied it—not enough that Billy could stick his head out and attract even more attention—but enough so that I could reach inside and remove a potato and an onion, which I offered to the Mulligan Brothers. They were more than happy to take it.

You never, ever walk into a 'Bo camp and not offer something to go with the evening's meal if you can help it. That's part of the code. Not that they'd let you go hungry—if there's a meal being cooked up in a camp, then that meal is for everyone there and anyone who might happen by. Just because there's a code, that in no way means that fellow 'Bo's would let a man starve.

The camp warmed up to me fairly quickly after that, and when I later pulled out some recent newspapers and detective magazines that I'd managed to pick up along the way, well, you'd have thought I was one of the Permanents there. The three things you can have in your pack which will always make you welcome in any camp are coffee (or tobacco), food, and something for the fellows to read. Life on the road is lonely— that's a given—but it can also be boring as hell and a recent newspaper or a story magazine can offer a man something to occupy his mind with besides the worry of where his next job and meal might be coming from.

It was only when we were sitting down to dinner that Billy woke up and started raising a ruckus inside my pack. I reached in and pulled him out and from the way the rest of the camp reacted, you'd have thought I'd produced a wad of greenbacks.

"Well, damn my eyes," said the bigger of the two Mulligan Brothers—who went by the name of Cracker-Barrel Pete (you never use your real name in a camp and never ask a man for his)—"Why didn't you tell us you had yourself a little fur-ball with you?"

"He was sleeping when I got here and he doesn't take kindly to being woke up from his beauty rest." The fellows laughed at this.

"You know, don't you," said Pete, "that there's a couple restaurants in town that'd be happy to give a day-old fish to a cat like your, uh—he got a name, your cat?"

"Billy."

Pete nodded. "Yessir. Never fails to amaze me, human nature, that is: Folks who wouldn't give you a slice of moldy bread would hand over something small and fresh for a hungry cat."

I knew that to be true enough; many was the time when Jack and I almost met with the business end of a proprietor's shotgun until they caught sight of Billy; then we almost always left with a tin of sardines or tuna. A can of tuna, mixed with some crushed cracker, sometimes lasted the three of us a couple of days.

Pete's words did not go unheard by the others.

"Say," he said, leaning over and refilling my coffee tin, "think you and Billy there might be up for a little excursion in the morning? Might find yourself a days' decent work, plus old Billy there might snag us some special goodies for tomorrow's dinner."

"Don't see why not," I said, letting Billy get comfortable in my lap. I picked a small square of potato from my stew and fed it to him. Billy liked potatoes—onions, too, which often made his breath a holy terror. "Folks seem to take a quick shine to him."

"Then it's settled," Pete said just loud enough that the others would know I was more than willing to do my share. "First thing tomorrow, we'll go into town with Billy and hit the bakery there, see if we can't get ourselves some day-old bread or pastries—he like pastries, does he?"

"Billy's a pastry fool."

Pete laughed. "Ain't that something? A cat that likes pastry!"

We all had ourselves a good laugh then at Billy's expense, but he didn't seem to mind; an animal of sweeter nature you'd be hard-pressed to find.

I couldn't help noticing, though, that the other Mulligan Brother—a thin reed of a fellow calling himself Icehouse Willie—wasn't laughing like the rest of us; oh, sure, he was chuckling away so's to fit in, but I caught something in his eyes as he looked at Billy that didn't sit right with me.

Maybe I'm just tired, I thought, and would not allow myself to think unkindly of anyone in the camp that night.

I read a few news articles to some of the men who couldn't read themselves, then we passed another hour or so passing around one of the detective magazines, taking turns reading serial chapters (and a juicy one this yarn was, too!), then, long about ten, with the stars above us in abundance, we found our spots for the nights and got as comfortable as the ground would allow.

Just before I dozed off, Billy's terrible breath on my cheek on account he'd decided to sleep on my arm, I heard a train whistle in the distance, echoing low and lonely, and I closed my eyes, wishing Jack a good night, as well.

As if to echo my sentiments in his own unique way, Billy sneezed in my ear, yawned, then dug in his claws and conked out.

Long about three in the morning (I checked the position of the stars, something Jack had taught me to do, in order to guess about the time) I woke up and pulled Billy off my arm, sitting him down next to me. He gave a grumpy, sleepy-faced look—you'd better have a damned good reason for this—then sat back on his hind legs and stared.

"Shh," I whispered so as not to awaken anyone nearby. "Just…just stay right there."

I reached into the bottom of my pack (which I'd been using as my pillow) and pulled out a small piece of smoked salmon wrapped in tinfoil—a little treat I'd bought for Billy with some of my Michigan wages at a Japanese place in Cedar Hill, Ohio the day before. I would've offered it to put in with the stew, but Billy had been a little out of sorts lately—Jack having only left us a week ago—and I figured the fellow would enjoy a little late-night treat.

That's when I heard the cry.

It wasn't so much a scream—it had been strangled in the throat before it could get to that point—but there was enough panic and underlying misery in the sound to let me know that whoever had made it was either being killed or in the middle of a right terrible dream.

I did a quick look-round the camp and saw Pete a few yards away with the other Mulligan Brother, Icehouse Willie—the one who'd been looking at me and Billy so strangely. Pete had Willie's head pressed against his chest and was covering Willie's mouth with one of his hands. Willie was crying fiercely, deep, body-wracking sobs, his eyes closed tight, his face getting redder and redder, and as I gently put Billy down and started over to see if there was anything I could do to help, I saw that Pete was rocking his buddy back and forth like he would a baby, and all the time whispering, "It's okay, Willie, there you go, there you, no fires, okay? It's a nice, cool night and you're out here in the open with me and you're okay, shhh, there you go, it's okay…"

It took a few more minutes of this before the other man finally fell back to sleep.

I hoped for his sake that it was a peaceful slumber.

Another quick look-round showed me that the man's cries had awakened a few of the residents, but they acted as if there were used to it and so simply rolled over and went back to sleep.

Pete came over to me, shaking his head. "Sorry about that. Guess we should've told you about Willie."

He gestured toward the far end of the camp and we set off walking. When we were almost to the edge of the camp he stopped for a moment, a sad look crossing briefly over his face. "I don't mean to sound cold-hearted, but Willie, he's…he's not quite right in the head, understand? Lost his wife, Carol, and his little girl, Sandy, to a boxcar fire about a year ago when they were riding to Chicago. I was riding that same train, only I was in a different car. Terrible thing. He tried to get to them, but they were in a hay car on account the train was hauling a lot of cattle, and the flames…well, you get the idea."

"…yeah…" I whispered.

"Sometimes he talks about 'em like they were still alive." He reached up and squeezed the bridge of his nose. "Damnedest thing, though. The folks who were ridin' in that car…well, shit, you just know better than to light any kind of match in a hay-car. I mean, light's a bad idea in the first place on account it can tip off the bulls, but in a hay-car!" He shook his head. "We had just pulled out from a stopover when the fire broke out, understand? And most of the people in that car had been asleep. Willie and his family, they were sitting way in the back of the car so's they'd face everyone…"

"Best way to protect a family, under the circumstances."

"That may well be, but I heard later from a couple of the folks who got out that a bull set that fire—just came running up alongside and tossed in a match. Someone hadn't closed the door all the way." He shrugged. "It happens. Them cars, they can get damned stuffy." He looked back to where Willie was sleeping quietly, then looked at me and lowered his voice. "Just between you and me, though, I always thought Willie must've gotten a look at the bull who done it, and maybe part of what makes him...not quite right anymore is that there just ain't enough room in him for both his grief and his wanting to get revenge on the sumbitch what set that fire."

By now we'd started walking back into camp. I looked at Pete and grinned. "It's really decent of you...I mean, taking him on like you have."

Pete grinned back. "That obvious, is it?" A shrug. "What the hell else was a God-fearing man supposed to do? Couldn't very well leave him to his own devices, not in the shape he's in. Yeggs'd make a meal of him and not even leave bones for the dogs. And lately—hell, ever since we came to this camp three, four weeks ago—he's been gettin' a lot worse. Not just the dreams, those're bad as ever, but he's...he's acting less and less...uh..."

"...rational?"

"—yeah, that's the word. He's been actin' less rational when he's wake. Scares me, y'know? Man's been a good traveling companion and I think of him as a friend, but if he gets to the point where I can't handle him no more..." He let the words and thought trail off. He knew I didn't need to hear him complete that sentence.

"How'd he come to be called 'Icehouse' Willie?"

Pete told me, and his answer damn near broke my heart.

I stopped by my sleeping spot where Billy was still sitting impatiently, waiting for his late-night treat.

"Cute little bugger, ain't he?" said Pete.

"Not so loud. He's full enough of himself as it is."

Pete smiled, reached down and petted Billy's head, then gave me a tip of his hat and went back to his spot beside Icehouse Willie.

I laid back down and got as comfortable as I could, then peeled away the foil wrapping Billy's treat and placed the chunk of salmon in front of him. "There you go, pal, enjoy yourself."

Billy sniffed at it, decided it was to his liking (why he always made of show of deciding he wanted to eat something I could never figure out), then dug in, savoring every bite.

I had to admit it looked sort of tasty and made my mouth water slightly—and it wasn't as if I'd never shared Billy's meals before—but I figured he deserved this special treat all to himself.

I stroked the fur on top of his head. "You're a good traveling companion, Billy."

He sniffed once in mid-chew as if to say, Yeah, yeah, yeah, I'm a prince and so're you, now can I please get back to the business at hand?

I laughed under my breath, then rolled over and fell back asleep.

The last thing I remember thinking was how I hoped that Willie could sleep the rest of the night without hearing the cries of his wife and daughter.

Damnedest thing, really, the trouble that little secret snack of Billy's caused later.

Jack was an old-timer on the road (he admitted to being "…in spitting distance of seventy, but I ain't gonna tell you in what direction."), and many was the night he'd regale me with tales of his adventures on the road before I hooked up with him.

One of his favorite memories was of a house in Portage, Wisconsin he'd spent time at a few years back.

"The mother there, her husband had died a year or so before, and what with a family to care for, she had to find a way to make herself a respectable living. She took in washing, cooked meals for others, and baked up something like forty or fifty pies a night for a little restaurant called the Pig-n-Whistle. All that pie-cooking, it took a powerful lot of stove wood.

"Now, her children couldn't keep up—poor woman had to have at least five long rows of stacked wood that needed to be split—so she was more than happy to offer a 'Bo a job splitting the logs. You could earn yourself a fine, fine meal splitting wood for her. The jungle we lived in was just a few hundred yards from her back yard, on the other side of the rail yard in a grove of trees by Mud Lake. 'Bo's tended to hang around that jungle for a good long while, not just because of the work and meals this lady'd provide us with, but because if it was your birthday and her kids got wind of it, she'd bake up a little cake and send it over, and her kids…well, they always managed to come up with sort of present for you, a magazine of book or old toy. Yessir, it was a good place. Many's the night, after the wood had been split and the pies baked and the evening meal served, she'd invite any 'Bo who wanted to come over and sit on her porch and listen to the radio. She always served something to drink on those nights. I remember her lemonade best, on summer evenings with the radio playing and the trains' whistles calling in the distance.

"Yessir, that's my idea of Heaven. In fact, that's where I first found old Billy here. He was one of a litter of kittens that someone tossed in the river one night, all tied up in a bag. If me and this other fellah—can't recall his name now—but if we hadn't been where we was and seen this happen, all them kittens would've drowned. Terrible thing, the way people treat their pets."

"What about the way they treat each other?"

He looked at me and shook his head, grinning. "You expect too much of others, son. Take my advice—if you expect no kindness, then you won't be disappointed when none is given; but, Lord, are you all the more grateful for it when it is!"

I was awakened from my pleasant dream of Jack and the Pie Lady when someone slammed a steel-toed boot into my hip. I came awake with a shout, grabbing my pack and spinning around on the ground, ready to swing at whoever'd done that to me, when I found myself staring up at one of the most unpleasant-looking bulls I'd ever seen. He stood there, big as life and three times as ugly, holding his club in his hands and looking all-too-ready to open up my skull.

And if he wasn't up to messing up his uniform with my brains, one look at the younger fellow with him told me he was ready.

A little too ready, from the glint in his eyes.

The big bull stared down at me. "Understand you came in here around six, six-thirty last night, that right?"

"Yessir," I said, looking around for Pete and the others. They were gathered together near the cooking area, trying not to be too obvious about looking at me.

I looked around quickly myself, wondering where Billy had wandered off to.

"Look, officer," I said, "I don't want any trouble. If you'd be so good as to tell me what this is all about—"

He snapped the business end of his club forward and thrust it into my chest. I took this as a request to shut up and listen.

"There's been rumors about a yegg moving through these parts," the bull said to me. "Don't get me wrong, boy—I got nothing against the likes of 'Bo's, but last night—early this morning, actually, around four-thirty, five—someone from this camp broke into a couple of stores and stole themselves a bunch of food, liquor, and a little bit of money."

He squatted down to get his face close to mine, still keeping the club in my chest. "Reason I know they were from this camp is because it wasn't enough for them to be happy with the stores. No—they had to go and break into some folks' homes." He made a quick sideways gesture with his head.

"Pete over there told me you're the only new fellah what's come around here lately. Sorry to say, but that makes you—"

"—your best suspect, yessir."

He studied me for a moment. "The only reason I don't have the sheriff out here with me is because, one, I didn't think you'd be stupid enough to come back here and, two, I think it would sit better with the folks who were robbed if I could go back and tell them that the 'Bo's took care of the problem in their own manner…if you read my meaning."

And I did, all too clearly.

You live in a camp, you don't rob from another hobo. You live in a camp, thievery of any kind was to be avoided outside the camp as well—or at least kept to a minimum; a pie lifted from its cooling spot in an open bakery window every now and then, some vegetables hurriedly snatched from a garden, or an old shirt clipped from an outside line, that was acceptable if the circumstances warranted thieving, but if it could be avoided, you did so. Townspeople were your only source of jobs and handouts, and you did not—repeat, did not—do anything to anger them. One dirty yegg could muck it up for everyone in the camp, and a good camp near a good town—especially one where the bulls didn't run you off on a regular basis, as this seemed to be—well, that was to be respected in the same way people respect the church they go into every Sunday.

The bull looked at his partner and said, "Watch him while I search his pack, Carl."

Carl's idea of watching me was planting one of his feet right into my chest and pressing down. Hard.

"Carl," said the other bull. "What'd I tell you about that?"

"Bastard broke into my house, McGregor."

"I know that your place was one that he hit, but until we find something of yours or one of the other folks—'" He stopped, then looked down as he pulled a half-empty bottle of whiskey from my pack. He followed that with some bread, cheese, and a couple emptied cans of salmon.

None of which had been in my pack the night before.

"Looks like we got our man, Carl." Then McGregor pulled out an envelope with some writing on it. He read it, looked at me, then his partner, and handed the envelope to Carl.

"What's this?" asked his partner.

"You tell me. It's got your name on it."

Carl glared at me—now I was sure there was a craziness barely hiding behind his eyes—and snatched the envelope from McGregor, tore it open, and removed the letter inside.

He tried to control it, that I could see, but whatever was written on that page rattled him something fierce.

"Well?" said McGregor.

"Huh? Oh—it's, uh…it's just a letter I got from, uh…my granddad." He folded the paper up in a hurry and stuffed it into his pocket. "You piece of—" he said to me, pulling back his foot to kick me.

"Carl!" snapped McGregor. "This ain't that Illinois rat-trap you moved here from. We don't strike a man without bein' provoked."

"I can't help it! It's bad enough to break into a man's house and steal his food and whiskey, but what the hell kind of yegg steals a man's personal mail?"

"The kind we just caught."

McGregor stood up and gestured that I should do the same. As soon as I was on my feet Carl spun me around slapped handcuffs on me—none too gently, I might add—then marched me into the center of the camp and sat me down a an old tree stump.

"One way or another," Carl snarled in my ear just low enough so only I could hear him. "One way or another you're going to the Lowlands."

My mouth went instantly dry. The violence in his voice was like nothing I'd ever heard before, and there was no doubt in my mind that Carl wanted to kill me with his own bare hands…and whatever was in that letter was the reason.

"Okay, fellahs," said McGregor loudly enough to get the camp's attention. "My shift ends at five. I got three other guys from the yard who're willing to sit on the jury. I'll stand in as bailiff. You got until then to pick out the other nine jurors."

Pete stepped up and said, "You be the one who calls Judge Carson?"

"I'll take care of it—and I'll make damned sure the people in town know that you fellahs are gonna take care of this problem. I'll offer apologies, if it's all the same."

Pete nodded. "And if it's all the same to you, McGregor, I'll be defending our friend here."

"Ain't no friend of mine." He turned to me real quick and said, "Nothing personal. If you're innocent, I'll apologize to you. Until then, you're as good as a crook in my eyes." He grabbed up a small coil of rope someone had scavenged from the dump and ordered a couple of men nearby to tie my legs and ankles to the stump.

"Be seeing y'all this evening," he said, tapping the end of his club against the brim of his hat.

Carl walked by me real slow.

Real slow.

Not blinking.

One way or another…

Everyone in camp watched the two bulls make their way over the hill and back toward the rail yard. Then Pete put a hand on my shoulder and said, "You know what the penalty is for that kind of thieving, don't you?"

I nodded my head.

If found guilty, they were bound by the code to either kill me or exile me.

You exile a 'Bo by marking his face; that way, he'll not find himself welcomed in any camp he comes across thereafter.

I have seen such marked men in my travels. Burned faces, faces missing an eye, an ear, a nose…a simple scar would be treasured as a symbol of mercy. But mercy was something you rarely found under these circumstances. Not only was a marked 'Bo not welcomed in a camp, damn few people will give him work or a handout.

Death or marked exile; wasn't much of a choice, when you got right down to it.

The rules of the road can be brutal when a bad element threatens to ruin it for the innocent.

I looked up at Pete. "You seen Billy?"

"No, I ain't. And that's how come McGregor went right for you."

"Beg pardon?"

"Whoever broke into them places had a cat with him. A couple of witnesses saw it. Guess the guy stole a fish or two from one of the markets to feed it."

"Oh, brother…there were a couple of empty cans of salmon in my pack.."

"Not yours, I take it?"

"No."

"Now let me ask you something."

"Anything."

"Am I the only one who's noticed that Willie is conspicuously absent this morning?"

I looked at his face and knew there was no need for me to answer.

The trial got under way a little after four p.m.

It didn't help my chances much that Eastbound Earl, the prosecutor, dumped the contents of my pack onto the ground to revealed the evidence that McGregor and Carl had found there.

It also didn't help much that Billy finally put in an appearance a few minutes before the trial started, his breath stinking of fish. He bounded right up to me and jumped into my lap, rubbing himself against my coat.

"I have to say in all fairness," whispered Pete, "that this does not bode well for your, uh...your—"

"—acquittal?"

"I was going to say something a little more colorful—mentioning a particular point on your anatomy—but 'acquittal' will do. Look, we both know full well that Willie's the one who snatched Billy up and took him into to town when he did all that stealing. I told you he ain't been actin' like himself since we got here. Probably figured things would go just like they have up to this point. Hell, wouldn't surprise me one bit if he actually made an effort to be seen."

"He knew that any witness would remember the cat more than his face?"

Pete nodded. "If there was even enough light for them to see his face."

"...yeah..." I whispered.

"Don't get me wrong, he's the one who did this, but the rules don't allow for his, uh, condition to be taken into account. Thief's a thief, and that's all there is to it."

We both searched the crowd of faces until we found Willie, standing way in the back of the spectators and looking for all the world like a man who was walking in his sleep.

"We'll hear the defense's arguments now," said Judge Carson, a hard-looking older gentleman whose voice sounded like he gargled with moonshine three times a day. Pete told me that Carson had ridden the rails once himself and had been treated well by the hoboes he encountered, and so always oversaw these trials. "He's as fair as you're going to find."

"Pete," said McGregor, our bailiff.

Carl stood off to the side, trying for all the world to look like he didn't want to slit my throat.

"If it please the court," said Pete, standing just a bit taller than usual, "I would like to call Mr. Icehouse Willie to the stand."

There was a murmur among the spectators, and when Willie didn't come forward right away, McGregor—our inspiring bailiff—said, "All right, Willie, let's—"

—and that's when Pete pulled me to my feet and led me up to the witness chair.

McGregor stopped and stared but said nothing.

He knew damned well—as did every other resident of the camp—that I was not Willie, but no one said a thing.

"What the hell're you doing?" I whispered.

"You remember our talk last night?"

"Yeah…?"

"Just try and follow my lead. And remember that Willie stammers."

I glanced in Willie's direction; he gave me a nervous, almost apologetic look as Pete started in on his questioning.

"Okay, Willie, why don't you tell us why you—"

"Thief!" someone shouted.

The camp crowd reacted with appropriate shock.

Judge Carson banged his gavel, calling for order.

"Would you please tell us," said Pete, "why it is you're called 'Icehouse' Willie?"

I was never much for play-acting, but I gave it my best try; can't rightly say why, but I trusted Pete. "Ah, hell, Pete…what's that got to do with—?"

"Answer the question, please," said Judge Carson.

"Pete here, he g-gave me that name."

Judge Carson stared at me, then at Pete. "I'm gonna assume here that this has some kind of bearing on the case?"

"It does, Yeronner; it might not seem, ah…uh…"

"Evident," I whispered from the side of my mouth.

"—evident right away," said Pete, "but it will come to bear on things."

Carson sighed and nodded his head. "Just don't go off on any tangents, understand? My daughter's bringing my new granddaughter over for supper tonight and I'll be damned if I'm gonna miss seeing them."

"Understood, Yeronner." Pete turned his attention back to me—but not before making a quick gesture with his head and eyes that told me I should look over at Carl.

I did so, and saw a 'Bo offering the bull a bottle of beer. Carl accepted—not gratefully, big surprise—and had a little trouble getting the top off. While he struggled with the bottle opener, the 'Bo who'd given him the beer brushed back behind him—

—and slipped something from his pocket.

I looked at Pete to let him know I'd seen it. I'd told him about the letter earlier that day. Evidently he'd taken it upon himself to obtain the thing without Carl's cooperation—Carl being so warm-hearted toward hoboes as he was. It probably would have seemed like taking advantage of the man's good nature to ask him for it.

I went on, remembering as best I could what Pete had told me of Willie's story last night. "…and after the fire, the bulls put all the bodies in this here icehouse near the yard. I…I, uh…I w-w-went in there to find my Carol and Sandy and after I f-found 'em I wanted to sit with 'em awhile, y'know? Sandy, she don't like to be left alone when she's sleeping, and Carol, sh-she'd give me h-h-holy h-hell if I went off while they was resting…" I made up this last part, which might have been stupid, buy by that time I found I was enjoying playing this part; so much so that I felt a tear slip down my cheek—wasn't hard to muster tears at the thought of how terrible Carol's and Sandy's last moments had been—then I simply sat there, staring at the ground and shaking.

"Go on," said Pete, softly.

"...you come in there after a bit and made me leave before I f-froze to death." Then I remembered something Pete had told me Willie once said: "Sometimes I wish I had. Least then we'd all still be together."

Judge Carson slammed his gavel against the wood table-top that served as his bench. Someone had scavenged the table from the dump earlier; it smelled of old and rancid food and decay and probably accounted for the pained expression the Judge's face had been sporting since this got under way.

"All right, Pete, that's enough," said the Judge. "Whether or not this has any bearing on your case, I don't care. It's damned depressing and I, for one, will not sit here and be made to listen to a man re-live something as terrible as losing his family."

"May I ask one more question, Yeronner?"

"Best make it a good one."

I saw Pete glance over in Carl's direction; that glance was not lost on McGregor, who, for the rest of proceeding, kept looking from Carl to Pete to me to Willie, then back again.

"Willie, did you see the man who set that fire in your boxcar that night?"

Carl froze, blanching.

I shot a quick glance in Willie's direction; he looked straight at me with one of the most lonely, scared, and pained expressions I've ever seen deform a man's face, then gave a short, sharp nod of his head.

"I'm a bit deaf these days," snapped Judge Carson. "You're gonna have to actually say something."

"Oh, yeah," I said. "I saw him real good."

Carl looked about ready to dump in his shorts.

I had just a moment before figured out what was in that letter and who had written it.

What I didn't understand was the why of the rest of it.

"O-kay," said Judge Carson, slamming his gavel once again, "that is more than sufficient for my tastes. We are here to try this man"—he snapped a liver-spotted hand in my direction—"for thievery and breaking & entering. I must gettin' soft in the head, lettin' you pull a stunt like this—"

"But, Yeronner—"

"But nothin', Pete." He looked directly at me. "Are you guilty of the crimes of which you're being accused?"

"N-nosir."

Carson smiled. "All-righty, then." He glared at Pete. "Now, we have heard the prosecution's arguments and seen their evidence, I have the statements of the townsfolk whose business and residences were broken into, so now it's your turn. That's how this works, Pete, it's called a trial. They go, then you go, I listen to all pertinent statements. Dull, I know, but I like dull. So…do you have any witnesses to call who might actually have something to say about the case that I'm supposed to be hearing, or should we just go right to the closing statements?"

Pete looked at me, then Carl, then Willie.

"One moment, please, Yeronner," Pete said.

"What the—?" I whispered to him when he came over to me.

"You a gambling man?"

"I don't—"

"Shh, hang on."

The 'Bo who'd picked Carl's pocket came up to Pete and handed him the letter. Pete made a fairly big show of accepting the letter, opening it, reading it, then considering what he'd just read.

"Yeronner," he said, "I have no other witnesses to call, but I would ask a favor of the court."

"Oh, hoo-ray," muttered Carson. "What is it?"

"A twenty-four hour recess."

Carson mumbled curses under his breath, then said, "If I ask you why, is the answer going to upset me?"

"Probably."

"I should've retired last year like Mildred wanted." A sigh, then: "All right, why do you want a recess?"

"Some new evidence has just come to light which might prove my client's innocence."

Carson was silent for several moments, then said: "You're kidding?"

"Afraid not, Yeronner."

"The man was discovered with several of the stolen items on his person—not only that, but several of the stolen items were either fresh or canned fish—and don't think I didn't get a whiff of his cat's breath earlier. Between its breath and the smell on its fur, it could knock a buzzard off a shit-wagon."

"It looks bad, I know."

"This is such a help" I said under my breath.

"We're talking not only about the thieving here, Yeronner, but a man's life, as well. I'm willing to personally vouch for my client. Twenty-four hours."

Carson looked at his pocket watch. "No...but I'll give you some time. It's just right now six. Even though it's gonna have Mildred spittin' nails at me, we will reconvene at this same spot at nine a.m. tomorrow morning. Is that sufficient time for you to gather and examine your new evidence?"

Pete's smile was almost evil. "That'll be more than enough time, Yeronner."

I looked back to where Carl had been standing.

He was long gone.

One way or another...

And Pete—with more than a little help from Willie—had just turned me into bait.

"Nine a.m." repeated Carson. "But after that, new evidence or no, some sort of action has to be taken, understand? If someone isn't punished, the town's gonna want me to have McGregor and his friends bust up this camp and send all of you on your way. I'd hate to see that happen. I know a lot of you fellahs—if not by name, then by sight—and find you a decent sort for the most part.

"Until nine a.m., then"—he cracked his gavel against the table top—"this court stands in recess."

Pete looked at me and winked.

"Please tell me you know what you're doing."

"I sure hope so."

I looked down at Billy, whose expression seemed to say, Me? I wanted to keep going, but you just had to stop and make some new friends, didn't you? If Jack was here he'd hit you on the head so hard you'd have to unzip your pants to blow your nose.

"Next time, I'll listen," I whispered to him.

Then Billy yawned. Easy to do when there's no chance your body'll be in the Lowlands come this time tomorrow.

It was close to midnight and I was freezing.

Billy lay curled up in my lap, fast asleep.

I had been moved outside the camp, to a special "holding area" that McGregor and one of the jury bulls had set up—according to Judge Carson instructions—before all the Law Boys left for the night.

I was still in handcuffs, though my legs had been untied so I could at least stand from time to time and stretch. McGregor and the jury bull had taken a group of 'Bo's down to the dump and hauled back a couple of discarded railroad ties which they proceed to set upright into a portion of soggy ground. The mud pulled the ties down about two feet before the things hit solid rock and stayed in place. Then one of the cuffs was opened and my arms were stretched behind my back and cuffed again behind the two ties—both of which extended to a good three feet past the top of my head. I didn't have a lot of room for moving, but at least it wasn't so tight that I couldn't relax my shoulders a little.

But only a very little.

Pete and Willie had made themselves pretty scarce after I was secured, and for the better part of the last four hours it'd just been me and Billy, sitting in the cold night air with little more than cricket-song and starlight for company.

Trees still surrounded me—in places pretty thick.

A man could hide himself pretty well in those trees.

I had a feeling I knew what was going to happen, and why it was that no one in the camp—McGregor included—had spoken up to say that I wasn't Icehouse Willie.

It was all a crap-shoot, and while I don't discourage a fellow from taking himself a big leap of faith once in a while, it feels a bit different when a possible snake eyes will come attached to a real snake of sorts, one filled with venom and ready to end your life in a heartbeat.

I looked down at Billy's sleeping form and jostled him with my legs.

Nothing.

I tried once more.

Billy made a little mewling sound in the back of his throat, dug his back claws in just a little bit deeper, but still didn't wake up.

"Wish to hell I could sleep like you," I said to him. "You have any idea how that used to burn Jack up when was on the road together? He used to say that you could probably sleep through a train wreck that was caused by an earthquake that took out an iron bridge." Then I laughed. "There were times he wondered whether or not you were deaf."

"What happened to your stammer, Willie?"

I snapped my head up just in time for my eyes to meet the business end of a .38.

"You should've known better than to try and catch a free ride on any line I worked for, Willie," said Carl, looking crazier than even before. He gave me the once over, then stepped back and gestured with his gun for me to stand up. "I don't like the idea of killing a man who's not on his feet, even though you goddamn tramps barely qualify as men, you ask me."

I thought that last remark should be left unanswered, so I shimmied myself up into a standing position, much to Billy's chagrin; he finally let go of my leg and dropped onto the ground, stretching, yawning, and hissing.

"Cute cat," said Carl.

"I get a lot of compliments on him, thank you."

Carl stepped forward again and pressed the barrel of the gun to the middle of my forehead. I was amazed that I didn't wet myself, I was so scared.

"Tell me one thing," he said.

"Anything to keep the conversation goin' as long as possible."

A smile slithered across his face like a worm. "Good that you can crack wise right now. Be a good idea if you kept a pleasant thought in your head."

In the distance I heard the whistle of a train.

Far off, from the opposite direction, it was answered—though not yet joined—by the cry of another train.

"How'd you see me, Willie? I mean, I was pretty fast on my feet and that door wasn't opened all that far, I just ran up and tossed in the lit book of matches…how'd you get a look at me?"

"I d-don't quite r-r-remember." The stammer this time wasn't play-acting on my part; I was scared right down to the ground.

Carl considered this for a moment, then shrugged, pulling back the hammer. "So I didn't get everyone in the boxcar. I guess I can live with that."

Billy had by now wandered over down by Carl's legs and was rubbing himself up against the bull's steel-toed boots.

Carl kicked out a bit but that didn't deter Billy; once he decides he's going to rub up against you, you just resign yourself to it and that's all she wrote.

"Dammit to hell!" Carl snapped looking down and giving Billy a more insistent kick—

—and that's when the gun slipped away from my forehead, a little off to the side—

—and that's when I heard a voice yell, "Duck!" from somewhere in the nearby trees—

—and then there was a blast from somewhere that sparked right above my head and sent Carl to the ground cussing and flailing and blew away a good foot of railroad tie above—

—and before I knew what was happening, I felt someone toying with the handcuffs.

"Don't make a sound," said Pete, who was in front of me.

"Who's messing with the cuffs—?"

"Willie," Pete replied. "Did I forget to mention that he used to be a locksmith?"

I twisted my neck so as to look beside me. "That true?"

"B-bad locks in t-t-town," said Willie, working the cuffs open with some sort of pin. "Bad and ch-ch-cheap, easy to break in, easy, easy, easy."

The cuffs came off and I took my pack when Pete offered it.

Carl still lay on the ground a few feet away, cradling his right hand against his chest. There wasn't any blood but his hand looked to have been burned pretty good. The cylinder of his .38 gleamed in the moonlight pooling near my feet. I looked around and saw the rest of his gun a few feet beyond that.

McGregor came walking up to Carl, holding a mean-looking pump-action shotgun in front of him.

"Helluva shot, ain't he?" said Pete.

"A true marksman," I replied, shaking so much I thought I was going to drop.

Trailing behind McGregor—and looking for all the world like the most cantankerous so-and-so you'd ever want to meet—was Judge Carson. Two sheriff's deputies flanked him.

I looked at Pete. "And…?"

"Okay, okay, sorry. Look, me and Willie, we been keeping close to Carl ever since Chicago. We figured it was only a matter of time before he wound up transferred to some little 'burg like this and we'd have time to…well, see if we couldn't do something about what he done. The trick was being able to stay in one place long enough to get the trust of the camp."

As he spoke, I noticed the other residents of the jungle, awakened by the gunfire and yelling, were shuffling toward us from down below.

"They had a helluva time convincing me," said McGregor over his shoulder. "I know Pete and Willie here fairly well, and I knew when Pete pulled a stunt like he did earlier today—you know, calling you up to testify like you were Willie…I figured something pretty serious must be going on."

I nodded. "That's why you didn't say anything?"

"That's why no one who knows the two of them didn't say anything. 'Course, that letter of Willie's that Carl had on him was a pretty convincing piece of evidence. That, and what he just now tried to do to you."

Carl was still, evidently fascinated by the barrel of McGregor's pump-gun.

"I'm real sorry that we did this to you," said Pete, putting a hand on my shoulder. "But we had to distract ole Carl's attention there in order to have time to convince McGregor and the Judge that Carl here's the fellah that set that fire in Chicago."

"Twelve people died in that fire," said Judge Carson. "Be they hoboes or not, it was murder. Some parts of this country still look poorly upon that."

"Judge," I said, nodding my head.

"That was quite a performance you gave this afternoon," he said. "Mildred's going get herself quite a laugh out of it when I tell her."

"How was dinner?" I asked.

Carson shuddered. "Oh, it was great, seein' my daughter and granddaughter, but my wife still can't make a decent gravy." He put a hand to his belly. "I was already up when McGregor came by with Pete and Willie. I figured even if this turned out to be a bust, I'd at least be out in the open when that gravy made me start sounding my horn…if you get my meaning."

The judge and McGregor, along with the two deputies, hauled Carl to his feet and cuffed him with the same cuffs he'd used on me. I'd be lying if I said I didn't get a certain amount of enjoyment out of seeing that.

I looked at Icehouse Willie. "Why'd you have to take Billy?"

"Sandy likes cats, that she d-d-does. Likes 'em a lot. Was always asking me for one. Her mother, though—" he whistled quick and low, "—can't stand the things. M-m-make her sneeze something terrible."

He was crying as he told me this.

"No one's g-g-gonna burn today, nosir, not while I'm around, nosir. No one's gonna burn. The Lowlands aren't g-g-gonna take anybody today, nosir."

Pete slapped my back. "C'mon, we got to get the hell out of here."

I heard the cry of the approaching train whistles.

"Where's Billy?"

Willie opened his coat. "S-snug as a bug."

Billy was nestled comfortably in one of Willie's massive inside pockets.

Judge Carson looked at us, then toward the train whistle. "You know, this here's gonna draw a lot of attention from folks for a while. Me and McGregor and the deputies, we all heard Carl's confession. The rest'll be fairly easy." He came up to Willie. "Justice will now be served, Willie. Your Carol and Sandy, they can rest easy now. So can you."

And with that, they hauled Carl away.

I turned and looked at the rest of the camp; they had stopped several yards away and were now making their way back to their beds, cricket-song and starlight accompanying them.

Life on the road is hard, but sometimes you make new and good friends.

"You in the market for a couple of extra traveling companions?" Pete asked.

"The more the merrier," I said as the four of us took off up the hill and over the rise toward the tracks.

We decked the rattler just outside the switch yard, disembarking a few hours later just a few miles from the Canadian border. From there we caught a lumber car.

We've been a team ever since.

Some nights Willie wakes up from his bad dreams about his wife and daughter. That's when Billy helps the most, soothing his night terrors while I tell him all about Heaven, and how Jack saw it. Then we smile at each other, finding peace in the thought of Jack and Sandy and Carol all sitting on that back porch under a summer night sky and sipping lemonade while the radio plays on. A good end to a good day's labors.

And no train whistles mourning.

The Lowlands can't touch us here.

MERMAID IN DENIM LONELY

*U*NDER THE WATER *life is long, life is hard; under the water life is long.*

Debra Mae Bishop stood alone on the nightbeach and watched as ocean returned the pebble she'd thrown out only moments before. Kneeling to pick up the tiny stone, she wondered if everything she ever tried to share or give of herself would be tossed back in her face with the same direct carelessness, but self-pity was never a land in which she journeyed for long, so she stood erect, arched back, and heaved the stone out into the damp night. She pulled a handful of change from her pocket, then—in a superstitious homage to the ancient Egyptian Trinity of Osiris, Isis, and Horus—bowed three times to the moon while making the loneliest of her lonely wishes. Half covered by the sand at her feet she saw the molding remains of a very small starfish, and wondered if the creature had been washed ashore against its will or if it had died while waiting for others like itself to rise from the depths and join it. Somehow the nightbeach made her think this way, and with each successive evening she had begun to hate it less and less.

She looked behind her, at the world of dry land, and asked herself, as she had every night for God knew how many weeks, what there was here that made it worth sticking around.

The soft whisper of the waves against the shore answered: *Nothing.*

She picked up the dead starfish and held it against her chest.

Under the water life is hard, life is long.

"I believe you," she said, her lonely heart no longer breaking.

Under the water life is long…

Some children found her clothes and jewelry the next morning.

"Told ya," said one to the other. "Told ya this is where the mermaids come when it's time for them to go home!"

TRISKAIDEKAPHOBIA

(Alfred Hitchcock, on the eve of *Frenzy*'s premiere)

1. *Number Thirteen*

Never finished that one, unfortunately; how the Jesuits would have laughed had they known. "So very much like you, Alfie," they'd say, knowing he disliked being addressed in that manner, by that name, with that tone. "But we, all of us, must learn our shortcomings, regardless of our age or station in life, mustn't we?" Dismissing him then with a smile full of pity and condescension, sometimes a pat on the head or cheek or – even worse – leaning over to ever-so-slightly straighten his tie (he loathed ties and the pressure they applied against one's throat; loathed the way they made it so difficult to swallow; loathed, above all, how it always felt as if the tie were wearing *him*): someday he would be able to proclaim his loathing of the beastly things to the world without fear of the schoolmaster's ruler, paddle, or slap in the face before the entire class.

A pity he looked so debonair when sporting a tie; patterns, he found, suited him better than solids; dots more than stripes.

—Are you a superstitious man?

—No, not at all, never, knock wood.

This always made the interviewers laugh.

"So very like you, Alfie," indeed. He would stand watching the backs of their Jesuit heads as they strode away from him, disappearing down the halls of St. Ignatius (though St. Indignant would have better suited the place; at least, as far as the treatment he and some of the others received), watching them grow smaller as they shrank into the glow of marbled tiles against which their shoes so loudly clicked, behind the shine of polished-wood doors that echoed like the explosion of a bomb when pulled so firmly closed. He was grateful for these noises: they masked the sound of knuckles cracking as he made a fist.

Impecunious.

Impecunious was the word one of the teachers had used when discussing him with another, unaware that he was passing by the room. Fancy word, that, one with which he was not acquainted, not then, not him, not the son of a poultry dealer and importer of fruit, not a boy who spent many weekends and holidays beside his father at the fruit and vegetable market, Covent Garden (a place against which he'd sworn vengeance for all the time lost there by both his father and himself).

Reflecting on such moments, now well over five decades behind him, he smiles a smile filled more with irony than bitterness as he tussles with the beastly thing in his hands. It will be worth it, he tells himself, catching a glimpse of his shadowy profile on the wall. It will be worth it. His ode to Covent Garden, neckties, and the bloody Thames (because of the ear infection it had given him when filming the trailer).

—Are you a superstitious man?

—No, not at all, never, knock wood.

It will be worth it, for this Impecunious son of a poultry dealer and importer of fruit. His smile fades as the beastly thing once again defeats his efforts to tame it. But he must look dapper, he must look dashing, he must look debonair for the premiere and the dinner to follow.

Still, as always before a premiere, he thinks of *Number Thirteen*. Never finished that one, unfortunately. Would like to have seen where it was going.

—Are you a superstitious man?

—No, not at all, never, knock wood.

A lie, that. He never began a film without thinking of the one left incomplete, never began a film without feeling a bit rattled (more than rattled, be honest – *afraid*) because, if he never finished that one, what guarantee was there that he would ever finish *this* one?

—Are you a superstitious man?

—No, not at all, never, knock wood.

"So very much like you, Alfie."

He thinks of his friend Michael Powell, about the disaster following the premiere of *Peeping Tom*, how the poor fellow's career never did recover, and wonders if Michael were here tonight, would he know that he was the one who helped to open this particular door.

2. "Mr. Rusk ... you're not wearing your tie."

"Everything that I put into that film, and all anyone cares to remember is that bloody backward tracking shot – down two curving flights of red-carpeted stairs, pulling out through the entryway, into the street, people and traffic moving into the frame as the camera reaches the other side and we look at this building where we know something horrible is happening inside and we cannot be of help.

"Actually, there are, I suppose, worse things that a film can be remembered for. Providing, of course, that one finishes the film his film."

—Are you a superstitious man?

—No, not at all, never, knock wood.

Would like to have seen where it was going.

3. *Family Plot*

Review: **

It has now become apparent that Hitchcock has forgotten how to tell a story. *Family Plot* stumbles along, having no idea where it's going, and too often relies on slapstick to take the place of wit. The final image of Barbara Harris winking at the camera and, by extension, the audience, is meant to tell us that we are in on Hitchcock's joke; unfortunately, Hitchcock forgot to tell us the joke, and all we are left with is the punchline. *Family Plot* feels somehow incomplete ...

—Are you a superstitious man?
—Not at all. Never. Knock wood.
(... *how the Jesuits would have laughed* ...)

I Never Spent the Money

"It is strange that the Mind will forget so much, and yet hold a picture
   of flowers that have been dead for thirty years and more."

—Richard Llewellyn, *How Green Was My Valley*

"I COULD DO IT, you know," said the old man, nervously cradling his tall whiskey and water. "I could just get up from this stool and walk out that door and go over to that damned bank and…yeah…" He took a few sips from his drink, winced as the alcohol hit his stomach, and smiled bitterly. "I know I could do it" His eyes filled with dispirited fragments of memories.

Elliot Richards took a drag off his fifth cigarette and turned toward the old guy. "You could do what?"

"Rob the place."

Elliot eyed his barstool neighbor with quiet amusement, wondering just how drunk the old geezer was. He supposed that everyone had the same fantasy at one time or another: throw on a ski mask, burst in with a gun, scare the bejeezus out of everyone, and make off with a few thousand. Probably sounded good to most people toward the end of the month when the bills were piling up and the TV was on the fritz and the insurance premium that it seemed like you paid just last week came due again. Hell, even bank employees had to think about it at least once; you could handle all that cash only so long before wondering how a nice thick roll of it would feel nestled in your pocket. Yeah, everyone fantasized about committing that one Big Robbery. Elliot had thought about it himself. Especially lately. Thought about it a lot.

"Just like that?" he asked the old man. "Just waltz in there like Butch Cassidy and clean 'em out and become a legend in your own time?"

The old man swirled his drink. "Sure. And I'm gonna do it. Take that money and…" His voice trailed off as the bartender sauntered over and asked if either of them would like another round. Elliot shook his head and the bartender—a slab of beef with a crewcut and longshoreman's hands—gave a quick but suspicious look to the old man, then wandered back to the end of the bar and watched the small black-and-white television mounted on the wall.

The old man set down his drink, cracked his knuckles, and cleared his throat. "I bet you don't think I could, do you?"

"How long have you been nursing that drink?"

"Long enough. You didn't answer my question—you don't think I can pull it off, do you?"

"I never said that, pal, I only asked—"

"And don't call me 'pal'! I got a name, and if you want to talk with me, you be courteous and ask what it is."

"Fine. What's your—"

"Nathaniel. And yours?"

"Elliot."

"Pleased to meet you," said the old man, extending his hand. Elliot shook it, surprised that the old guy's grip was rough yet friendly, thick with callouses, not weak and frail and sponge-soft like he'd expected; this Nathaniel had done some mighty manual labor in his time.

Elliot crushed out his cigarette and immediately lit another.

"You smoke too much," said the old man.

"You sound like my wife—my ex-wife. Soon-to-be ex."

"Maybe them smokes are why she called it quits. No sense sittin' around watching somebody commit suicide on the installment plan."

"I've heard enough lectures, Nate, and—"

"Nathaniel," snapped the old man. "I hate it when folks take a right proper name and trim it down 'cause they don't like the feel of all them extra syllables in their mouth."

"All right; Nathaniel it is." Elliot studied him and Nathaniel stared right back. This Nathaniel wasn't so old as to be thought ancient but the cracks and lines and discolorations in his features betrayed that he'd seen better days. His eyes were every lonely journey Elliot had ever taken, every unloved place he'd visited, every sting of guilt he'd ever felt. He didn't tremble at all, though, which Elliot found refreshing; it seemed that every old dude you ran into these days had the shakes like some lush going through the DTs. This Nathaniel had a hardness about him that drew Elliot's interest and held it.

"You ain't from around these parts, are you?"

"Just driving through," replied Elliot. "My divorce becomes final in three days and I just had to... well, you know... get away from things." He didn't know why he said it. Maybe he just needed someone to talk to. Didn't everyone?

"How come she left, if you don't mind me askin'?"

"How do you know she did the leaving?"

"You're still wearing your wedding ring."

Elliot looked at his left hand. Nathaniel was right.

"Got a livelihood, son?"

Elliot shook his head. "I'm what you call 'between situations' at the moment"

"That why she left?"

"No. She was pretty good about it. I just got kind of crappy about her having to support us."

"Bruise your ego, did she?"

Elliot turned to face him. "Not that it's any of your business, but, no."

"Liar."

"Yeah, well … it sure sounded full of conviction, didn't it?"

"Not particularly."

Elliot rubbed his eyes and sipped at his drink. "The goddamn plant just up and shut down. Happens all the time in this glorious land of prosperity. We had to make do with what I got in severance pay, which wasn't a whole helluva lot and—ah, just forget it!" He turned away and cursed himself under his breath. Two weak drinks and he turned into a copy of *True Confessions*.

"You know what I don't understand?" he said. "I don't understand why it is that if you're broke and unemployed at twenty-one, people'll smile and tell you that it's okay, you're young; if you're broke and unemployed at seventy, people'll smile and tell you that it's okay, you're old; but if you're broke and unemployed and thirty-five, these same people don't smile or say anything to you because you're just a failure."

"You must've worked pretty hard to polish that self-pity routine of yours."

Elliot laughed but there was no humor in it. "Oh, you bet I did. But Sandy—that's my wife—ex-wife—soon—"

"—to-be," said Nathaniel. "I was listening."

"Sandy was really patient with me. Then I started to just get… mad about everything. Losing my temper over nothing and… breaking things."

"Didn't lay a hand on her, did you? I can't tolerate a man who raises his hand against a woman."

"No—God, no. I couldn't live with myself if I'd done something like that. No, I just stewed all the time and never talked to her—yell at her, yes, but that was the extent of our marriage; her being patient and supportive, me throwing fits about it. She finally had enough and left. That simple. Case closed." After a moment he sighed, crushed out his cigarette, and said, "So you're gonna go across the street and take that bank, are you?"

"Why the hell not?"

"Prison might be a good reason."

Nathaniel grunted. "Judge'd take one look at how old I am and give me community service."

"I wouldn't count on that."

"Then how's about I don't care."

"How's about telling me why?"

Nathaniel got off his stool and shuffled over to a rusted jukebox in the corner. Elliot noticed, then, how the bartender watched the old man with something like pity in his eyes, and wondered how much of the conversation the guy had overheard.

A soft, sweet voice came out of the speaker, singing "When I Grow Too Old to Dream."

Nathaniel returned to his stool and said, "I just want to finally do something."

"There'll be security guards, you know? Don't take this wrong but you don't strike me as the type who'd have quick reflexes under fire."

"My ass did all right under fire at Omaha Beach, boy!"

"They could shoot you. Probably will if they get half a chance."

Nathaniel gave him that bitter smile again. "Don't matter none to me anymore. When you get right down to it we're all being shot. It just takes the bullet sixty years or so to hit you. Meantime, you still pay on the mortgage and take medicine. Doesn't make sense somehow." He hoisted his drink.

That's when Elliot saw the thin, white, plastic bracelet with blue computer print hanging around Nathaniel's wrist

He walked out of a laughing academy.

He was sitting here having a drink with a looney.

Nathaniel caught sight of where Elliot was staring and pulled back his sleeve, inviting closer scrutiny. "I walked out of that goddamn nursing home at eleven-fifteen this morning. Been there goin' on two years now. Couldn't take it no more."

"What do you plan on robbing the bank with, an IV needle?"

"No," said Nathaniel, reaching into the pocket of his coat. "I intend to use this." He produced a Deutsche-Werk 7.65mm pistol, VMI model. "Only war souvenir I got left. And it works, too. I kept real good care of it." He slowly jacked back the slide to show how smoothly it operated. "Took it off a dead German soldier in France. Those dummies at the nursing home—I've had this thing in the bottom drawer of my dresser all this time and they never knew it." He leaned in and lowered his voice to a whisper. "Snuck it in wrapped up in a bag of my underwear. They ain't too swift over there. Damn nursing home." He slipped the gun back into his pocket. "I only get twenty-five dollars a month out of my DAV check—that's all the more allowance they'll let a person have. Rest goes for the bills and for tissues and…stuff like that. I been squirrelin' it away, my allowance. I got close to a hundred dollars in my pocket. Bus money to Mexico when I make my getaway. I'm gonna finish this drink, then I'm gonna go do it."

Elliot swallowed hard as he lit another cigarette—with shaking hands, no less—and looked toward the end of the bar, hoping that the bartender—

—no good. He'd seen the gun and was already dialing a number on the phone.

Elliot spun around and said, "Don't do it, Nathaniel, it's not worth it."

"Whatta you care? Calling me Butch Cassidy and shaking your head at me?"

"I told you about my wife! I'm having a drink with you! That should count for something."

"Yeah, son, that's right. Everything ought to count for something." He exhaled, lowered his head, and cupped his hands around the nearly empty glass in front of him. The song on the jukebox finished playing. There was a loud squeak and a couple of clunks as the record changed, then another sweet voice, this one a little sadder than the last, began singing "What'll I Do?"

The bartender replaced the handset, glanced at the old man, and turned away. Elliot was certain he'd seen pity in those eyes.

"I used to be quite a specimen," said Nathaniel. "Was not an ounce of flab on this form, nosiree. I worked honest and hard all my life, I served my country well, and I married a right fine woman who bore me three daughters. We never lived like no royalty but we done all right. My wife's been dead for six years now and I never…never once did anything to surprise her."

"Committing armed robbery isn't exactly like giving her a diamond ring for your anniversary."

"I ain't talking about giving her stuff, I'm talking about showing her that I had some nerve…" He took out his wallet and flipped to a couple of pictures. He gently touched one old black-and-white photograph of a lovely, tiny, frail-looking woman whose hair was tied back in a bun. Next to it was a photograph of a small boy who Elliot assumed was Nathaniel as a child. He wondered why Nathaniel didn't carry any pictures of his daughters.

"No, my wife didn't have much need for stuff. I just always wanted to show her I wasn't all talk. 'Got yourself a head crammed full of notions, Nathaniel,' she always said. And I did. I had me some right powerful notions about all the things I wanted to do with my life. None of 'em ever really panned out."

Elliot felt a thin bead of perspiration form on his upper lip. He kept glancing toward the front window, expecting to see a squad car or two come driving up, visibar lights flashing. Sandy would get a kick out of that, probably say something like, See? The minute I leave you, you fall in with felons. And you'll still probably insist that you don't need me, right?

Wrong.

Elliot had never wanted to see someone so much in his life as he wanted to see his wife, his ex-wife, his soon-to-be ex-wife right now.

"My daughters're all moved away now," said Nathaniel, looking down at the pictures. He seemed confused for a moment, then shook his head and continued. "I suppose they got too much to do, what with their own families and all. Probably don't have the time to come visit the old man in the home. Just as well. Seems like every time I get a visitor, they run out of things to say after fifteen minutes, then spend fifteen more apologizing because they have to leave so soon on account of their bein' so busy." He closed the wallet and laid it on the bar next to his nearly empty glass. "My body just don't want to cooperate no more. I cough too much, been dropping weight something terrible. Sometimes I get the pains so bad I can't move and the nurses, they have to… wipe me and such. I have to wear this goddamn thing that's like a big diaper—got it on right now, matter of fact. I hate it. They all talk to me like I'm some damn three-year-old who can't remember his name from one minute to the next—'course, they got their reasons. There's this one fellah comes to see me every so often and try as I do I just can't seem to… recall his name or where I know his face from. Seems to know me well enough, though." He let out a long, heavy breath. "That's how come I'm gonna rob that bank. If I'm getting too old to remember what my friends look like, then I probably ain't got too much longer left. Time to take the bull by the horns—how's that for a right powerful notion? I always…" He drifted away for a moment.

"You always what?" asked Elliot, looking at the bartender who was crouched under the counter. Maybe the guy had a shotgun stashed down there in case there was trouble. Elliot fired up another smoke and turned back to Nathaniel, who was saying, "…always had the same damn dream, had it again last night, matter of fact. I find me a ton of money, or someone gives it to me, or I win it in the lottery, or I steal it and don't get caught. Don't matter. Point is, there's a load of cash and I got it. And I'm on my way home with this money and I'm all excited because my wife's still alive and my daughters are still in grade school and I can't much stand the wait because I'm gonna buy 'em all them things we couldn't ever afford before." He was alive now, his gestures sharp, his eyes wide and glittering, thirty years younger and no longer beaten down by a world he hoped was going to give him a fair shake but didn't. Elliot couldn't help but get caught up in Nathaniel's excitement. "My wife, I'm gonna get her some real nice clothes and the best damn hi-fi they make so she can play her Elvis records until I can't stand 'em no more. And no one's going to laugh at my little girls because they each only got one pair of shoes to wear to school, nosiree. My family's going to have the best stuff there is and no one'll dare look down their noses at them like they was trash and—" he stopped, his mouth hanging open, hands parted in mid-air, posture strong and confident, trying to find just the right words to express the rest.

Then his eyes darted back and forth as if searching for some image, some memory, some right powerful notion; not finding it, they turned downward to stare at the bar. His shoulders slumped, his mouth closed, his hands drifted down to cup around the glass, and as the jukebox gave out with "There Will Never Be Another You" he was an old man again, broken by the storms, who'd come to rest his weary bones among the bottles and cigarette smoke. "Thing of it is," he whispered, "I always wake up just before I get home. All the times I've had that dream I never once got to use it; I never spent the money. And I should have been able to. Just once. Is that so much to ask for?" He lifted the glass, drained what little whiskey was left, put it down on the bar, tossed down some wadded singles, and stood. "So you see, Mr. Elliot, I'm gonna do it and I don't much care what happens to me after. This damn notion's all I got left and I don't want to die wondering if I could've pulled it off."

Elliot glanced over his shoulder and saw that the bartender was moving toward them slowly, with extreme caution.

He gripped Nathaniel's arm. "Look, even if you do, through some miracle, get away with it, there's a million"—he lowered his voice to a whisper— "ways they can catch you later. Fingerprints, pictures from hidden cameras, marked bills— they could put one of those stain bombs in with the money, or—"

"Save your breath son. You're right. I might get caught, might even get myself killed for trying—but at least I'll have tried. Butch Cassidy went down trying. Nothing wrong with that. Probably died with no regrets."

He pulled away and, giving a quick, two-fingered salute to Elliot, turned and went out the door.

Elliot saw that Nathaniel had left his wallet on the bar and reached for it but the bartender got to it first. Elliot looked up and saw that the man's eyes were red-rimmed and moist. He opened the wallet and flipped to the two pictures Nathaniel had been looking at.

"We have to stop him before the police get here!" said Elliot, panic rising in his chest.

The bartender reached out one beefy hand and gripped Elliot's forearm. "I didn't call the police," he whispered. "You might say old Nathaniel there is a…a regular. Though I doubt he remembers it."

Elliot felt confusion swim up to mingle with the panic that had jumped into his throat. "W-what?"

The bartender closed the wallet and shoved it in his pocket. "I called CHH. They got someone on the way out to get him." He gave a short, disgusted laugh. "The security there's been a joke for awhile now."

"But the bank!" shouted Elliot, jumping to his feet.

"Come on, mister. I want you to see something." He guided Elliot to the large front window. "There's your bank."

Elliot looked out the window and across the street to a large stone archway with the words CEDAR HILL SAVINGS AND LOAN chiseled on it.

The bank was little more than a half-gutted building with grimy, broken, boarded-up windows.

He swallowed. "How long's the place been that way?"

"Going on six years now," said the bartender, wiping some sweat off his face. "You know, it's funny that you called him Butch Cassidy like you did. He likes to tell stories about how he used to play Butch and Sundance with his little boy."

Elliot stared as Nathaniel reached the front of the bank and stood at the rotted doors with his legs wide apart and his hands on his hips in a sad imitation of the classic Western Outlaw stance. "But he said that he had three daughters…"

"No," said the bartender, shaking his head. "Mom died when I was born. That was close to forty years ago. He never remarried. He changes the story every time this happens—but he believes it, you'd better bet."

"What about the gun?"

"Oh hell, it don't have any bullets. Doesn't even have a clip for that matter. Never did. This is the fourth time he's done this but…it's the first time he ever brought the gun with him. Isn't that interesting?" He leaned against the window and watch Nathaniel kick open the bank doors. "I always wondered what happened to that damn gun. I have all of his medals, you know? Bought him a real nice wood case to put 'em in."

Elliot turned away when he saw the first tear slip from the bartender's eye.

"Helluva disappointment to live through once," said the bartender, "let alone over and over again. Man works his whole life long with only a few notions to keep him going, then one day it turns out he can't remember anything except those notions so he has to make the rest up. Strange, isn't it? Some men want to build ships and end up slinging booze; he wanted to be Butch Cassidy and ends up in diapers. I wish just once that he'd remember who I was. Just long enough so I could say good-bye."

Elliot couldn't take any more. He threw some cash onto the bar, grabbed up his cigarettes, and stormed out to his car. As he started the engine an official-looking vehicle with the words CEDAR HILL HEALTHCARE CENTER—EMERGENCY VEHICLE painted on its doors pulled up across from the bank. Two burly attendants and a nurse got out, spoke quickly and quietly among themselves, then—evidently deciding to wait until Nathaniel came out—walked toward the bar.

As Elliot pulled away he thought of Sandy and how she always said he wasn't a disappointment to her because he had a good heart, even if he didn't think so.

He looked at his wedding ring and wondered if she'd be at her apartment tonight. Maybe they could talk things over before it was too late.

He made a U-turn and was driving past the bank when Nathaniel came out. He tried not to watch as the old man stumbled into the street toward a final showdown that no one would be able to save him from.

"I hope you get to spend some of it this time," whispered Elliot; then, rubbing something from his eye, he drove toward the road home and the woman he hoped was still waiting there.

WHEN IT IS DECIDED THAT THE WAR IS OVER

• • • A ND FOR THOSE OF YOU who might not have been born yet, in September of 1945 the General Headquarters of the Occupational Forces issued a statement so flat and emotionless in its content and intent that it still leaves one absolutely speechless. This statement—I can't remember the exact wording, it's been well over half a century and I was only five years old at the time, but my uncle, Robert Pearson, was a correspondent with CBS at the time, and so had access to a copy of the report, which said, in essence, that those civilians of Hiroshima and Nagasaki who were likely to die from A-bomb afflictions should be left to die. The official attitude was that people suffering from radiation poisoning were not worth saving, and that any attempt to do so would be an inexcusable waste of time, money, and medical supplies. What was understood but of course unwritten was that the General Headquarters of the Occupational Forces did not want to risk the lives of U.S. military personnel by sending them into the quote affected areas unquote. They were just beginning to understand the wide-ranging effects of what had been done, of how long those effects were going to last, and how they had, in our zest to end that damned war, unleashed their version of Frankenstein's Monster on the entire world. Perhaps calling it 'Oppenheimer's Monster' would be more precise, but I never agreed with that, not entirely. I had the privilege of interviewing J. Robert Oppenheimer in December of 1966, shortly before his death a few months later. Even then, he could not stop himself from railing against the 1954 hearings that resulted in his security clearance being revoked.

I was 26 years old, it was my first really important assignment, and put me 'on the map,' as the saying goes.

"The man who is now in referred to as the 'Father of the Atomic Bomb' was, in his own way, broken by what he had helped to create. His outspokenness against the bomb before, during, after the hearings is well-documented, and I have no doubt that those records—now in the form of computer files—are tucked securely away on several hard drives scattered about through the two dozen or so underground cave bunkers where the men and women who once governed us are now making their preparations for when it is decided that the war is over. Those computer files, like those whose duty it was to assemble and organize them, are safe and sound, along with those three thousand U.S. citizens who were chosen for their skills, or their knowledge—or were among the seventeen-hundred-and-fifty who were given a place by lottery drawing. After all, while it's all well and good to have the politicians, the doctors, the physicists, the scientists, poets, writers, newspersons, composers, actors, painters, and others without whom American culture would vanish from the face of whatever will be left of the Earth, there must also be a place for those who perform the invisible tasks that the others cannot be bothered to think about. There must be a place for the cooks, for the dishwashers, for the construction workers, janitors, plumbers, maids, electricians, the butchers, the bakers, the candlestick-makers…

"I was told by the technicians who helped me to set up this broadcast that the network has picked it up for a national feed, so there may be millions of you watching me right now…or maybe no one is watching. I don't suppose it matters, since everything is being recorded, stored away on digital files, preserved for posterity…or maybe not. I have no idea if this broadcast will be saved or even remembered, but I will not stop talking to you until the choice is taken out of my hands.

"If you'll look behind me, you'll see that I am standing atop a television station building in a typical, bland, white-bread Midwestern city. You can see the roofs of houses in the distance, just past the section of now-deserted freeway. The panic is over, the rioting has stopped, the looters have taken all there is to take. If my calculations are correct—and I base these calculations on those issued by the Pentagon—then I have a little over thirty-six minutes before the first missile strikes the air force base a few dozen miles from here.

"Do you like this tie I'm wearing? I actually spent five minutes this morning choosing it. It is the tie I wore when I made my first news broadcast over fifty years ago. My late wife knew how to take care of such things—ties, shoes, suits, all manner of clothing—and it seemed only appropriate that I wear this tie for my final broadcast. The morning of my first broadcast, Carol—my late wife—chose this tie for me. I do this for you, my love, my heart, and hope that you can hear me, wherever you are. You've no idea how happy I am that you are not here to witness these final minutes of the human race—the human race that has been abandoned above-ground, I should clarify. The human race who didn't have enough money, education, talent, or skill to rate a place in one of the underground bunkers. The human race that has been left to face its own extinction with the same matter-of-fact dispassion that deemed the survivors of Hiroshima and Nagasaki not worth saving. I never thought I would say these words my love, my heart, but I am so grateful for your being dead right now. I don't know if I could have found it in me to…

"I'll get to that in a few minutes. Right now, I want to talk briefly about how all of this came about—not only for whatever historical record of this broadcast may or may not remain, but for my own…understanding, if that's the correct word. I *still* can't believe that we, as a race, allowed this to occur. To destroy the world because one nation tried to help another that was starving to death by the millions each day. Until seven months ago, most of us had never heard of Zapheristan — or if we had, it was just another poverty-stricken, disease-laden, revolution-wracked Third World place where starvation and sickness was a way of life.

"Our late president, James Ryan, as you'll recall, sent in ground troops when anti-government rebels blocked all ports in and around Zapheristan and began using anti-aircraft guns on any planes that attempted to drop medical supplies and food. As a result, nearly half a billion dollars' worth of food and medicine was either being sold on the black market, distributed among the rebel camps, or simply left to rot and expire. The UN Peacekeepers were having little-to-no effect, even when combined with U.S. ground forces, and so President Ryan had little choice but to send in even more troops, much to the ferocious outcry of the public.

"The worst of it came ten days before Ryan attempted to send in those troops. Not only had the U.S. ground forces lost another twenty-seven soldiers to rebel attacks, but sources inside the Zapheristan capital were reporting that a large shipment of arms intended for government forces had been intercepted by the rebels and that U.S. soldiers were facing the very real prospect of being fired upon by American-made weapons as well as Kalashnikov rifles of Russian, Eastern European, and Chinese manufacture, Soviet RPG-7 rocket-propelled grenades, AT-3 anti-tank missiles, Chinese "Red Arrows," and mortars ranging from 82-millimeter to 102-millimeter. Though possessing far less manpower than the combined U.S. and NATO forces, the rebels were now nearly as heavily armed. They blew up three main ports, making supply drops even more dangerous than they had been in the first place. Outbreaks of cholera and other diseases in the migrant camps had wiped out nearly all the medical supplies that had managed to get through in the early days of the conflict; even basics such as bandages and peroxide were scarce. Another supply drop was scheduled, but whether or not U.S. military vehicles would be able to get safely through the blockades rebels had placed on the road which linked Zapheristan to the Uganda-Kenya railroad system—the only viable option, since the port of Mombasa had fallen—remained to be seen.

"It didn't look very promising—unless, of course, U.S. soldiers staged a full-scale offensive to take back the main supply road—an action that would leave, conservatively, at least three hundred American soldiers dead. President Ryan fought tooth-and-nail for the authorization from Congress, calling in every political marker he had, and after one of the longest and most vicious sessions in Congressional history, was given the authorization by only a narrow margin.

"Do you remember, at the 'Town Hall' meeting Ryan insisted on having two days later in Philadelphia, when one of the people in attendance asked him point-blank: 'Why are you doing this? Why are you willing to risk the lives of hundred of American soldiers to deliver *groceries*?' Do you remember his answer? He looked right at that woman and said, in a voice as calm and assured as any I've ever heard: 'Because no one else is, and I don't know about you, but I have trouble sleeping knowing that for every hour I'm asleep, a minimum of one-hundred-thousand men, women, and children—mostly children, in case anyone gives a damn—will die from disease or starvation before most of us switch on *Good Morning America*.'

I would have liked to have heard that woman's response, but as those of you who were watching know, that's when the bullet took off half of President Ryan's head. How the assassin was able to smuggle in the gun used to kill the president was never discovered—unless, of course, as was hypothesized, it had been placed there beforehand by someone connected to or working directly with the Secret Service. God knows President

Ryan had made some powerful enemies during the days of the Zapheristan conflict. And as much as I hate to admit it, it no longer seems like such a fantastical notion that a U.S. president could be killed by members of his own government…but any further speculation is pointless. The vice-president was sworn in and shortly thereafter, a nuclear missile was launched at Zapheristan, making Ryan's efforts, as well as his death, futile. To this hour we're still uncertain as to who it was who made the strike—though some would like us to believe it was either China or Iran, both countries now having been fired on by the US. I could rattle off all the theories and data that were made public, but what's it matter now? Our new president, given almost absolute power due to the state of war that now existed, immediately appointed the Secretary of Defense as his new V.P. The new V.P. was aboard an aircraft carrier at sea, was sworn in over the radio, and given his orders. Every position in the government was filled by the person next in line. Re-shuffle the deck, cut the cards, and hope for the best because there's no time for red tape or meetings or discussion. How were we to know that some of those now in power would be madmen, wielding scepters?

"I liked Jim Ryan. He was a moral man who had the misfortune of allowing his morality to sometimes override his political savvy. I well remember the famous line that many credit with winning him the presidency: 'All problems confronting the human race are and always shall be at their core *moral ones,* matters of conscience, human decency, and compassion; they only become *political issues* when someone or a large group of someones can gain wealth, power, fame, or real estate—preferably all four—by exploiting them.'

"How right he has been proven. Except who will buy the real estate when it is decided that the war is over? Who will buy any piece of land from the nations of ash that will greet them when they finally emerge from their underground havens and walk out into sunlight again? Who will even have the money, wealth, fame, and power—illusions that they have now been revealed to be?

"I have seen too much war in my lifetime. Yes, some of these wars were called 'police actions,' but when bombs are dropped, villages and cities reduced to rubble, when bullets are fired that take the lives of men, women, and children, it's a war. And it is not kind, despite the debated irony of that famous poem.

"I remember, when I was covering Vietnam, standing with a film crew on a road outside a Montagnard village that had recently been bombed. The surviving villagers were stumbling and crawling away from the destruction. A few of them had managed to find wagons in which to place their dead or wounded. One old woman was pulling such a wagon, and her strength struck me then as it does now as the kind of superhuman strength one finds in oneself during times of war, for inside this wagon was a young man or perhaps fifteen who was using a sewing needle and some kind of terrible thread to try and stitch up the chest and groin of a child—I couldn't tell if it was a boy or a girl, only that it was a child. The child's innards were spilling out, and the young man was trying to hold them in place with one hand while he used the other to push the needle and thread through the child's flesh.

"The child was still conscious and screaming, but it did not try to move or push away the young man's hands, as if it understood that he was trying to save it. Both were covered in blood and burned skin, their clothes—what remained of them—still smoldering. But what stays with me above all else is what happened when that child saw us as the old woman pulled the wagon passed. Its eyes widened, and the expression of anguish on its face softened for just a moment, and then… excuse me…and then…*dammit!*

"…and then it *smiled* at me, one of its small, ruined hands rising up from its blasted body to point at the camera. It understood that it was being filmed, that it was going to be on television. Somehow that knowledge—however the child had acquired it—took the pain away for just a few seconds, and it waved at the camera as the wagon was pulled by.

"That footage was never aired, and it was my fault because I was in tears…not unlike the pathetic spectacle you're witnessing now. But that was Vietnam. Since then I've witnessed similar scenes in the Gulf, in Israel, Nicaragua, Afghanistan, Iraq and Iran, I've seen the 'dying rooms' in the mountains of China where sick and deformed children are abandoned to suffer a slow, miserable, lonely death, I've seen bodies floating in rivers of blood and intestines through the center of Rwanda, I've seen corpses piled as high as the sun in El Salvador, and I have seen too many screaming, wounded, terrified children running through bomb-blasted streets crying for their mother, or their father, or brother, sister, *anyone* to come and hold them, to make them safe, to take away all the pain and fear and make everything all right again and I am here to tell all of you who might be watching that this time, *this time* there is no making everything all right again. For those of us left above-ground, there remains between fifteen minutes and ninety minutes of life, depending on where in this country you live. California is gone, as is Utah and Nevada. Was anyone there to record those screams, I wonder. Is anyone there to open their arms to the radiation-scorched children who are crawling through the debris, crying for someone to come and hold them? And when it is decided that the war is over, will those children, should they still somehow be alive, find it in their war-ravaged hearts to forgive? Or will forgiveness be nothing more than an abstract concept to them, like freedom and compassion and God?

"Forgive me for raising my voice like that. It won't do to have my final minutes spent with you remembered for my having done nothing but scream. For over fifty years you have—if I am to believe the *Newsweek* poll done a few years back—looked to me as the 'voice of reason.' A reasonable man would not scream at you, not with so little time left, so, again, please accept my apologies.

"I came back here to the city where my career began so that I might see my daughter, my son-in-law, and my grandchildren. They were so happy to welcome me into their homes, even knowing how terrible things had become. My son-in-law, you see, was not one of the people deemed 'of use' for the bunkers and caves and mine-shafts where now America functions and will continue to do so for years to come. My son-in-law, you see, is a factory worker whose only 'useful' skill is cutting saw blades. My daughter is, by choice, a stay-at-home mother. I could not possibly be more proud of either of them, or of my wonderful grandchildren. They took me into their home at this worst of all possible times and made me feel a sense of being loved again, of being needed, of being *necessary*.

"They didn't know that I had been offered a place in the bunkers, in the caves, in the mine-shafts, in America Below. They didn't know that I had told the military officials who came to 'collect' me that they could go straight to Hell—which should be easier for them, since they'd be so much closer than I. I had watched these same officials literally pull a physicist away from his wife and children, telling him that they were not 'on the list,' that they were 'acceptable losses.' I watched these officials knock that physicist unconscious because he refused to leave without his family. And I watched as his family, screaming and in tears, chased after the vehicle into which he was thrown.

"When it is decided that the war is over, perhaps it will also be decided that there is no such thing as an 'acceptable' loss. I don't know where that physicist's wife and children are now. Maybe they're watching this broadcast. If they are, I want you to know how sorry I am that the government and the military in all of their collected wisdom somehow found it 'acceptable' to offer a place in America Below to an old newscaster in his seventies who's dying of cancer, rather than allow you to remain a family.

"My daughter and her family did not know about my cancer. Nor will they. You see, my doctor is an old coot, like me, who knows there are better and more peaceful ways to shuffle off this sad mortal coil than to be consumed in slow degrees by a disease that leaves you without any dignity in the final hours. And so my doctor, he gave me something. I don't suppose it will matter much to tell you about it now. What he gave me were two vials of Potassium, enough for several sixty milli equivalent doses. Death is instantaneous and painless when it's injected.

"Last night, as I made the preparations for this final broadcast, I doped my daughter and her family with sleeping pills that I had crushed up and mixed in with her homemade chocolate pudding—last night's dessert. It wasn't enough to kill any of them, just enough to make certain none of them would come awake while I did what needed to be done.

"I moved from room to room with the vials and a single hypodermic. I administered the exact doses of Potassium and then held each of their hands as they died. None of them suffered, none of them went into convulsions, there was no screaming. And this morning I showered, shaved, chose this tie from the three I'd packed, and came here to the roof of this local television station.

"The sentimentalist in me, the little boy who believed and embraced the idea of God and heaven and Peace Eternal, hopes that my daughter and her family are with Carol at this moment, and that there is no more suffering, no more pain. As sad as I am that they are gone, I feel not one whit of regret for my actions. I have that hypodermic in my pocket now, with twice the needed dosage in it. If I choose to do this, I'll be dead before the plunger if halfway sunk.

"But I won't do that to you, because right now we're all we've got left. So in these last few minutes, let's not talk about what is or what was. Let's talk about what's to come—much later. Let's talk about what will happen when it is decided that the war is over, shall we? This is Lowell Douglas Pearson, broadcasting from not-so high atop your favorite local television station, and it's time we spoke directly and honestly.

"Can you see it in your imaginations? The day when the nuclear winter is past, when the radiation levels have dropped to an 'acceptable' level, when the sealed solid-steel doors of the American Below are opened and the survivors walk into the new day?

"When it is decided that the war is over, they will all embrace one another and shake hands and kiss each other's tears away. When it is decided that the war is over, they will pour one another celebratory drinks and organize parades. When it is decided that the war is over, they will gather in public places and sing happy, spiritual songs, even if it is raining or well above ninety degrees. They will feel good about themselves and all they've managed to protect and save, because feeling good will be the first step toward doing good when it is decided that the war is over. And they will believe in doing good, just as J. Robert Oppenheimer and everyone who worked on Fat Man and Little Boy believed they were doing good. 'It's good to feel good,' they'll say. 'It's good to *do* good,' they'll say, then all join hands and sing 'Shall We Gather at the River' or 'Teach Your Children' or 'Michael Rowed the Boat Ashore.' Their pets will eat only organic food along with them when it is decided that the war is over. And all of their artists, all of their composers, their philosophers, their poets with their visions and their novelists constructing new visions and all their lyrical essayists who have been busy scribbling or typing or recording their thoughts and memoirs will all rethink their stances and outlooks and viewpoints when it is decided that the war is over. Their leaders will all assemble and say to one another, 'This must never happen again,' while their assistants secretly gather the sticks and stones that will be needed to fight the next war that no one wants to think about but knows is coming.

"And what of us, we who will never savor the joys and safety of America Below? We will be the bodies they have not seen and so do not speak of as they step into the light of the new day. When it is decided that the war is over we will still be here: mud, rot, dust, bones, sleeping peacefully beneath the soils of their nations of ash, and they will hear our bones crunch under their feet and smell the faint scent of our charred flesh and perhaps a few of them will imagine that they can still hear our final cries wafting by on the breeze, a paper cup tumbling in the wind when it is decided that the war is over.

"But we'll be beyond all that, you, your families, and I, because when it is decided that the war is over we will not be the ones in need of forgiveness, or comfort, or a way to fall asleep at night without the faces of the dead marching across our memories.

"I don't know how much time we've got left, so I'm going to tell you the thing you most need to hear, the thing we all want to hear, the only thing that can perhaps be that warm hand reaching out of the smoke from a death-stinking battlefield to pull you in and enfold you in understanding arms. And maybe, just maybe, when it is decided that the war is over, some part of this broadcast will remain, and they'll know that we who were not part of America Below spent our final minutes caring for one another, soothing the fears of our children, giving thanks that our loved ones would not leave this world alone.

"So come closer, my family, my friends, all of you. Come closer and look into my eyes and listen to the sound of my voice as you kiss your wives and husbands and brothers and sisters and children and grandchildren. Listen to me, listen to the sound of my voice.

"Don't be afraid, everything's all right, it will all be over soon. Don't be afraid, everything's all right, it will all be over soon. Don't be afraid, everything's all right, it will all be over soon. Don't be afraid, everything's all right, it will all be over soon. Don't be afraid, everything's all right, it will all be over soon. Don't be afraid, everything's all right, it will all be over soon. Don't be afraid, everything's all right, it will all be over soon. Don't be afraid, everything's all right, it will all be

Esmeralda; No Fanfare, Please

WHEN QUASIMODO AWOKE he found that sometime during the night he'd turned back into Gene Cooper and the woman who was his Esmeralda had broken into particles of dust that drifted before his eyes like so many unattained goals.

He dragged himself out of bed, stoop-shouldered, and made his way down to the kitchen where, for the umpteenth time, he prepared himself a breakfast of toast, tea, one strip of turkey bacon, and half a grapefruit. He ate in silence, trying to recapture the scent of Esmeralda's skin, the soft fullness of her lips, the sparkle in her eyes that promised passion. No good; gone but not forgotten.

Gene finished his breakfast, started the day's first cigarette, and thought about his life, all thirty-six years, four months, two weeks, six days, seven hours, and—he looked at the clock— eighteen minutes of it. It was not an extraordinary life—he was no poet, no visionary, no heroic leader of men—but it was usually a good life, if a bit solitary; but what else could an acne-scarred, slightly overweight, prematurely balding bachelor who was still technically a virgin expect?

He crushed out his cigarette and went into the bathroom where he showered and shaved. As he stood in front of the mirror drying what was left of his hair, he studied his average face. It was a pleasant if unmemorable face (and if anyone *did* remember his face, they remembered only the terrible acne scars), and he decided—as he always did during this morning ritual—that he was happy with it and the man who accompanied it. If only he could find someone who would feel the same—

—ah, the hell with it. That's why he had Esmeralda at nights, or in the afternoons, sometimes during lunch, but she was always with him, more a part of his memory than those few people who were actually a part of his life.

And so Gene Cooper, perceived by those around him as an average, lonely, unimaginative but decent man, dressed and left for work, still trying to recapture the scent of his dream lover's skin.

Just another day.

No fanfare, please.

DUTY

"There are some mistakes too monstrous for remorse."
—Edwin Arlington Robinson

MOM WOKE UP just as the priest was giving her Last Rites.

(Is this part of the penance? you asked of the Guests. *Isn't it all?* was their reply. Smug fucks.)

For six days she'd lain unconscious in the ICU at Cedar Hill Memorial Hospital, kept alive by the ventilator which sat by her bed clicking, puffing, humming, buzzing, measuring her blood, inspiratory, and baseline pressure, waveform readouts showing the fluxes of tracheal and esophageal pressure, proximal pressure at 60 to + 140 cmH2O, 1 cmH2O/25 mV, output flow at 300 to 200 LPM, 1 LPM/ 10 mV, the whole impressive shebang running smoothly at maximum system pressure of 175 cmH2O, the ribbed tube rammed securely down her throat into her lungs, ensuring that she continued to breathe at the acceptable rates of 250 milliseconds minimum expiratory time, 5 seconds maximum inspiratory time. Details. Specifics. Minutia. Like the other tube, the one running out of her nose into the clear container hanging on the other side of the ventilator; this tube is emptying her lungs of the blood filling them, but you've noticed, haven't you, that there's much more than blood flowing through the tube; there are flecks of things, black flecks, some tiny, others so big you're surprised they don't clog the flow, and when these flecks are released into the container they swirl around with an almost deliberate precision, dancers executing masterful choreography, and you remember a phrase spoken by one of the EMTs: *swirling the drain.* Yes, that was it: when they're about to lose a victim, the EMTs say that they're swirling the drain. That's what the black flecks are portraying in your mother's blood, and for a moment you wonder who would compose the music to this ballet; more likely Mahler than Copland, you're willing to bet. *Drain-Swirl of the Black Flecks.* Like the title of a bad 50's horror movie, the kind you used to watch with Dad on Friday nights when you were a child and there was no sibling to compete for his attention. All of this comes to you as you stand there studying the details, the specifics, the minutia. Things to look at and memorize because you can no longer look at the pale, pinched, collapsed ruins of the face and body lying motionless on the bed. A glowing number changes, a monitor beeps softly to register the new data, the pump presses down, expanding the lungs, raising the chest, and all is right in God's techno-savvy world. Except.

(Except, say the Guests; ah, there's the rub, as Willy S. once wrote, right, pal? 'Except.' What a word that is, so much disaster and heartache and ruination and disappointment and pain and all of it always follows one little two-syllable word. Very dramatic, don't you think? Yes, we thought you'd agree, so what say we get back to things and see what follows that word of all words that you seem incapable of getting past right now so, as usual, we have to do it for you. Be a Good Boy and say it with us, now.)

Except that she never should have been here in the first place. Her DNR order had ceased to be in effect at the hospital when she was transferred to the nursing home, but some stupid nurse over there panicked and called an ambulance when Mom went into respiratory arrest, so she was brought back here and immediately placed on life-support; the last thing she'd wanted was to be hooked up to some goddamn machine at the end of her life— she'd told you and your sister that often enough when her emphysema had entered the advanced stage, this a full year before the double pneumonia now snarling inside her— and the two of you had promised you wouldn't let that happen. But it has happened. You wonder if she blames you.

But doesn't she realize it isn't your fault? Someone should have called you, should have made sure that the DNR order was attached to her chart at the nursing home, should have been paying attention to the fucking records when her name was entered into the computer and her information came up in the ER, but all of this is for lawyers to deal with later. Right now a duty needs to be performed. You and your sister have already tracked down Mom's doctor and told him what you want; you have shown him the living will and he has nodded his head solemnly, he has picked up the phone and called the ICU; you and your sister have shown the living will to the nurse in charge, have called various friends and family to tell them what you are about to do, and have contacted Father Bill at St. Francis. The two of you have agreed to wait until everyone is present before giving the order. That's everything so far, right? Well, no, but that's *most* of it. Even now as you stand here witnessing these events, you're already replaying their beginning in your mind, as if by doing so and focusing on the details, the specifics, the minutia, you might find a way to alter the outcome which hasn't even been determined yet. To wit: Father Bill was the first to arrive, all soft words and sympathy— "This must be terrible for the two of you, so soon after your father's and grandmother's deaths,"—as he donned the garments and uncorked the vial of holy water and found his place in his book of blessings. "In the name of the Father, the Son, and the Holy Spirit: 'O God, great and omnipotent judge of the living and the dead, we are to appear before you after this short life to render an account of our works. Give us the grace to prepare for our last hour by—'"

And that's when Mom woke up.

She blinked a few times, then looked up, saw Lisbeth, and smiled as best she could with that tube in her mouth and throat.

Father Bill continued: "—a devout and holy life, and protect us against a sudden and unprovided death.'"

(Bummer, say the Guests. *Hadn't planned on this turn of events, had you, pal?)*

Mom's eyes grew wide and she began to shake; at first you thought she was having some kind of seizure, but she tore her hand from Lisbeth's and began to shake it in the air: No. Stop this. Stop it now.

"'Let us remember our frailty and mortality,'" continued Father Bill, "'that we may always live in the ways of your commandments. Teach us to watch and pray, that when your summons comes for our departure—'"

Mom started shaking her head and making wet, querulous, awful sounds as her hand shook more violently, the index finger trying to uncurl from its arthritic brethren to point at someone or something; her head jerked to the side, then back again, her eyes staring into those of your sister.

*(*The Guests again: *She'll cave. She will. Sis always does wherever Mom's concerned. Next stop, Cave City. And you know it.)*

"'—from this world, we may go forth to meet you, experience a merciful judgment, and rejoice in everlasting happiness. We ask this through Christ our Lord. Amen.'"

Father Bill then placed his hand on Mom's forehead—or *tried* to, rather. She was having none of it. "It's all right, Mary," he whispered. "It's all right, Frank and your mother are waiting for you, there's no need to be scared. God's love will ease your fear and carry you home."

He whispered something to her that you couldn't understand, then with a nod to you and your sister, made his way out.

You didn't want to turn around and look back into the room because you knew what you'd see, but eventually Father Bill disappeared from view and you had no choice.

There. All up to date now, yes? Yes. The outcome was determined even as you were trying to alter it by your observation at the time. And you didn't notice until it was too late. What's wrong with this picture? Too many black flecks, dancing.

Okay, so what now?

Duty.

You turn back into the room and there's Lisbeth, looking at you with a surprised smile and a "Maybe-Everything-Will-Be-Okay" gleam in her eyes. She's holding Mom's hand and trying to look happy while all the while silently asking: Should I be happy or not? She's back with us, we didn't think that would happen but here she is. Maybe this is a sign, her coming awake when she did. Maybe. Maybe?

(Cave City—this stop, Cave City.)

You shake your head. The gleam fades from her eyes for a moment, appears again as if she's thought of an argument against this, then leaves completely. She knows what you shaking your head means.

And so does Mom.

She's looking right at you, and you know what this look means. Oh, the lids are droopier than they've ever been, and the eyes are both dull and bloodshot, but the look is a classic: How can you do something like this?

How often in your forty-one years have you seen that look from her? Or, for that matter, from everyone else in your life? *Yes, Mom, look at me. I'm no longer your son—I'm what* became *of him. Forty-one, divorced, living alone* (well, sort of, but you wouldn't understand, *no one* would understand about the Guests), *no real friends, and here I am about to kill you—because that's what you're really thinking, isn't it, Mom? "My son is going to kill me." Because you know if it were just Lisbeth, she couldn't do it. You could always talk Lisbeth out of anything, but me? I inherited your stubborn streak, and you hate that. Does that also mean you hate me right now? Or maybe you always have, who knows?*

"I'm glad to see you," Lisbeth whispers to Mom, squeezing her hand and kissing her cheek. But Mom is still shaking, still trying to point a finger, still objecting.

"There's a lot of people who want to see you," says Lisbeth. "We called everybody. You're going to be real popular today."

You pull in a breath and cross over to the bed. "Hi, Mom," you say, but it doesn't sound like your voice, does it? When did you start speaking with someone else's voice? Odd—Lisbeth and Mom seem to recognize it. "I thought you were gonna stay asleep on us."

She continues to shake her head, and you notice for the first time how wide her eyes are. (*'Deer in the headlights' is the simile you're looking for,* say the Guests.) For the first time you let yourself acknowledge that she's scared. She knows what's going on and she doesn't want it to happen but one look in your eyes and she knows she's toast, that maybe she'd have a chance if it was only Lisbeth but with *you*…oh, yeah: toast. Browned on both sides.

Tears form in her eyes as her mouth works to form words but she can't speak, not with that tube, so what emerges is a series of squeaks and whistles and deeply wet groans, a vaudeville of language but it's all she's got, that and her shaking head and pointing finger and tears.

You reach out and grab her shaking hand, squeezing it gently. "I love you, Mom," you say, and this time the voice sounds a little more like your own; an echo, yes, distant and thin, but yours nonetheless. "I'm so sorry you've been so sick for so long. But the doctor's told us that you…you can't breathe on your own anymore. You have to be hooked up like this, it's the only way you can breathe, you see?"

Her eyelids twitch as a single tear slips out from the corner of her left eye and slides a slow, glistening trail down her temple into her ear. You pull a tissue from your pocket and wipe the tear away before it drips into her ear canal. That's always irritated you whenever you've been on your back and crying so it must be twice as awful for her because she can't raise that arm, what with all the IV needles decorating it like a seamstress's pin cushion. So you wipe away the tear just like a Good Boy should do for his Mom.

"Please don't cry," you say, hating the hint of desperation that's suddenly there in the echo of your voice, but Mom's wrinkling her brow and every last line in her face, the short ones, the long ones, the deep and not-so deep ones, all of them become so much more pronounced, each one looking more painful than the one next to it, or over it, or crisscrossing it: the map of a face, the topography of a life: *This is from the night when your spleen burst and we had to sit the emergency room, your dad and me, wondering whether or not you'd make it out of surgery or if we were going to lose our little boy; this one here, under my right eye, is from all those nights I spent squinting over grocery store coupons when your dad was on strike at the plant, we had to watch every penny so the coupons were a big help but, Lord, there were so many of them, and maybe I wouldn't have this line if I'd admitted to myself that I needed glasses, but even if I had admitted it we couldn't afford them, not with the strike and all, so I squinted...* and there are no rest-stops on this particular map, are there? No, not a one that you can find.

"You'll wear yourself out," you say, squeezing her hand a little tighter. "You don't...you d-don't want to do that because everyone is coming over to see you."

Her private vaudeville of language continues, and every squeak is wrapped up in sandy, sputtering, wet rawness that makes your stomach tighten and your throat constrict. Her hand in yours is cold and leathery but she's trying to squeeze back, to let you know *Please don't do this, please don't do this, I know I'm sick and I know it's hard on you kids but I don't want to die, not yet, I don't want to die not yet not yet not yet please don't do this pleasepleaseplease.*

You let go of her hand as a nurse comes into the room and asks if she can speak to you or your sister. You nod at Lisbeth and walk out into the hall, but not before bending down and kissing Mom on the cheek; it still tastes of the tear you wiped away earlier, and the saltiness is unexpected; it tastes of flavor, of something being prepared, Christmas dinner where Mom always used just a little too much salt in her stuffing, but you loved that smell, didn't you? The way it wafted up the stairs and tickled your nose to wake you: *It's Christmas, come on down, sleepy-head, and see all the goodies Dad and me have got for you!*

"I'll be right back," you whisper to the tear's trail, hoping Mom hears it, as well.

Outside, the nurse pulls closed the glass door separating Mom's room from the rest of the ICU. "Is there anything more you'd like us to do?"

"I think she might need a sedative of some kind. She's really scared and—"

"—doctor already wrote the order for a sedative and morphine, as well. I can give it to her any time you say."

You nod your head and chew on your lower lip for a moment.

(Handling things just like the Good Boy we all know you are, say the Guests. You can't tell if they're making fun of you or not, so before you get too caught up in this moment you tell them to fuck off and simply jump to the outcome without benefit of observation.)

"I don't want her knocked out, understand? She'll want to say g-good…good-bye to everyone and I want her to be conscious."

"It won't knock her out, I promise."

"Then please give it to her now."

The nurse nods her head and looks at you—she has very pretty grey eyes, doesn't she? They look just like your ex-wife's—but here you are observing the moment while it rides right on by, and have to ask the nurse to repeat what she's just said.

"Is there anything we can do for you or your sister?"

"No, thank you. I just want Mom to feel…I mean, she's been so sick for so long and we—Lisbeth and I, we…"

The nurse puts a hand on your forearm. Her fingers are soft and warm, the first time a woman's fingers have touched there in—what?—a year-and-a-half? Two years? Who remembers?

(*We do*, say the Guests. *We remember everything, pal. That's why you invited us here.*)

"Is everything the way you want it?" asks this nurse of the warm soft fingers on your arm.

What you want to say is: *No, everything is not the way I want it, so if you'll pardon me, then, I think I'll just go over here and scream for lost things, throw back my head and open my mouth and just scream. For a smile I haven't seen in years, or the chime that's missing from a laugh, or the noise not made by a child now ten years in its grave, for the toys my ex-wife and me don't have to pick up; I'll scream for all the school pictures that aren't decorating a mantel, then maybe for songs no one but me remembers of cares about, songs from dead singers that make me smile or cry when I hear an echo of their choruses from a passing radio accidentally tuned into an Oldies station, and finally I'll scream for my only living parent whom I am about to kill. Yes, that sounds good. Sounds* splendid, *in fact. So if you'll just excuse me for a moment, I'll go take care of this. Sound okay? Good. If you need me I'll be right over there. Can't miss me. I'll be the one screaming.*

That's what you want to say (as you observe in the moment that hasn't quite gotten away from you yet), but what actually comes out of your mouth is: "Yes, thank you, everything is fine…as fine as it can be under these circumstances, I guess."

Nurse of the warm fingers lingers for just a moment longer, maybe longer than is necessary or even professional, and the sad smile on her face is echoed by the one in her eyes.

You both release a breath at the same time. She blinks, squeezes your arm, and with a soft swish of shoes against the polished tile, heads off for the syringe.

(*Were you just flirting?* the Guests inquire. *Oh, pal, what stones you've got. Mom lying in there choking to death on the ruined slop of her insides and you're making time with Florence Nightingale. Show of hands: spit or swallow?*)

"Shut the fuck up!" you growl through clenched teeth. An older gentleman passing by you snaps his head in your direction, his offense at your language all over his face.

"Sorry," you mumble. "I wasn't talking to you, I was—"

But he's gone, turned into another room a few yards down.

(*A flirt* and *a charmer. What self-respecting nurse wouldn't want some of this action?*)

Shaking your head, you go back in to Lisbeth and Mom.

"She's *scared*," Lisbeth whispers. You wonder why she bothers. Fer chrissakes she's standing right there next to Mom, holding the woman's hand, and Mom might be hard of hearing but she isn't deaf and she may not have been the ideal parent but her life's going to be over—repeat that, turn up the volume, OVER—in less than two hours and the woman deserved to not be spoken of in Third Person.

"I know you're scared, Mom," you say, taking your place by the bed. "But this is what you wanted."

The shaking of the head again.

You reach into your pocket and remove the copy of her living will, unfold it, and hold it up for her to see. "You made us promise you that if this time ever came, we'd go through with it. Even if you said 'no,' we'd go through with it."

Lisbeth snaps your name and you give her the Glare. The Glare has served you well over the years, hasn't it? The Glare scares even the Guests sometimes. Burns right through a person, makes it damn near impossible to maintain eye contact with you. You know this, and you use it to your advantage whenever you want to be left alone, which is most of the time, so many have known the terror of the Glare.

Lisbeth looks away almost at once. You feel terrible for having looked at her this way, but dealing with that is for later.

(You got that right, pal. We'll just add that to the list, shall we?)

You grab Mom's hand away from Lisbeth and hold it tight. You look at your sister—who's still not returning your gaze—then directly into Mom's eyes. You have looked into her eyes this intensely maybe three times in your entire life. "Listen to me, Mom. You will *never* be able to function without this machine, do you understand me?"

A slow nod. Another tear.

"Even if we were to call this off right now and leave you hooked up to this thing, you're not going to last another week. You're on borrowed time, Mom. You should have been dead six days ago."

Once again Lisbeth says your name, this time spitting it out as if it's some rancid chunk of food.

"You're here with us now," you continue, "and you're awake, and you're getting the chance to do something Dad didn't get to do. You're getting a chance to say good-bye to all the people who love you. They're all coming, and they're all going to stay right here with you until you fall asleep for the last time. The nurse is going to give you a shot so you'll be comfortable, and all you have to do is just let us say good-bye and tell you that we love you and then you can rest. You're tired, Mom. You've been tired for so long—" your voice cracks on these last two words, and you have to turn your head away for a moment to get a grip on yourself.

(*Aw,* say the Guests, *look at this. Widdle baby cwying faw his mommy. Little late to feel sad about this now, isn't it, pal?*)

You ignore them and turn back, "—and you need to rest. You've earned it."

Her hand squeezes yours.

"I have no idea how scary this must be for you, but we're going to be right here, however long this takes. But I'm—*we're*—going to keep our promise to you, Lisbeth and me. Because this is what you wanted. But there's something you need to do for me, Mom. You need to let me know you understand. Can you do that? Can you squeeze my hand and let me know that you understand so I don't have to go through the rest of my life feeling like I've killed you?"

She looks in your eyes.

And for some reason you remember something from twenty years ago: you were still living at home and had picked up the phone one day, just to make a call, but Mom was talking to someone so you started to hang up when you clearly heard her say the words: "I love you."

Phone in hand, staring.

Dad was raking leaves in the back yard.

You lifted the receiver to your ear and listened. Details. Specifics. Minutia. Three years this had been going on. They laughed. At your dad. At you. But not Lisbeth, not the light of everyone's lives, not her.

You hung up loudly and waited. It didn't take long. Mom at the door to your room, her eyes wide and frightened by the headlights.

"How much did you hear?"

"Enough," you said.

Her face took on many forms in a very few seconds; sadness, shame, anger, indifference, confusion and, finally, resignation. "Go ahead and tell him. I don't care." Bullshit bravado, that.

"I figured out that much from what I heard. So you really think I'm useless?"

Shock, for just a moment. Then: "Sometimes."

You nodded your head. "It would kill Dad if he knew."

"I'm not going to tell him."

"Neither am I."

She'd smiled at you, then, and for a moment you thought it was a smile of love and appreciation, but it was in her eyes, wasn't it?

You were now in it with her. If Dad ever found out, she could deflect part of his hurt and anger and anguish by saying, "Your son's known about it almost the whole time." And that *would* kill Dad.

There are times you wonder whether or not it *did* help kill him, just as much as the diabetes and high blood pressure and prostate cancer. Had he somehow found out? Then just let his heart break along with everything else so he could die alone in the toilet of his room at the nursing home? That's where they found him—dead in the crapper.

You never found out what happened to the other guy, never asked his name, never kept an eye out for a strange car or truck parked near the house.

Dad's gone. Grandma, too. Now it was Mom's turn; not because you want it this, because it has to be this way.

"Please squeeze my hand," you whisper, and the begging in your voice disgusts even you.

Mom looks at you the same way she had after that phone call twenty years ago.

"*Please?*"

Mom does not blink, does not try to speak, does not shake her head.

After a moment you look at your sister. "She squeezed my hand," you say. Softly.

Lisbeth releases a breath, her shoulders slumping, then smiles and weeps at the same time. The relief she feels is palpable even from where you're standing.

(She bought it, pal. Very nice, very smooth.)

You look back down at Mom. She will not look at you.

"I love you, Mom." And you do. That's the terrible part. If she's going to hate you for this, so be it. It's what she wanted, and you promised.

(That you did, pal.)

You were her son. You were a Good Boy. And it was your duty.

The first of the friends and family begin to arrive, and you're relieved to step back from the bed and give the rest of them the chance to say good-bye.

The warm-fingered nurse comes back in, smiles at you, then gives Mom the shot. "This will help you relax, Mary. You'll feel better here in just a minute, I promise."

Mom smiles at her, a smile full of gratitude and affection. Part of you wishes she'd look at you like that, just once, just for a moment, but the rest of you

(And us, pal. Don't forget us, we'll take it personally!)

knows damn well that you've already gotten the last direct look from her that you'll ever know, and there you were in the moment, observing the event while not being a part of it so now all you've got is the impression of something that may or may not be a memory of an experience you weren't really a part of in the first place.

(Let's hear it for our Fearless leader, folks! Nothing gets by him, nosiree!)

The room fills quickly; aunts, uncles, Mom's co-workers from the cable assembly plant, friends of the family you haven't seen in years, and a few people you've never seen before. You wonder if one of them is Him. You wish you could figure out which one He might be so you could follow him out to the

parking lot and slit his throat with your car keys, then pull
back his neck and expose the wet tissue and shit right down
his throat.

(*Now, now,* say the Guests. *Is that any way to think at a
deathbed?*)

Mom smiles at all of them, squeezes their hands, gestures for
them to bend down so she can hug them and they can wipe
away her tears. Warm Fingers comes back in and give Mom
a shot of morphine, then stops beside you and whispers, "I
have orders for two morphine shots. The second one is much
stronger. I'll be at the desk, so when you want the second shot,
just let me know." She touches your arm again, and this time
there's a definite intimacy to her touch. You nod your head
and place your hand on top of hers. For a moment her fingers
entwine with yours, then she is gone.

A few moments later two technicians come in and ask for
everyone except you and Lisbeth to clear the room. They
wander into the hall. The first technician—a girl no older than
Lisbeth, twenty-six, twenty-seven tops—closes the glass door
and then pulls the curtain across it. The room becomes grey
and shadowed; Death pausing to check his schedule: Here, is
it? Ah, yes, I see. Okee-dokee; back in twenty minutes.

"Are you ready?" asks the technician.

You look at Lisbeth, then at Mom who still won't look at
you, and say: "Yes."

She turns off the ventilator.

The sudden silence sings a sick-making sibilance of final
things that cannot be taken back.

"Now, Mary," says the technician, "we have to take out the
tube now. Are you ready?"

Mom smiles around the tube and nods her head.

You look away for only a moment, hear the terrible sound of
medical tape being peeled away, then decide this is something
you have to see.

Mom's already wrenching upward from the force of the tube being pulled from her, her face collapsing forward, becoming a reddening gnarl of flesh as her body locks rigid and her tears stream down and her fingers shudder (somehow that is even more terrible to you than her face, the way only her fingers and not her hands shudder) and the veins bulge in her head and temples and her eyelids spasm—

—*make it stop*, you think. *OhGod I didn't think it would hurt this much, it's my fault, I'm so sorry, Mom, I'm not mad at you, I understand, I never hated you, never,*

please make it stop, please make it stop, please make it—

"Don't swallow, Mary," says the technician, her hands moving gracefully, one over the other, as she pulls and pulls and pulls.

It takes only ten seconds but it seems like ten minutes, and when it's done, when the tube has been pulled free Mom slams back against the bed with such force she actually bounces a little, and when she bounces a spray of thick black-flecked spit scatters across her face and down onto her chest and even onto your own hand even though you're standing a couple of feet away. Her face is covered in sweat but it's not quite so red now, and her chest is moving up and down as she pulls in breath and you feel the tears on your own face now, goddammit, and the snot running out of your nose but you don't move to wipe away any of it because look at her, she can't wipe the muck away so you won't, either, you'll stand here covered in your own fluids to show her that you understand, that you want to feel something of what she's going through now because this is the last thing you'll ever share, the last thing, the very, very, very last thing and you want to remember it, every specific, every detail, every minutia because you're a Good Boy and that's what a Good Boy does

(And noble, to boot. Look at all this fucking nobility. It makes you want to openly weep sensitive manly tears, it does.)

The ventilator is rolled into a corner, the tubes rolled into coils and deposited into the medical waste bin, Mom is wiped clean, and the technicians leave, opening wide the room to light and sound and the waiting throngs.

You move toward a corner and stand there, no longer trusting your legs.

Looking out of the glass, you see Warm Fingers and nod your head. She nods hers in return and runs to fetch the last syringe.

Bit by bit, Mom's eyes close—but not all the way. The light fades, the readouts become erratic, the last shot of morphine is administered…and then all of you wait.

No one in the room will look at you. At Lisbeth, yes, but not at you. You were the one to give the orders. You were the one who didn't get off at Cave City. You were the one with Mom's stubborn streak and the living will folded neatly in your pocket and the memory of the phone call and your ex-wife's tears when the police called about your little boy who you shouldn't have let ride his bike to the movies that day but, jeez, Dad, I'm almost ten and it's not that far and the screams in your ear of You Fucking Bastard How Many Times Have I Told You I Don't Want Him Riding That Bike Outside The Neighborhood and the fists against your face again and again and again and Dad whispering No Son of Mine Would Ever Put My Ass In A Nursing Home but you're a Good Boy, aren't you?

(*Well,* say the Guests, *about that…*)

It takes Mom two hours and seventeen minutes to die. It is slow and painful to watch, but you never once look away.

When it is over and everyone begins to leave, you are the one who closes her eyes the rest of the way.

You wait until you are alone in the room with her, then lean down and kiss her. "I will miss you every day for the rest of my life," you say. "I loved you, Mom. I'm sorry for every bad thing I ever said to you. I'm sorry for all the times I forgot to do something for you, for all the times I could have called you but didn't, for every time you felt lonely and forgotten. Is that all right? Is it all right for me to say these things to you? It's just the two of us now, so I think it must be all right." Then something small bursts inside you and you're crying again. "I'm sorry I wasn't a better son, a better man, a better husband and father. But Lisbeth and Eric, they gave you two wonderful grandchildren, didn't they? And they never let them ride their bikes too far from the house, you can count on that. They never get so busy with work that they just tell their kids it's okay, ride wherever you want, it'll be fine. They never do that. They never leave the bottle of prescription sleeping pills setting out open so that their Dad can sneak them into the toilet at the nursing home. They never will. They'll never disappoint you. Never.

"I have to go now, Mom, because there's a lot to do for your funeral. But I just wanted you to know that I always had the best intentions. In my heart, I always meant well. I love you. You should rest now, you've earned it."

You make sure no one is watching from outside, and you observe the moment as it passes; you can do this now, because the outcome is given. You move to one of the corners, and you take something, and then you leave.

Warm Fingers smiles sadly at you as you walk past the desk. She looks like she might cry herself. You wish she'd touch you again. Warm Fingers would forgive you all your trespasses and mistakes. Warm Fingers would understand.

You park outside your house and see that all the lights are on. You look up at the windows and see the Guests moving around. One of them is playing the stereo. NIN. "Head Like A Hole." Too loud for this hour.

You smoke three cigarettes before going inside. The Guests don't like it when you smoke inside, and you are nothing if not a gracious host.

They're all waiting for you when you come inside. All of them have their props at the ready. None of them speak to you now. They never talk to you when you're here, only when you're gone, only when you're performing a duty like the one tonight.

One of them comes up to you, empty-handed. He's the new one. The one behind him, he arrived the day you buried Dad. His is the face you wore the night you walked out of the nursing home knowing what Dad intended to do with those pills.

Lurking in a corner near the stereo is another guest. He showed up the night your ex-wife came over after little Andrew's funeral to slap you in the face yet again. You had been brewing water for tea and after she slapped you, you pushed her away and she fell against he stove and spilled the scalding water all over her arm. This Guest is holding the boiling kettle and wears the face you wore that night. Just like all of them. Wearing the faces you happened to have on when committing your trespasses.

The new Guest is still standing there, holding out his hand. You reach into your pocket and remove the coiled ventilator tube. He takes it with a smile and points to the chair. You remove your coat and sit down.

Other guests—the one who arrived after you had that brief affair with that temp before Andrew was born, for instance— bind your wrists and ankles to the chair.

The music changes. The James Gang. "Ashes, the Rain and I." The saddest song you've ever heard. It's important that you have sad music now.

One Guest has the pills. One the boiling water. One has the dart you stuck Johnny Sawyer with when you were six and you got mad because you thought Johnny was cheating.

There are pins. And burning cigarettes. And pieces of broken glass.

You wish you didn't remember what every last one of these items means, but you do, you remember so very, very clearly.

The phone rings. No one moves to answer it.

The answering machine picks up, gives its banal greeting, then a beep. A woman says your name. Her voice is soft and warm, just like her fingers. "This is Daphne. I'm the nurse who gave your mom the shots today. Listen, we're never supposed to do this—call patients' families personally like this—but, well…I just wanted to make sure you were all right. You didn't look good when you left and I was…oh, okay, I was worried. I hope you're not angry. I just thought that maybe you, y'know… needed to talk to someone. So I was wondering…"

Joe Walsh's voice drowns out the rest of the message. You almost smile. Maybe after all of this is over—a few weeks or however long it takes for you to heal this time—maybe you'll give her a call. Warm Fingers would be sympathetic. Warm Finger would listen. Warm Fingers would understand and squeeze your hand.

The new Guest stands in front of you, reaches out, and forces your mouth open. He has lubricated the ventilator tube with Vaseline. You remind yourself that it's important to swallow as the tube goes down. You just hope the Guest with the boiling water remembers his proper place in line.

You open wide your mouth and close your eyes. It is important for a Good Boy to remember things. Remembering, that's a duty, as well.

And you are nothing if not dutiful.

Nothing at all.

She So Loved Her Garden

AFTER THE DEATH of her husband the old woman spent countless hours alone in the house for the purpose of making it emptier; it was a game to her, like the one she'd played as a child, walking on the stone wall of the garden, pretending it was a mountain ledge, not daring to look down for sight of the rocks below, knowing certain death awaited her should she slip, a terrible fall that would crush her to bits, walking along until her steps faltered and she toppled backward, always thinking in that moment before her tiny body hit the ground: *So that's when I died.*

When, after four days, her son hadn't heard from her, he packed his family into the car, ignoring the children's protestations that "Grandma's too weird," and drove to her house for a surprise visit.

They found her in the back yard, slumped against Grandpa's old wheelbarrow—which was filled to overflowing with unmixed cement powder.

In front of her was a pile of medium-sized, multi-colored stones. She had used a garden spade to dig a small trench around the perimeter of the garden and had even managed to put several stones in place.

The police and EMTs, without meaning to do so, trampled most of the marigolds. Her son didn't notice until after they had taken her away, then asked his wife to pick the ones remaining.

After those marigolds died, he pressed them between the pages of a book, but if you were to ask now which one, he isn't quite sure.

Rose of Sharon

"There are some mistakes too monstrous for remorse."
—Edward Arlington Robinson

WHEN I WAS A YOUNG BOY and sick with fever, my mother would sit at my bedside and read stories. She liked mysteries the best—especially Sherlock Holmes and Mickey Spillane—because they were, she said, like a flower. "Imagine that the solution is what's at the center of the flower, but you can't get to it yet because the bell has to bloom and the petals have to open one by one. I always like to think of it that way: the truth is the fruit in the middle of the flower."

I forget who suggested going to the club, I just know it wasn't me and that's how I needed it to be. We were a bunch of guys at their twenty-year high school reunion, a collection of receding hairlines, expanding waistlines, and deepening worry lines who made the mistake of comparing today's mature responsibilities with yesterday's youthful dreams only to discover that none of us had known what it was to fly above the heads of mediocrity; we smiled at each other (but not too broadly), shrugged, reminisced while plying our memories with hearty doses of liquor in order to make the past seem grander than it really was, and eventually someone half-jokingly mentioned "male entertainment" clubs and off we went to watch a bunch of shapely, sad, Sweet Young Things bump and grind and expose engorged nipples and if we were lucky reveal their pink, perfect sex so that maybe, just maybe, we as a drunken whole could for one night forget about the whispering tumor in the pit of our stomachs that turned everything into bile and anger and disappointment. Old, the tumor whispered: Ineffectual.

Every day the tumor in my gut blossoms, whispers, then dies.

I imagine it to be bell-shaped, with a five-pointed calyx surrounded by a set of colored bracts growing just beneath it. In full blossom, it has five petals, a column of fused stamens with kidney-shaped anthers, and countless pistils. Its fruit is a many-seeded, five-celled pod shaped like a newborn's face.

I don't matter, it says to me. If I did, you wouldn't have.

The club was called Rose of Sharon, its name spelled out in tacky, sputtering red neon above the doorway, and I laughed when I read the words but was too drunk to get my tongue around the syllables and syntax to explain to my tumored brothers of yesteryear what was so funny.

Not that they would have understood.

Inside, the place was dark, cramped, and humid, the subtle scent of jasmine incense overwhelmed by the cumulative stench of cigarettes, stale beer, piss, puke, and pussy—this last bit of pathetic alliteration courtesy of One Of Our Own, a recently tenured English teacher in the midst of his second divorce whose opinion of women could be accurately surmised by his boasting that he knew how to say twat in sixteen different languages.

Shame on you, the tumor whispered. Shame on you all.

I reached inside my jacket, pretending to scratch my back, and felt the reassuring coldness of the Mauser tucked between my pants and the base of my spine;

7.65mm of nerve.

The cover charge was outrageous, but the giant at the door assured us that our experience inside would be worth every dollar. "Just remember, you can't touch 'em. They can touch you, unless you tell 'em not to, but if you touch them you're gonna get hurt." He displayed a set of spiked brass knuckles to ensure we'd remember to behave as responsible gentlemen should.

There was no proper stage, only a dais of raised wood perhaps twenty feet in circumference, flanked by gaudy turquoise curtains and enough above floor level to guarantee we'd have unencumbered eye-contact with the dancers' knees when they came down the runway.

We ordered our drinks, an MC twenty years too old for his hair coloring introduced the next dancer, and tinny music squawked from hidden speakers as she emerged.

She wore a feathered, multi-colored three-quarters mask that allowed only her eyes that glittered promise and full rose-petal lips and sharp chin to be seen. Her neck was long and luxurious, merging with the center of her collar bone in a perfect 'V' of flesh that made you want to trace it with your tongue—providing you looked no farther down her body.

Her breasts, from a distance, were large and smooth, pendulous perfection with light brown aureoles and nipples the size of your thumbnail, but if you watched closely as she slithered about the stage, those breasts never moved; not a jiggle, not a wobble, not a bounce. The number of tummy tucks or ass lifts that she'd had was unknowable. Worse than anything else was her body as a whole—or, I should say, the remains of her body; any high school girl or supermodel wannabe with anorexia would have been jealous. This woman stood a little over five seven and could not have weighed ninety pounds. Whatever natural beauty she had once possessed had atrophied in a series of sputtering little agonies, then been reshaped and mummified with stretched flesh and silicone standing in for bandages and tannin.

I wriggled slightly in my seat as I realized that she was stepping down off the dais and moving toward our tables. I casually reached back to feel the hard lump of the pistol against my spine.

Though we'd kept in contact through occasional letters and the rare phone call (the latter usually because she'd been left stranded somewhere by the current Dickbrain of the Month and needed me to wire money to her now), it had been ten years since I'd last seen her. I'd put on almost thirty pounds, grown a salt-and-pepper beard, watched my dark brown hair turn almost totally grey, and exchanged my glasses for tinted contact lenses.

Still, whispered the tumor, its bell opening, petals blossoming outward, she might recognize you.

True Love never dies.

I looked down on the table. A small conch-shell centerpiece was filled with huge, showy red flowers—shrubby althea, *Hibiscus syriacus*.

Also known as Rose of Sharon.

I smiled, knowing the irony would be lost on my companions.

She stopped in front of our English teacher and threw one of her legs up on the table top, her skeletal fingers going to work on her thong; pulling it out, letting it snap back, slipping two fingers under the leather to rough her sex as she arched her back and rolled her hips, her tongue moistening her mouth while her rich, abundant, expensive breasts moved teasingly closer and closer to Teacher's mouth.

"Can't touch that," croaked one of the guys in a bad imitation of some hip-hop song that'd been popular a decade ago, then bust into uproarious laughter at his snappy display of envious wit.

The music grew louder.

Something in the way she moved suggested that we were about to get our money's worth.

She leaned forward and whispered something, Teacher smiled and nodded his head, then she knelt down and unzipped Teacher's pants, took his erection in his hands, and with a deft, expert neatness of touch, a dramatic subtlety I have seen no other woman exhibit, sucked at it until he shuddered, groaned, and was drained. The elastic grace of her hands, the variety of physical rhythms moving in synch with the music, the way she changed from gripping his erection with her entire hand to gently touching the tip of it, from roughly kneading all of the parts to tenderly teasing his pubic hair with her tongue before sliding wetly down his length once again—all of this was more effective than any hallucinogenic: We sat there, painfully stiff inside our pants, staring at the way she took Teacher's erection into her magnificent mouth between flashes of slightly discolored and crooked teeth while her phony breasts heaved and her lifeless, bleach-blonde hair lay splattered across her sweaty back like the seared remains of a moth fused to the glowing surface of a light bulb.

The muscles in her throat did a dance of their own as she gulped down the rest of Teacher's bliss, and somewhere in the back of my head I could hear a young girl's voice say, I could swallow you whole.

She pushed back on her knees, legs spread wide, and began to feel herself for our enjoyment, thrashing and twisting, sliding along the length of the floor with such liquid grace that you'd almost swear she was remaining still while the rest of the club shifted position to accommodate her.

She at last came to me: leg up on table, fingers under her thong, tongue moistening lips, then she leaned forward and whispered, "You want my lips?" I could smell the stink of Teacher's bliss on her breath. When I didn't say anything, she pulled back and wriggled a bit more, working herself (or so it was supposed to appear) into a frenzy before throwing herself forward, hands gripping either side of the back of my chair, her face less than an inch from my own, her hair fanning out enough to conceal both our faces from everyone else. "C'mon, baby, you know you want me to."

Not daring to break eye contact with her, I whispered—so low that none but her would hear—"Do you still want to live in a song?"

Her shriek was more vibration than sound.

Shame, whispered the tumor.

"S-Scott?" she croaked.

"Hello, Kim."

She gave me a look you could iron clothes with, then threw my tie over my shoulder, ran her hands over my chest (stopping just long enough to pinch my nipples), then did a couple of seductive twirls around me before moving on to the next customer.

I stared at the flowers on the table. I didn't want to see what she was doing to him.

A Rose of Sharon flower, when plucked, will live only one day.

She told me this long ago; it is one of my few untainted memories of our time together.

Over the years I have come to the conclusion that the Rose of Sharon is a fitting metaphor for women who are growing old. How many of them, I wonder, would gladly accept the flower's fate if given the choice? To achieve a moment of absolute, ethereal beauty, to become something nearly angelic and fly above the heads of mediocrity, knowing others can only gaze up in wonder; to reach this level of the miraculous and then simply stop, vanishing forever, leaving only mystery and the jealous memory of wonderment in their wake.

But instead, too many women simply grow old and misused, offering their hearts and dreams to men who take them only for their bodies and then, once satisfied, leave them to look in lonely mirrors and see a face made hard and tight and ugly from fighting against bitter thoughts, knowing they will never be loved in equal measure because they will never again know what it feels like to be held in awe and so must settle for finding, hopefully—dear God hopefully!—someone who treasures them not for the perfect beauty they no longer possess but for those remnants they might still have but can't see.

I have known many women like this.

They are part of me.

I pity them, and they forgive me; they understand that different women, in different situations, seem to create a different me. I gladly oblige but, eventually, cannot tolerate their not being a different them; one them, in particular.

Each should have been a Rose of Sharon; their beauty achieving perfection—snip!—a day of unadulterated worship, and then...

And then.

Always I look for some sign of Kim in each of them when they blossom under the care of the different me; and always I am disappointed, and always what should be tenderness and lovemaking becomes just fucking.

It took a long time for me to learn that there was a difference between sex and intimacy. Not that it matters now.

Every day the tumor in my gut blossoms, whispers lonely, why shouldn't you be, then dies. Two of its petals are me—the man I have become and the boy I once was; two of them are Kim—the girl she was and the woman she has become; the fifth petal is what we were when we were together; and the truth that is the fruit at the center of the flower is the awful thing we did one night that killed us both but left our bodies and conscience intact.

But that came later.

Much later after the first time ever.

It was 1975 and I was seventeen the first time I told Kimberly Wilder that I loved her. It was a little before eleven on a Friday night and we were in the living room of my parents' house listening to an album on the stereo, the volume as low as the lights. Kim had come over around eight with her book-bag in hand under the pretense we were going to work on an extra credit school project.

I had been fumbling around her body for the better part of an hour, daring to touch one of her breasts, then another, then haphazardly sliding my hand under her blouse to unhook her bra. I broke away from her kisses only long enough to gulp down air and occasionally wipe the sweat off my face and the saliva (hers, mine, ours) from my chin.

Without either of us having to say so, we knew that this was going to be it.

She pulled away from me, one hand on my chest, the other squeezing the back of my neck, and looked at me with her pale green eyes as if she were a kindergarten teacher facing a sad, slow-witted child. "Do you like the flowers?"

"Yeah," I said, not knowing if I meant it or not. She'd brought me a bunch of huge red flowers that she said had to immediately be put in water because they were red hibiscuses and they only lived for a day.

No girl had ever given me flowers before.

"I wanted you to have them so you'll remember how… special this evening has to be. There'll probably be better times than this, maybe even a best time, but there's only one first time. Do you understand?"

The delicate vulnerability in her eyes—eyes with sad, dark places around them that gave the impression when she laughed that she was hiding an oft-broken heart behind a scrim of gaiety—was enough to kill you.

Mustering all my self-control, I touched her face and said, "More than you know."

She stood and began to disrobe in a slow, promising way. "Don't touch your clothes," she said. "I want to undress you."

Her fingers went to work on my shirt and belt, my socks and shoes, my pants and underwear as if they were playing a glissando over piano keys. The ninety or so seconds it took for her to strip me naked me were agony; exquisite agony.

Then we lay down on the floor and made unhurried, quiet, intensely satisfying love, careful not to make even the slightest sound; the secrecy of the sex, the jittery silence because my mother and father were asleep upstairs and it was an old house and sound carried like you wouldn't believe, the threat of being caught at any second, the underlying Is-this-where-that-goes-and-are-you-sure-it-doesn't-hurt panic—all of it had added to the urgency and made the sex even steamier. Throughout all of it she had chewed on piece of strawberry flavored bubblegum like it was sweet sacred mouthful of forbidden dirty. (To this day I can't see a teenaged girl chew gum without getting a raging hard-on.) For a few astonishing moments, as Greg Lake's richly resonant voice rolled from the speakers and sang of love that would flood darkness with light, we melted into the natural rhythms of our bodies, a rhythm that was ours and ours alone, Scott and Kim, my body and hers, in the clearest physical connection one body can make to another; I sank deep between her legs, pounding my erection into her wetness, her breath the humid warmth of sunlight against my bare shoulder as her pelvis thrust and her nipples hardened and her hands clamped together at the base of my spine and Lake sang and she sighed, then softly groaned and I swallowed a scream and we felt each other writhe and buck and shudder as we spread out warmly from the center of our bodies to become something grander than we'd been before, a thing unseen in a place unknown where we were no longer alone behind our flesh.

Afterward we lay facing each other, fingertips touching, bodies lacquered in sweat, voices barely more than spirit-whispers among the shadows, and spoke of the secret things that two people who have just savored the moist, vulnerable intimacy of each other's bodies feel compelled to reveal.

I told her I wanted to freeze the world in this moment forever; that way, her flowers would never die and we could stay just as we were. She smiled, brushed my lips with hers, then draped one of her legs over my hip and held my face in her hands.

"I could swallow you whole," she said.

"I might like that." I eased her onto her back and began kissing her everywhere, endlessly, and just as I was parting her legs, tongue at the ready, she gently gripped a handful of my hair and stopped me.

"Don't want too much," she said.

"I can't get enough of you."

She traced along my jaw with her index finger. "Be careful. With some people, even a little bit is too much."

"You sound so serious."

"And you look so wrecked. The sweat on your face looks like tears. That's why I said that. Don't ever cry for me, okay? Promise me that—that you won't ever cry for me?"

Even then it seemed she knew her life would take a downward spiral, but that thought flashed across my mind only briefly; I was too horny to think about anything other than the moist, inviting treat only inches from my mouth.

"I promise." I started in on her, but she jerked back and sat up, pulling her knees up against her chest.

"Listen to me, okay? I know this's going to sound weird, but…okay, you lose things along the way, right? I don't mean stuff, I mean other things, things"—she touched the part of her chest where her heart was— "in here. And you can feel the empty spaces sometimes and it hurts." She looked at me. "You have no idea what I'm talking about, do you?"

"No."

"You know what I want? I want to live in a song. Does that sound stupid? I know most people want their lives to be like a movie or book but I want...I want 'Drift Away' and 'The First Time Ever I Saw Your Face' and 'Join Together'. I want tenderness and romance and poetic proclamations of love, I want to dance in the rain at midnight in Paris. I want to be like the music I love. To be Maggie May and Layla and Julie-Julie-Julie Do You Love Me. But I know that's never going to happen. Because I'm not pretty. I'm not even cute enough. I wish you could freeze the world right now. The flowers would never die and I'd never grow any older than I am right now, I'd never have to worry about watching everything...fade."

I tried to take her hands but she wouldn't let me touch her. "What's wrong?"

She wiped her eyes, then stood up and began putting on her clothes. "Don't think I don't know what the other guys say about me. You know that I've done this before with other guys—lots of other guys. It's the only way I can get them to keep paying attention to me. Mom and Dad, they always tell me that a girl like me— 'Face it, hon, you're kind of plain and you're not that bright.'—the only way I'll ever get a guy to like me is to give him what he wants whenever he wants it. So I do. And then they go away. You were the first guy who didn't try to get into my pants on the first date—hell, you didn't even try to get into them on the tenth date. You're the only one who ever came back." She finished buttoning her blouse, then came over and put her arms around my neck. "Was I all right? Did you like it?"

She sounded so mournful, so lonely and scared, that all I could say was, "I love you, Kim. I always will."

She kissed me, long and tenderly, then pulled something out of her book-bag: a Polaroid camera, the instant kind. She turned on one of the table lamps and I saw how happy, how joyous she looked.

At that moment, I knew that I would never see anything so beautiful as she was right now.

"You're the first guy who's ever said he loves me." She handed me the camera, stood back, and began straightening her hair with her fingers, then stopped. "No. I want to capture this just as I am right now. Will you take my picture so I'll always know what I looked like the first time someone said they loved me?"

"We'll put it in a photo album," I said. "We can even write a caption beneath: 'The First Time Ever I Saw Your Face.'"

Her smile was starlight. "You really meant it, didn't you?"

"Yes," I said, getting her in frame. "I love you, Kim Wilder."

Starlight, starbright; Kim-there, Kim-now: Oh my sweet Rose of Sharon.

The camera flashed, grumbled, and whirred. The photo came sliding out.

She snatched it away and held it against her chest, then quickly plucked one of the red hibiscuses from its stem and wrapped it in a fresh Kleenex.

"What're you doing?" I said. "I want to—"

"No," she said, laughing almost giddily. She reached into her bag and took out a thin hardback book, *The Poems of Christina Rossetti*, flipped to a specific page, then carefully placed the flower and undeveloped photo inside and snapped it closed.

"But I—"

"Shh," she said. God, she was so radiant. "No, you can't see it, and neither can I. Don't you understand what you've given to me, Scott? Do you have any idea what you've done?"

"...uh, no..."

"You've frozen the world for me, and I'll always love you for it. From now on, regardless of what happens, I'll always have this time, preserved just the way it was—the way it is right now. And someday, when I really need to feel good again, when I need to have something to look forward to, when I need to be reminded that there was a time when everything was perfect and I was loved, I will open this book, and I will take out the flower and the picture, and I will see for the first time what I looked like on the night you told me that you loved me, and maybe that will be enough to make everything new again so I can go on."

She knew; even then, she knew.

Plain girls who aren't that bright often do.

Every day the tumor in my gut blossoms, then whispers, then dies at night.

Every morning when I rise there's a new one there to take its place.

The Tumored Brothers of Yesteryear left the club about fifteen minutes before the next show was supposed to start. All of us understood that we'd not only been diminished by our little adventure, but had diminished the women, as well. Not that it mattered.

Halfway back to the hotel where the reunion was being held we began to break away from one another, each man going his separate way to ponder the delicious perversity of this evening's indulgence and decide in his own heart if he had sinned or not.

I went back to the club and waited at the "performer's entrance" in the alley, careful to keep myself in the shadows.

A little after three a.m. the door opened and two of the dancers came out, followed by the bartender and the three waitresses. A few minutes later another of the dancers left with the MC, and as they hurried out of the alley I managed to get to the door just before it closed.

I was in a narrow, musty, dimly-lighted hallway. The floor was covered in fuzzy green carpeting that looked like fungus you'd find on the underside of a rock.

The hall branched in two directions at the end, one way leading into the club, the other leading farther backstage.

It wasn't hard to find her. I could hear the sound of the giant man with the spiked brass knuckles hitting her and shouting, "You fuckin' knew that guy, didn't you?"

"I t-told you, Bernie, h-he just reminded me of someone I used to—"

Her words were cut off by an ugly, sharp slap, followed by the unmistakable sound of a body walloping into furniture.

"Don't you lie to me, you worthless ball-busting-son-of-a-cunt bitch!"

"I'M NOT, I SWEAR!"

Another slap. An ugly thump. A glass shattering against a door.

Then the muffled sounds of weeping.

"I'm sorry," said Knuckle Man.

"I know."

"I just get mad sometimes."

"I understand."

"Guess I'm still a little upset about the other night. You breaking it off with me and all."

"I know."

"Can I get anything for you? You want some water?"

"No."

"You need some aspirin or something? A little toot, maybe? Make you feel better?"

"No."

"At least let me get something to clean that cut with. I mean, c'mon; I paid good money for that work. Won't do to have me damaging things."

"No, I suppose not."

"Let me help put you back together, okay? For old times' sake?"

"All right."

He came out a second later and headed straight out into the club. The dressing room door closed behind him of its own volition, as if it knew the tableau which lay behind was too ugly to be seen.

I moved quickly, following him into the club and grabbing one of the overstuffed pillows from the stage that the last dancer had used in her Mata Hari routine.

Holding the pillow up in front of me, I pulled out the Mauser and pressed its barrel against the fabric and stuffing, walked up behind Knuckle Man as he made a beeline for the bar, and said, "You shouldn't have hit her."

He whirled around, wide-eyed, and started to say something but I shoved the pillow into his face and slammed him against the wall and kneed him in the balls and said, "She's too delicate. She always was," then plowed two shots into the pillow, scattering down-filling and blood and bits of viscera in all directions.

The sound made by the gun against the pillow was little more than a muffled *whumpf!* that I'd barely heard myself.

Knuckle Man slid slowly down to the floor, striping the wall in red on his way.

I stood back, brushed away some of the filling whirling through the air, and took a deep breath before turning around and heading backstage once again.

Here is the truth that is the fruit at the center of the flower:

We stayed together through high school and the first year of college, then she dropped out because of low grades and took off with a vanload of self-centered "artists" for New Mexico to live the Bohemian Way. They moved into a "creative community" where everyone experimented with a number of drugs and Kim quickly discovered that she possessed no talents whatsoever outside of a bed, and for a while, her self-esteem in the toilet, she stayed on as the court whore, sleeping with whichever "artist" (actors, painters, poets, sculptors, whatever) fancied her for the time being. Eventually all had their turn, and she was taken away and dumped at an Arizona truck-stop one night with six dollars in her pocket. She called my parents, who gave her my number, and the sound of her crying, her desperation, sent me first to an all-night banking machine, then to a Western Union office to wire her enough money for a motel room and food until I got there.

I drove for thirty-one straight hours and was a zombie by the time I pulled into the parking lot of the shabby motel down the road from the truck-stop, but I didn't care. She needed me.

True Love never dies.

When she answered the door and saw me she didn't say anything or even touch me; she put her hands over her mouth and began to shake her head as her eyes filled with tears and then she crumbled inside, I could see it in her eyes. I came in and closed the door behind me and took her in my arms and kissed her cheek and held her tight as if that alone would be enough to squeeze the pain out of her.

The baby shouldn't have surprised me, but it did.

It was lying on a blanket on one of the beds, and when I went over to get a closer look at it I had to hold my breath in order to keep from crying out.

It looked like something that floats. I had seen Down's Syndrome children before, but the extent to which this child had been afflicted defied description. I had to turn away.

"I know," said Kim, sitting on the bed and taking the sad thing into her arms, rocking it back and forth. "I know."

The baby's breathing sounded like someone trying to suck congealed grease through a straw.

"How sick is it?"

"She," snapped Kim. "Her name's Sharon. And she's really sick. She has been since she was born. It's one of the reasons they asked me to leave. None of them could stand to look at her. The first baby born in their precious fucking commune, and it wasn't perfect."

"Do you know who the father is?"

"No."

"Were there that many?"

The disgraced look she gave me was all the answer I needed.

We were almost out of the state when the baby started getting worse. Kim sat beside me holding Sharon in her arms, both of them softly whimpering.

"Ohgod, Scott. I don't know what to do. She's so sick and I don't have the money for doctors—"

"—I can get money."

"I know, but…"

We looked at each other, and in her face I could see that she knew whatever promise the rest of her life might hold would be spent caring for a sick, retarded child who, odds were, would never have a good day on this earth.

I pulled off the highway and got onto a winding road that led deep into some hills.

Kim said nothing, only stared at me with an odd combination of disgust and admiration.

I stopped the car.

Sharon snuggled her bloated face into Kim's chest.

Kim put her hand on the back of Sharon's head.

I put my hand on top of Kim's.

We looked into each other's eyes, not daring to blink.

And we pressed.

We buried the baby under some bushes alongside the road. Kim didn't think I saw her toss her copy of the Rossetti book into the grave before I started pushing the dirt in with my hands.

It was only as we were getting into the car to leave that she looked back at the bushes and said, "She's buried under some red hibiscus blooms. I didn't think they grew out here."

Then she fell apart and stayed that way for a very long time.

She lived with me for a while, and we tried to recapture things but it didn't work. Our relationship crawled along for a few months, a pathetic thing, back-broken and spirit-dead, before ending in bitterness and harsh words and poison.

We never mentioned the baby.

I came home from work one night to find that she'd gone, leaving no note, no numbers, no address.

That night, I took her Rossetti collection from the back of one of my dresser drawers where I'd hidden it after we came back from Arizona and almost opened it to see if the picture and flower were still there.

Almost. But I didn't.

She might need it someday.

I opened the door of the dressing room and just stood there staring at her as she daubed the blood from her lips with a tissue. This close, without her mask, she looked almost sepulchral with her sad and weary eyes glowing like those pictures you see of starving children in nameless Third World countries and the skin of her face pulled drum-tight over her cheekbones. I saw the healing cigarette burns, the bruises that the makeup couldn't quite hide under the harsh lights, and the faintly discolored patches on the inside of her arm that could only have been track marks.

She was only thirty-four but appeared fifty—and not a kind fifty.

She looked up at me, her face expressionless, and said, "I didn't think you'd come."

"Why wouldn't I? Haven't I always been there for you before?"

"Yeah," she said, tossing aside the tissue and lighting a cigarette. "You've always been there for me."

"It was quite a message you left on my answering machine."

"I meant every word, Scott. I can't...I can't anymore, you know? Everything's gone. Ruined. I can't even get angry or feel guilty—that's the worst of it. For so long I lived on the guilt. It was all I had."

"I know."

"What about you?" She cast a quick glance at the gun in my hand but showed no reaction.

"It comes and goes."

"Lucky for you."

"I'm sorry things turned out this way."

"Me too." She nodded toward the gun. "Did Bernie see that?"

"No. But he knows now that I had it."

She spit out some smoke. "He was a worthless piece of shit, anyway. Got his kicks from beating me up when the mood took him."

"Did you ever fight back?"

"No. I figured I deserved it. Not for anything I did to him, though."

"I know." I reached into my coat pocket and took out the Rossetti book and handed it to her.

She almost smiled when she saw it.

Almost.

"I always kind of figured you dug this back out after I went back to the car."

"Thought you might like to have it." I moved over next to her and began to stroke her hair with what I hoped was tenderness—or a reasonable facsimile.

She stared at the cover for a moment, tried to brush off some of the caked-on soil, then tapped her fingers against the spine.

"Did you ever look at it?" I asked.

"No."

"Then why don't you now?"

She reached up and touched my hand. "Only seems right, doesn't it?"

"I suppose."

She opened the book and the yellowed tissue fell out, scattering bits of dried red hibiscus. The photograph fell into her lap, face down.

She closed her eyes and took a deep breath. "You were the only guy who ever said he loved me."

"For what it's worth, you're the only woman I ever really loved."

"So much for romance, huh?"

"Yes. So much for it."

She lifted the book close to her face and read: "'I will shelter thee from harm,/Hide thee from all heaviness./Come to me, and keep thee warm/By my side in quietness./I will lull thee to thy sleep/With sweet songs—we will not weep.'" She lay the book on a table, then picked up the photo but did not turn it over. "You never cried for me, did you, Scott?"

"No."

"Good. Because you promised."

"I remember."

A slight shudder ran down her back and I felt something hitch inside her, then she lifted her head, pulled in a deep, strained, phlegmy breath, and said, "I know you still love me."

"Yes."

"Only someone who loves you would do this."

"Yes."

"Will you say it to me one last time, Scott? Not now, but in a moment? Will you tell me one last time that you love me?"

"Yes."

She nodded her head. I saw a tear slide down the side of her nose.

"I really messed up, didn't I? I never should have left you."

I traced the slant of her cheekbone with my finger. "I never should have let you go."

She pulled in another wet breath, held it, then kissed my hand and turned the photograph over. "Huh. So that's what I looked like."

"Not what you expected?"

"No. I look like a teenage girl who just got dressed after a really good fuck. That's all."

"I froze the world for you."

"I know. I should have died right then."

"Me too."

"Say it. Say it now." She pressed the photo against her chest and closed her eyes.

"I love you, Kim Wilder."

She released a breath filled with the grief of ages and smiled. "I've got it back now, that moment."

"Good."

I put two bullets through the side of her skull, then turned around and walked out of the dressing room and through the stage door, out into the cold, dark, rainy night where I was only shadows and footsteps.

Release, whispered the tumor as it lay down to die with the coming of night.

I stepped into a small doorway between a pawn shop and a florist's. I lit a cigarette with shaking hands and glanced in the florist's window.

They carried no red hibiscuses.

And then I broke my promise to Kim. I started crying. There in the emptiness between the raindrops, under shadow and guilt.

I cried for six minutes; one minute for each petal, one for the truth that was the fruit in the center.

There would never be anyone else.

Oh my sweet Rose of Sharon. The day is done.

I wiped my eyes, blew my nose, and stepped out of the doorway into the coldness and dark and the sad sudden silence.

THE ORDERED, THE NECESSARY, THE UNAVOIDABLE

IN SLEEP HE SURRENDERED to the chill timelessness that always accompanies the denial of grief. The place in his heart where once existed the love for his wife was replaced by a lonely aching that filled every crevice of his body.

He awakened to look down upon his sleeping self. He saw a man isolated, apart; ineffective and meaningless. A blink, a sigh, a shiver, and he was lying in the bed once again, reunited with his flesh.

He stared at the ceiling, feeling overwhelmed and invaded, as if another Self, a sad, broken thing that had lain dormant for so long, impatient and inaccessible, was insinuating itself into his psyche. Pale moonlight like a beam from a projector shone through the window, alighting on the full-length mirror hanging on the closet door.

In this bed, he was alone.

But not so in the mirror's reflection.

His wife, her wide gray eyes radiant, was lying next to him there.

He wondered if he should chance touching her—the Self in the mirror did the same things he did, their movements and gestures synchronized like two Olympic swimmers; if he were to make that Self caress her, would he himself feel the warmth of her lips, the smoothness of her skin, the ordered, necessary, unavoidable erotic truth that was her body? He'd always felt that way. Every time he saw her, every time they kissed, every time he caught a scent of her perfume that entered a room just before she did, he was amazed at the rush of emotions within him. Being with her wasn't like having a fantasy come true before he was ready for it; it was like having a fantasy come true before he'd even had the fantasy.

In the mirror, he put his arm around her, and they slept as one.

He heard the first plaintive morning song of a bird filter in. Stumbling like a drunkard, he lurched out of bed and to the window, rolling up the blind.

Outside it was purple-gray; dawn just creeping in, night not quite finished with the world yet. A thin layer of mist enshrouded the yard as a dispirited breeze sloughed its way through the trees. Dewdrops glistened on every surface, shimmering at the tips of leaves.

She had always loved this time of night, this time of morning.

He closed his eyes and pressed his head against the damp window glass. The contrast of its icy temperature against his own feverish one jarred him and he pulled away, snapping open his eyes.

She stood behind him in the window's reflection; naked, her hair tumbling down over her shoulders, a dark velvet cradle, laying gently against the slope of her breasts. He watched as her arms slipped around him, her fingers twirling patterns into his sparse, matted chest hair, then gliding down, down, her fingertips brushing over his nipples as they swept down, slowly down, teasingly down, pausing playfully as she lay her cheek against his bare shoulder, then rolling her head around so her lips kissed the nape of his neck, then one of her hands reached below his waist with craving and purpose; he arched his back to make it easier for her, not daring to turn around because he knew she'd be gone, only in this amorphous reflection could they be together, so he was content to watch as she kissed his neck and rubbed his stomach and massaged his cock in a way that always drove him into a frenzy—

—watched, but didn't feel any of it.

At all.

God help him, he couldn't feel anything at all.

LONG RED AND THE NEEDLE PATROL

YOU'LL FIND HER DOWNTOWN, usually. Her favorite place is the iron bench on the courthouse lawn, the one that has the sculpted figures of two old women doing cross-stitch sitting on it. Good thing it's a big bench, because Long Red needs a good deal of room, she does, for her bags and blankets and such. They call her Long Red because of the magnificent mane of fiery hair that spills over her shoulders and down her back. You get close enough, and you'll see the gray streaks that betray her years; even though, judging by her face, she's not a day over fifty, she claims to be well into her seventies. Nobody knows her real name, or where she lives—if she has a home at all.

Some days, if you catch her in the right mood, she'll tell you all about her husband, Ronald, and about the magic that has followed her all the days of her life. If you're like most folks and don't think you could much stand having a conversation with one of the street crazies, then you can just walk around the little garden a few yards behind the bench and listen to her tell the story to her chiseled-marble companions there on the bench, who never seem to tire of hearing it:

"Ronald got himself shot overseas during the war and it did something to the bones in his leg and the doctors, they had to insert all these pins and build him a new kneecap and calfbone—it was awful. Thing is, when this happened, he only had ten months of service left. He was disabled bad enough that he couldn't return to combat but not so bad that they'd give him an early discharge, so they sent him back home and assigned him guard duty at one of them camps they set up here in the states to hold all those Jap-Americans.

"Ronald guarded the gate at the south end of the camp, and I guess it was a pretty big camp, kind of triangle-shaped, it was, with watchtowers and searchlights and barbed wire, the whole shebang. There was this old Jap tailor being held there with his family and this guy, he started talking to Ronald during his watch every night. This guy was working on a quilt, you see, and since a needle was considered a weapon he could only work on the thing while a guard watched him, and when he was done for the night he'd have to give the needle back. Well, Ronald, he was the guy who pulled 'Needle Patrol.'

"The old guy told Ronald that this thing he was working on was a 'memory quilt' that he was making from all the pieces of his family's history. I guess he'd been working on the thing section by section for most of his life—'cording to what he told Ronald, it'd been started by his great-great-great-great-grandfather. The tailor had part of the blanket his own mother had used to wrap him in when he was born, plus he had his son's first sleeping gown, the tea-dress his daughter had worn when she was four, a piece of a velvet slipper worn by his wife the night she gave birth to their son...

"What he'd do, see, is he'd cut the material into a certain shape and then use stuff like paint or other pieces of cloth stuffed with cotton in order to make pictures or symbols on each of the patches. Ronald said this old Jap'd start at one corner of the quilt with the first patch and tell him who it had belonged to, what they'd done for a living, where they'd lived, what they'd looked like, how many kids they'd had, the names of their kids and their kids' kids, describe the house *they* had lived in, the countryside where the house'd been...I guess it was really something, all right. Ronald said it made him feel good, listening to this old guy's stories, 'cause the guy trusted him enough to tell him these things, you see? Even though he was a prisoner of war and Ronald was his guard, he told him these things. Ronald said it also made him feel kind of sad, 'cause he'd get to thinking about how most people don't even know their great-grandma's maiden name, let alone the story of her whole life. But this old Jap—'scuse me, I guess I really oughtn't use that word, should I? Don't show the proper respect for the man or his culture—but you gotta understand, back then, the Japs – I mean, the *Japanese* — they was the enemy, what with bombing Pear Harbor and all…

"Where was I? Oh yeah—this old tailor, he knew the history of every last member of his family. He'd finish talking about the first patch, then he'd keep going, talking on about what all the paintings and symbols and shapes meant, and by the time he came round to the last completed patch in the quilt, I guess he'd covered something like six hundred years of his family's history. 'Every patch have hundred-hundred stories.' That's what the old guy said.

The idea was that the quilt represented all the memories of your life—not just your own, but them ones that was passed down to you from your ancestors, too. The deal was, at the end of your life, you were supposed to give the quilt to a younger member of your family and it'd be up to them to keeping adding to it; that way, the spirit never really died because there'd always be someone and something to remember that you'd existed, that your life'd meant something. This old tailor was really concerned about that. He said that a person dies twice when others forget that you had lived.

"'Bout six months after Ronald started Needle Patrol the old tailor came down with a bad case of hepatitis and had to be isolated from everyone else. While this guy was in the infirmary the camp got orders to transfer a hundred or so prisoners, and the old guy's family was in the transfer group. Ronald tried to stop it but nobody'd lift a finger to help—one sergeant even threatened to have Ronald brought up on charges if he didn't let it drop. In the meantime, the tailor developed a whole damn slew of secondary infections and kept getting worse, feverish and hallucinating, trying to get out of bed and babbling in his sleep. He lingered for about a week, then he died. My Ronald, he almost cried when he heard the news.

"The day after the tailor died Ronald was typing up all the guards' weekly reports—you know, them hour-by-hour, night-by-night deals. Turned out that the three watchtower guards—and mind you, these towers was quite a distance from each other—but all three of them reported seeing this old tailor at the same time, at exactly 3:47 in the morning. And all three of them said he was carrying his quilt. Ronald said he read that and got cold all over, so he called the infirmary to check on what time the tailor had died. He died at 3:47 in the morning, all right, but he died the night *after* the guards reported seeing him—up till then, he'd been in a coma for most of the week.

"Ronald tried to track down the tailor's family but didn't have any luck. It wouldn't have mattered much, anyway, 'cause the quilt come up missing.

"He didn't tell me about any of this till our twenty-fifth wedding anniversary. He took me to New York City so's I could see a real Broadway show. On our last day there we started wandering around Manhattan, stopping at all these little shops. We came across this one antique store that had all this 'Early Pioneer' stuff displayed in its window. I stopped to take a look at this big ol' ottoman and I asked Ronald if he thought there were people foolish enough to pay six-hundred dollars for a footstool. He didn't answer me right away so I asked him again and when he didn't answer this time I turned around to see him all white in the face. He let go of my hand and goes running into this store, climbs over some tables and such to get in the window, and he rips this dusty old blanket off a rocking chair.

"It was the quilt that Japanese tailor'd been working on in the camp. They only wanted a hundred dollars for it so you bet your butt my Ronald slapped down the cash. We took it back to our hotel room and spread it out on the bed — oh, it was such a beautiful thing. All the colors and pictures, the craftsmanship ... I got teary-eyed when Ronald told me the story. But the thing that really got to both of us was that down in the right-hand corner of the quilt was this one patch that had these figures stitched into them. Four figures. Three of them was positioned way up high above the fourth one, and they formed a triangle. The fourth figure was down below, walking kind of all stooped over and carrying what you'd think was a bunch of clothes. But Ronald, he took one look at knew what it was — it was a picture of that tailor's spirit carrying his quilt, walking around the camp for the last time, looking around for someone to pass his memories on to because he couldn't find his family.

"See here, in this bag? That's it, that's the quilt. And this here needle? Ronald gave it to me. It was the one that old tailor used. I been adding things to it, 'cause it seemed to me that's what my Ronald would want me to do if he was here. See this? This is part of the suit Ronald wore when we got married. And this here come off the baby gown that my mom made for Cindy when I had her. Them things there? — those're the dog tags that the Army sent to us after Jimmy was killed over in Vietnam. The way I figure it, Ronald was like family to the tailor, so it's only right that I do this. It's only right.

"Thing is, I'm not as sprightly as I used to be, and except for Cindy all my family's gone — she don't much want to have anything to do with me. I'm not even sure where it is she and her husband are livin' these days. And if — oh, Lord, look at me, will you? Getting all teary-eyed again.

"I don't know what's gonna happen to this after I'm gone, you see? And that scares me something powerful, it does. Right down to the ground."

Saviour

"Madness is the first step towards unselfishness."
—Kahlil Gibran

I LAID OUT THE RIFLES.
Loaded the shotguns.

Stacked up the cartridges along the wall.

It occurred to me that, when this was over, the authorities would expect to find some kind of a note. An explanation of sorts. *Why did he do it?*

I looked down at the yard where my family was gathered and knew what people would say: *It must have been his family's fault. You have to pay attention to your loved ones or else—*

—or else, indeed.

(*Monsignor Kappes at the seminary: "If you don't stop disrupting studies with your outlandish questions, we shall have no choice but to take severe disciplinary measures. I know that an inquisitive mind is priceless but you raise questions that border on the blasphemous. You must learn to cooperate or else—"*)

I opened the window, checked the focus on the scopes, then grabbed a piece of paper and began writing.

Why did he do it?

It began, I suppose, as all things must, with seeds.

A man came into the store around three a.m. carrying a large brown paper bag. For a while he contented himself with losing money in the pinball machine and annoying what few customers there were. I stood behind the cash register and watched them all.

From 11:30 p.m. until 8 a.m. I am their watcher, their onlooker, their sentinel. With their tired and bloodshot eyes, chain-smoking filterless cigarettes, never looking at one another, the dead of spirit wander into this store for snacks, beer, cold cuts, and sometimes just to play the pinball machine. They never smile, never stand very straight, and their sex is of little consequence. They shamble in from the darkness to this house of light, supply themselves, and then vanish back into the night with the same familiarity one displays when walking up the steps toward one's home. I often wish I could do something to help them.

"Would you like to buy some flower seeds?"

I snapped out of my reverie and looked at him. I expected him to stink of liquor but he surprised me by smelling of talcum powder. His clothes were old but well-kept. His cheeks sagged and he could have used a shave, but I knew almost at once that he'd been at this all day and hadn't had the time.

"What are you selling them for?"

"I'm selling them for my daughter," he said (pronouncing it *dodder*). "She's a Girl Scout and they, well, they got this contest, see, and whoever sells the most seeds wins a scooter."

"A scooter?"

He looked worried by my question. "Look, I know this must look kinda weird, me bein' in here at this hour and trying to sell flower seeds, but she's been really sick lately and…well, she was doin' so good before and I just don't want to see her lose out again, y'know?"

I did see. And I believed him.

It was the "again" that did it. Not a simple, *I don't want to see her lose out,* no; it was the "again" that told me all I needed to know.

Standing before me was a man who'd probably worked damned hard his entire life to provide for his family but never managed to give them anything they *wanted*, only the necessities – and perhaps sometimes even those had to be cut back because the paycheck was a little short. I knew this by simply looking at his gaze. There is a certain sparkle that drifts across the eyes when desperation sets in, and Seed-Man's eyes had it.

"How much?" I asked, reaching for my wallet.

"Seventy-five cents a package. I know that might seem a little steep, but—"

"—it's for a good cause, I know." I began counting through the bills. "Tell me about your daughter." I genuinely wanted to know about her.

He smiled, full of pride. "Her name's Pamela."

Pamela. What a pretty name. Gentle, lyrical, maybe a velvety laugh that sounded older than her years, perhaps she wore glasses, small, thin but not frail…

"She's ten, and she's been a Girl Scout since her mother died four years ago." His voice was soft and musical, not at all what you'd expect from someone of his rough appearance, and I thought that if satin could speak it would sound like a man pitching seeds for his dodder at three in the morning.

He spoke as if he were composing a poem to be written down for the ages yet to come; a turn of the page as he told of the fishing trips the family used to take when his wife was still alive, the way his mother used to put her hand against her bosom whenever she laughed, the certain look Pamela would get when she told a fib, another page, a new stanza to his poem of satin and seeds, the way his wife died of lung cancer when she'd never had a cigarette in her life, another verse, a new line composed, the hidden ridicule he saw behind the eyes of people when he tried to sell them the treasures from his bag, the sounds his dodder made when she was a baby…I listened, enraptured, as he carefully chose his words, finishing the verse, completing the meter of his existence, one last line, there: he folded the sweet, golden, sad, bitter, triumphant memories of his life into a perfect paper diamond and gave it to me for safekeeping.

He looked at the clock on the wall. "I'm sorry. I didn't mean to go on for so long. How many would you like?"

"How many do you have left?"

"Fifty-eight."

"I'll take all of them."

He asked me if I was serious, I assured him that I was. I gave him the money, he gave me the seeds, smiled, thanked me for his dodder, and turned to leave.

"She'll be so proud of me," he said.

She should be, I thought. Of all the sights in this world, of all the valleys and temples and forests and pyramids and mountains, there is nothing so eternally powerful as the sight of a human being doing something out of love.

I waved at him as he left—

—then his back was to me—

—so I made my hand into a fist, stuck out my index finger, lifted my thumb, and snapped it down.

"Bang," I whispered. There. You'll never know hurt again, never taste humiliation, never feel like a failure. I love you. Your dodder will be proud.

Anima Christi, sanctifica me. Corpus Christi, salva me. Sanguis Christi, inebria me. Aqua lateris Christi, lava ma.

I said the prayer in thanks.

Seed-Man had given me my answer.

I suddenly recalled the look on Monsignor Kappes' face the day I left the seminary. He looked genuinely sad to see me leave; who would he have to argue with now?

As I was loading the last of my luggage into the taxi, I turned to him and asked, "Tell me one thing, Monsignor. Your brother has made a nice fortune manufacturing weapons for the government. How do you reconcile that?"

"I don't understand."

"How can you teach us the love of God, the holiness of forgiveness, the sanctity of life, while members of your own family provide the world with tools of death and destruction?"

"Decided to leave on a cheery note, eh?"

"I'd like an answer, please."

"So would the rest of us," he said, not making eye contact with me. "If we had the answers, none of us would need to be here."

"Oh, that's just *great*," I said, slamming closed the trunk and opening the rear passenger door. "I should've expected as much from you. I asked you a carefully considered question and you give me a 'Damned-If-I-Know.' What's next in the repertoire, 'Shit happens'?"

"Please," said Kappes. "I feel bad enough about this as it is. I don't want things to end like this."

"Fine, I'll let that one drop, but—hang on." I leaned in and told the driver to start the meter, I was going to be a minute or two, then I face Kappes again and said, "What say we at least finish our little argument about what is and what is not miraculous. As far as I'm concerned, you never did get out of that one. Consider it my going-away gift."

Kappes almost sneered at me. "I shouldn't *have* to 'get out of it,' as you say. Your arguments about miracles are perhaps the most cynical and offensive I've ever encountered."

"So as a good Man of God you should just ignore them?"

"No, I'm saying that—oh, all right. Have it your way, then. It's been a while since that day, you'll have to refresh—"

"You said that miracles are the supreme proof of God's existence."

"Yes."

"But that's not fair. You can't offer up miracles as evidence of God because that makes your argument circular. 'Miracles prove the existence of a God who produces miracles.'"

"Then what about Jesus walking on the water?" he said. "What about the loaves and fishes?"

"Parlor tricks. How can you claim to be an intelligent human being and still believe a bunch of tall tales written thousands of years ago by a group of zealots who were only interested in promoting their own brand of spirituality?"

Kappes shook his head. "Dear Lord, how can you *exist* from day to day with that kind of cynicism?"

"You're avoiding the question."

"Then be specific."

"Fine. If this taxi were to suddenly rise nine feet in the air, would you call that a miracle?"

"That's an absurd—"

"Step lightly. I'm sure a lot of folks in the loaves-and-fishes crowd thought the same thing when Christ announced he was going to feed all of them."

"There is a great difference between a floating taxi and Jesus Christ."

"There's a sentence you don't hear every day. Okay, I'll bite — what is this great difference?"

"Jesus was the son of God and possessed supreme power."

"And *that* was a miracle?"

"Yes."

"And as such proved God's existence?"

"Of course. God moves in—"

"Next question. If God is the Supreme Being, possessing of Supreme Power, why does he need miracles to prove His existence?"

"Because mankind's faith is weak and—"

"You're paraphrasing the textbooks—which, by the way, are about a decade out of date. You're also not listening to me, big surprise there, so I'll try this again. Why does God need miracles to prove His existence if His power is absolute?"

Kappes blanched. "I'm not sure I understand what you're getting at."

"Follow me on this. An omnipotent God, Who created and rules the entire universe, a God Who can do anything, make anything happen or not happen, Who gave us the stars and dreams and astrophysics and Kool-Aid and compassion and Vietnam and cheeseburgers and Elvis and UFOs, an omnipotent God Who is so majestic and wise, *this* God would have no *need* of miracles. If He doesn't want some infant dying of AIDS, He could prevent it from contracting the virus from its mother in the first place. If He doesn't want a couple of thousand people dying in a terrorist attack in New York, He could stop it from happening. If He doesn't want hundreds of thousands of people to die of starvation in Third World countries, He could pick up the cue from His kid and do a bigger-scale variation of the loaves and fishes routine. So why shouldn't I regard so-called 'miracles' as evidence that God has lost control of the universe and is stumbling around in a panic trying to patch up the damage?"

"Because He's not trying to 'patch up' anything! He is demonstrating His divine love through these miracles."

"Then why be so fucking *vague* about it? Why not just burn a proclamation into the sky or turn the moon tartan or something irreversible like that? Why not stop the spread of all epidemics? However wonderful a few freak cures at Lourdes may be, the stockpile of human misery is still enormous! The pain is still there, we're still bleeding and starving and freezing to death and lonely and angry and heartbroken and feeling like there's nothing we can do to make it any better! What you define as a miracle seems to me to be unworthy of such a majestic, loving, all-powerful God. Walking on water and a little mojo-man action with a loaf of bread and a couple of dead carp looks like a tacky conjuring act."

"Did you ever stop to think," said Kappes, "that maybe He *is* averting disasters all the time?"

"Bullshit. Anyone can claim the same thing. If I say that by standing on my head each morning while naked and chanting the words to 'M-m-my G-generation' I prevent aliens from outer space from landing in Hoboken, who's to say that I'm wrong? I could cite as my proof that aliens have indeed *not* landed in Hoboken."

Kappes glowered at me. "Why can't you be content with the bald fact that God and His miracles exist? Why do you always have to question everything? Everything has to have a concrete explanation for you or else it's just so much smoke and mirrors—and if someone doesn't agree with you, you mock them. I am sick to death of you looking down your nose at the Church and its beliefs, beliefs that *I* happen to wholly embrace. I believe that God exists and that He reaffirms His existence through miracles. In most cases He does this in small, commonplace ways—gravity, the light from the sun, a baby's laugh, *The Firebird Suite*, a really hot Charlie Parker sax riff—but sometimes He departs from the norm and has to employ more dramatic means. It's not a matter of your not being able to believe in miracles, it's a matter of your being too damned arrogant to accept anything that doesn't fit into your cynical little world-view."

I stared at him for a moment, then clapped my hands together, slowly, three times, in a lampoon of applause. "I guess all it takes is a little faith, right?"

"Yes."

"And God will do what He will do."

"Exactly."

"In other words, 'Shit happens.' Beautiful, Monsignor, just beautiful." I climbed into the taxi. "And just so you know, my 'cynical little world-view' has no room for judgmental half-assed theologians who are content to waltz blithely through life dropping platitudes like some kind of cosmic Noel Coward. And it sure as hell has no room for their relatives who provide the world with the means of further pain and destruction— unless of course you're willing to reverse the Church's stand on, say, suicide and euthanasia. I'd love to stick around and explain to you why I think the Church's stand on abortion is stuffed full of wild blueberry muffins, but the meter's running. Don't forget to renew that NRA membership."

And with that, the Church and I parted ways.

I had chosen to leave because my father had been injured in an industrial accident at the steel mill. A series of maddening complications set in, his sick pay and Workman's Comp ran out, he was denied unemployment benefits because he didn't fit the bill of being both available and *able* to work, and what my mother brought in from the dry-cleaning shop where she worked wasn't quite enough to cover all the necessities.

On the night Seed-Man gave me the answer to the question I'd asked of Kappes, my father had been out of work for sixteen months. It was killing him. When I collected my paycheck every two weeks, I left the store, waited down at the bank until it opened, deposited my check into my parents' account, and took the bus home where I handed the deposit slip to my father, who always accepted it with a sad shame in his eyes. Once a month, at his insistence, I kept one half of my paycheck for myself. I'd just given Seed-man one-third of it, but I didn't care.

At the diner the waitress smiled at me with tired eyes— always there are the tired eyes—and served my breakfast. Her pale skin had too much makeup and told me how much she wished she were beautiful, just a little. She told me a joke as she refilled my coffee, and it was a good joke, and I laughed, and she laughed, and something might have passed between us at that moment but I'll never really know. Too often laughter is mistaken for the sound of happiness.

As I left she told me to have a nice day. I wished her the same. Once outside I pointed at her through the window but she didn't see.

Bang.

There.

You'll never have any more nights longing for the warm body of a lover next to yours, touching you. You'll never again have to smile when you don't feel like. I love you. Thanks for the joke. It was a good one.

Passio Christi, comforta me. O bone Jesu, exaudi me. Intra tua absconde me. Ne permittas me separari a te.

The bag of seeds tucked under my arm, I began the long walk home. I needed to walk today. There were plans to make.

By the time I passed St. Francis on Granville Street, I'd already scattered a dozen bags of seeds. Outside the church, an old priest was crouching down, tending to a small garden in front of the statue of the Virgin Mary. I stopped to admire his flowers.

"They're lovely," I said, because they were. He thanked me for my kindness in noticing, I told him there was no kindness involved, that beauty creates its own reward.

"That's a nice way to look at it," he said, returning to his work.

"Father?"

"Yes?"

"Might you be interested in some more seeds for your garden?"

He waved me away. "I don't have the money to buy anything from you."

I set down Seed-Man's bag next to the old priest. "I don't want to sell you anything. I just want to give these seeds to you for your garden."

"Well, then, I apologize for jumping to that conclusion, and I thank you kindly."

"I only ask that you listen to a story I have to tell."

He considered this for a moment, then gave a slow nod if his head.

"I'll be able to make the place quite lovely with these," he said, looking through the different types of seeds inside the bag. "Please, then. Your story."

I knelt beside him and began:

"On a Florida beach one afternoon, while everyone was sunning themselves or swimming or playing volleyball, a figure in a flowing white robe descended from the sky. He said that he was Jesus. The fun-in-the-sun crowd didn't believe him and asked him to prove it. 'Feed all of us with this bottle of mineral water and these two fish sticks!' said one girl. So Jesus blessed these items and soon everyone was munching happily away. But still the crowd needed more proof. 'I can't swim because my left leg is lame,' said a little boy. 'Can you heal me, please?' So Jesus touched the boy's leg and restored it to health. Still the crowd wanted more. 'Walk on the water!' someone shouted. So Jesus got into a rowboat and went out several hundred yards to where the water was deepest. Everyone watched breathlessly as he stood up in the boat and touched the surface of the water with his big toe. 'I do this so that your faith may be restored,' he said. 'I do this so that hunger and sorrow and loneliness and pain and despair will never again taint your spirits.' Then he stepped out of the boat and immediately sank.

"He swam back to shore and walked back onto the beach where everyone was laughing at him. Jesus looked at them for a few more moments, then began ascending back to Heaven. Before he disappeared from view, he looked down at the crowd and said: 'Give me a break. The last time I did that I didn't have holes in my feet.'"

The priest fixed me with a cold stare. "I don't think that's very funny, young man."

"Neither do I, Father. I happen to think it's rather sad." I rose to my feet. "Maybe you'll understand someday."

"Understand what?"

"That even the greatest failures are born out of love."

And with that, I left him in his garden.

I have no idea how long I walked, the places I went, the people I smiled at, waved to, spoke with. All I could see was the sparkle in their eyes, the same sparkle, the one you learn to recognize when working nights. They all needed something so much, a sense of comfort, of belonging, of being loved and having that loved returned in equal measure.

I pointed at them—*Bang!*—took it all away, gave them peace.

Sometime later I passed a small retarded girl who was playing with a doll in her front yard. She seemed utterly content. There was no pain in her life for me to take away and I immediately felt an affinity for her, a special love. I wanted to embrace her, to kiss her cheek, to tell her of all that I had learned. Only she would have understood.

From across the street I waved at her, and she smiled.

"Dolly," she said, holding up her treasure. "Dolly dress."

"I love you, Dollydress," I whispered. Then walked the rest of the way home.

My father was in the back yard, hobbling around on a pair of metal arm crutches, trying to start the coals for a cookout. He liked cookouts, considered himself to be something of a backyard gourmet chef. I stood by the broken fence and watched him; the way he stacked the charcoal, the way he measured the fluid, the way he tossed the match in *just so*. Things like this were his big projects now. Skilled hands going to waste, attached to a broken body that was never going to properly heal. He saw me and smiled, so proud.

"Hope you're hungry, workin' man," he said.

"No problem there," I replied.

My sister was setting out paper plates on an old card table behind him and trying to arrange the lawn chairs so everyone would have enough elbow room. She'd recently lost out on a cheerleading position at school. I could see that it still hurt.

Do you weep? I wondered. Do you cry at night because you listen to all the latest music, read all the right magazines, and thumb through paperback books that tell you How You Can Be More Popular, but your weekends are still spent in front of the television with the rest of the family? Do you lie in bed wishing for a boy to call you, someone who's noticed all your efforts and wants to be your friend?

She looked at me and stuck out her tongue, then laughed. I could always make her laugh, though I don't know how or why.

Inside the house, my mother was sitting in front of the television folding freshly-cleaned clothes. All day long for the past twenty years she worked pressing clothes at Cedar Hill's only dry-cleaning shop, and here she was on her day off doing basically the same thing. She looked so tired, so worn and sad, but at least she had her favorite programs to look forward to.

Why, mother? I thought. Do you dream? Do you? Do you imagine that someday you'll get lucky and hit the lottery? Is that why you always manage to scrape together enough to buy ten dollars' worth of tickets every week? And in this dream, is your family happy? Do we all smile and embrace you and tell you how the money doesn't matter because you've *always* been so good to us? Are these the things you dream about while pressing clothes and breathing steam? Does it help when your lower back is killing you? Does it comfort you when you go to the grocery store knowing that your family will again have to eat macaroni and cheese three times this week?

I don't know what I felt as I stood there watching her. I just hoped it wasn't pity. I leaned over and kissed her cheek. She seemed so interested in the television program.

"What're you watching?"

"Huh?" She looked at me, then at the television. "I don't know, just…some show." She looked at her hands, cracked her knuckles, and then sighed. "Did you remember to get some of that new kind of aspirin for your dad? You know, them capsule ones with the flag on the label? His hip's really been bothering him and those pills seem to be the only thing that help."

I produced them from my pocket and she smiled.

"Oh, you're so thoughtful. Your dad was just saying the other night how proud he is of you. You didn't say no when we needed you."

"I love you, Mom."

"I love you, too, hon. Where have you been, anyway? It's almost noon. I was getting' worried."

"Just out walking. It's a nice day for it."

"I guess. I been folding clothes all morning. Isn't *that* a pisser? One day off a week, and I spend it…" She shook her head and laughed, but only a little. "I shouldn't complain. I'm lucky to have a job."

How do you thank someone for caring for you? I don't mean for loving you, I mean for the little things—the laundry and food and the toilet paper that's always there and the extra bit of change when you're a little short. How can the words 'thank you' erase the ache of a lifetime's work that you feel has come to nothing?

I started up the stairs. At the top of the landing hangs a charcoal sketch of Christ. This picture has been in the family for so long that no one can remember where it came from, or who originally purchased it. The eyes of this picture follow you everywhere, and until I was fifteen I avoided going anywhere near it.

Now I stood directly before it, hating the peaceful expression on the Saviour's face.

"Why?" I asked it.

If we had the answers, none of us would need to be here.

Tell me.

They've tried, they really have, we've all tried to get by and keep alive a faith in something bigger, the idea that it will all work out in the end.

How do you reconcile?

...and beneath it all is the hope that one day you'll hit on the lottery, nothing spectacular, mind you, just enough to help even things out. You wash the clothes, you stack the charcoal, you sell seeds for your dodder, and you try to believe. But every time you're lost in a pleasant reverie or dream something happens that snaps you back, and you find yourself sitting in your living room on furniture that needs to be replaced but you can't afford it, and, hell, some of it's not even paid for yet, just like the television and the house and everything else around you, and you realize that your accomplishments are fleeting but by God there has to be a reason...

"I'm waiting," I said.

The charcoal eyes stared at me.

No Dollydress scooter for the garden because love is a failure...

...to work all your life to provide for those you love, to do this thing, this seemingly inconsequential but ultimately selfless and remarkable thing, to do this and ask for nothing in return, to work like that without complaint or much hope of getting ahead with the next paycheck, to say your prayers at night and hope that someone somewhere is listening as you ask for courage and strength because your children gave up their education just so you could afford *to live*, and you want for them to have all the things you never could but now they can't even have less because the union turns its back on you when you're hurt and people get rich from selling death and the only person who could understand is cooing over her dolly, so you sit there in front of an 18 x 20-inch box, hoping that something good is going to appear on the screen and make you laugh, make you think that maybe life isn't the dumper it seems, but it is and you know it because God, the Saviour, GreatSaviour, greatsaviour who loves you and gave you gardens and dollydresses and weapons and televisions and unions, this greatsaviour is also a sadist but doesn't even know it.

...border on the blasphemous...

I knew now how one reconciled.

I went to my father's room and unlocked his gun cabinet. He used to go hunting with his brother every year but dear brother didn't come around anymore. Dad always kept the guns cleaned and oiled in the hope that he'd get to go hunting again someday. I took the weapons to my room.

I laid out the rifles.

Ab hoste maligno defende me.

Loaded the shotguns.

In hora mortis meae voca me.

Stacked up the cartridges along the wall.

Et jube venire ad te...

A note.

The authorities would look for some kind of a note.

I searched the bookshelf until I found the collection of famous quotations. I thumbed through the pages until I found the one I was looking for, the one that had created a great deal of friction between Kappes and myself. I wrote it down, and then taped it to the window overlooking the back yard:

> *"Regarding my actions in this world, I care little*
> *in the existence of a heaven or hell; self-respect*
> *does not allow me to guide my acts with an eye*
> *toward heavenly salvation or hellish punishment.*

I pursue the good because it is beautiful and attracts me, and shun the bad because it is ugly and repulsive.

All our acts should originate from the spring of unselfish love, whether there be continuation after death or not."

I smiled at the quote from Heinrich Hein's *Das Bader von Lucca*, picked up the rifle, and opened wide the window.

Mom had joined my sister and father in the back yard.

I felt a tear brimming in my eye.

I wanted to take it all away and make the reconciliation flesh. To erase your sadness and loneliness. To make you forget about all the ways you've lost out in life. To give you something golden and true.

I took a deep breath as I focused Mom in the scope.

(—so proud of you—)

Forgive me, all of you.

Ut cum Sanctis tuis laudem te…

I wanted to save you.

(—didn't say no when we needed—)

Hold your breath, that's it, focus, steady, steady, c'mon…

I wanted so much for you.

In saecula saeculorum…

But I've got holes in my feet.

Amen.

The first shot was easy, just squeeze the trigger snap back and the recoil feels so hard like the Confirmation slap, the smoke spit out, threw the greatsaviour's kiss, this is how I reconcile, and I saw something register on Mom's face and for a moment she looked just like—

—like—

—like the time she lost twenty dollars from her check after she'd cashed it to go to the grocery store and I remember, Mom, how you cried because your feet had been hurting so much that week and that was money you'd had to stand for three hours to earn and now there you were having to put stuff back in the checkout line and three hours of your work and pain was for nothing because your family couldn't have some of the extra goodies like you'd wanted and even though I was little I cried just like you did Mom and your tears were seeds and I saved one for you, here—

She caught it just below the base of her skull, my kiss, and fell forward over the table, wine spilling from her mouth, flowing wine, dark wine, come, all of you, and drink from this cup, this cup of my blood which shall be shed for your sins, but then my sister was screaming, so—

—so—

—so what if nobody asked you to the homecoming dance? You can go by yourself a lot of people do *I always go by myself I want to have a lot of friends even just one* but you never did, Sis, because you're plain, just like me, and the world doesn't embrace the plain to its bosom, we have to make do with the powdered milk of human kindness so I give you—

—the smoke of a dozen blackred roses. She took them to her chest and clutched them there, the first roses she'd ever received from anyone, calling out, her mouth opening and closing but there was no sweet sound because suddenly my father, no fear in his voice, brave old broken man, was stumbling toward her as I took a deep breath and sent—

—sent—

—sent me to the store on my birthday because you knew how much I liked to roast marshmallows in the fireplace, so I went because I knew you were planning something special, and I got the marshmallows but you surprised me by meeting me when I was halfway home, and we walked together, and you had your arm around me, so proud of your boy, and I knew there was going to be a big, roaring fire waiting for us when we came through the door, but when we got home there was nothing left of your fire but smoldering ashes and you looked so ashamed because you'd tried to do something special and failed again and you looked at me and said I wish—

—I wish—

—and I sent him his wish, sent right to his face, all over his face, through his face, and then there was smoke and the heat from the guns and soon nothing but peace and silence and I knew I was forgiven because even in the bitter smoke of failure there is still beautiful, fulfilling, triumphant love.

I fell back, sweating. I had done it.

I had save them. I had made the reconciliation.

I sat up, removed my shoes, and then pulled off my socks.

Perfect feet. No holes at all.

Neighbors were screaming then, someone was pounding on the front door. The yard was filling up with people, so I grabbed the nearest rifle and began sending all of them peace and roses and kisses as sirens came screaming in from the distance and the pounding downstairs gave way to an explosion and the sound of many footsteps running up the stairs toward my room—

—getting closer, they were getting closer, be here any second now, so I turned one last time toward the scene in the back yard, blew my family a kiss, chambered a round in my father's favorite rifle and began turning it toward my face—

—screaming, yelling, getting closer—

—I looked toward the sound, waited for them to enter, I had to time this exactly right—

—I took a deep breath—

—and the door flew open.

"Are you coming down to eat with us or what?" Mom stood there, out of breath. She shouldn't have climbed the stairs. Her feet hurt so much.

"I was on my way."

"Didn't you hear us all yelling for you?" She noticed the rifles and shotguns laid out around me. "What in the world are you doing with those old damn things?"

"Dad said he'd really like to start hunting again. I figured if I got these out and cleaned and oiled them he might, you know...feel like getting out one of these days."

Mom shook her head. "One of these days, my foot. Now put them things away before you hurt yourself."

"Yes, Mom. I just thought maybe I'd go along with him. We haven't had time to do anything together for so long. *None* of have, not really."

Down in the yard my father and sister were hollering at us to hurry up before everything got cold.

"Oh, hon," said Mom. "You wouldn't like hunting. You don't got it in you to hurt a bug."

I shrugged. "I suppose."

But I knew.

In saecula saeculorum. Amen.

She reached out and patted my cheek. I put down the rifle.

"I don't know about you sometimes," she said.

"I love you, Mom."

"I love you, too...you little weirdo."

We started down toward the feast.

Mom looked back at the rifles. "I swear, hon, things'll be better ... maybe one of these days."

"I know," I said, putting my around her to help her down the stairs. "One of these days..."

In the Direction of Summer's Coming

"It's the question of the last act before man-made dying
that hundreds of blossoms shout a final triumph
for earth and sky to behold."

– Peter Blue Cloud, "Dogwood Blossoms"

CHIEF WETBRAIN DREW a chalk circle around him, scooted into its center (he had to scoot everywhere because he didn't have any legs), and started playing his saxophone. Every morning, every afternoon, every evening, those who had given him this White Man's Title passed by, listening as he freed his music to soar through the air around him, asking a question that none ever heard:

Who will take me?

His real name was Jimmy Night-Eagle but he had long ago forgotten it. Here, they called him Chief Wetbrain because rarely was there a day he couldn't be seen bending his elbow, a bottle of cheap whiskey clutched in his hand. No one cared (if any of them had known) that the drinking was his only way of numbing the near-constant pain of his aching stumps; they saw only a soused conversation piece, something to pity or mock but mostly ignore, never once considering the genuine sadness of the question hidden in the heart of his music.

Who will take me?

Once, his question would have been heard by *Matotipila*, the eight stars of Gemini, answered by *Tayamni*, the glorious Orion, and remembered in the heart of *Wanagitacanku*, the bosom of the Milky Way, so when his music was finished at day's end he could look into the heavens and know that Some Being had acknowledged his existence.

Once, when he was younger and his faith was stronger; yes, perhaps then.

But no longer.

Still, his question remained constant; sometimes stubbornly so.

And surrounding the question was a song that rang out a tale composed of notes that became Kachinas and Crow Mothers and They Who Breathed The Land Into Being; it turned round in the breeze and caught a few of the soon-to-come raindrops that held memories of nights on the plains, future storm clouds rolling unseen above the heads of the people as they passed, sprinkling them with hints of things he still knew and they had long ago forgotten, secrets of the Earth and Time hidden in the silences between the notes; a breath, a beat, songs of the Elders and their tales of the Fiery-Sky Ones, another breath, another beat, and the notes multiplied like the birds of the sky after solstice, power, strength, and courage in his grip as he pulled the sax closer to his ruined body, breathing his soul into the reeds like a fine medicine man should–and over there, a glint in a passing pair of eyes, yes, as the song banked on the winds and came back to him, more than it was before, making him feel that he was once again among his people, where he should have been all along, grace covering him like tree-fallen leaves in autumn, so good, yes, I am ready: The time is upon me to fly.

A young man dressed in a handsome three-piece suit walked by and tossed something down into the medicine bag that Chief Wetbrain kept by his side.

He stopped playing and picked up the shiny object.

Sokela–a quarter.

"And my folks used to worry that I couldn't make a decent living as a jazz musician," he muttered to himself.

He smiled, gave a silent thanks to the young man, and resumed his playing.

Across the street, a group of young, rough-looking boys watched his every move. One of them kept opening and closing a serrated-edged switchblade as he stared at the medicine bag.

Chief Wetbrain played on, his question rising so high it could no longer see the sun rise on the Earth; it arced into the wind, traveling ever upward, until it passed the place where beat the soul of the *Mahpiyas,* the True Heavens, where all questions were finally answered. His music paused, asking its question again, then waited as something born on the yellow light of the eagle began its flight back down toward Earth.

He closed his eyes, set the saxophone by his side, and picked up his medicine bag.

Eceyanuniya, he thought: *I am the fool now.*

He opened his eyes. The boys were still watching him.

There was no fear in his heart. The circle would protect him.

He picked up the medicine bag and gave it a good shake: the money inside went *cha-chink!*

It was a good sound, a happy sound—happy enough, anyway—that reminded him of the coins his grandmother used to carry in her pockets, and that took him back to a time before the city with its towering monoliths, before the White Schools, before the desert and cacti and moonflowers were a mere wisp of wishfulness, before he found himself trapped in a place where the stars could not find him.

He remembered, then, the prayer his grandmother had taught him:

They that are born are destined to die; and the dead to be brought to life again; and the living to be judged, to know, to make known, and to be made conscious that He is the Great Spirit, the Maker, the Creator, the Discerner, the Judge, the Witness, the Complainant; He that will in future judge, blessed be He, with whom there is no unrighteousness, nor forgetfulness, nor hatred of persons. Know that everything is according to reckoning; and let not your imagination give you hope that the grave will be a place of refuge for you. For perforce you were formed, and perforce you shall be One with the Great Spirit upon the moment of physical death.

Beat the living shit out of "Now I lay me down to sleep" any day.

He muttered the prayer to himself, then decided to follow it through with the Ritual of the Four Directions, his way of giving thanks for another day of life.

He turned to the East and shook the bag.

Cha-chink, cha-chink!

He whispered something then, something eternal in the Circle, something that would have sounded like gibberish to the young men in their handsome suits. The wind listened to his chant:

"We dance in the Eastern direction of the sun's rising
We move in the yellow light of the Eagle…"

Somewhere in the distance his question paused again, waiting while something born on the green light of the Mouse attached itself, then journeyed onward.

The boys across the street began to stand, curious about this sudden change in the Chief's activities.

One of the young men, the anxious initiate, walked in front of the others as they made their way over. He stared at the medicine bag full of money. He held the serrated knife that had been shoved into his hand only moments before by the gang's leader.

Chief Wetbrain was living a fable from his heritage behind his closed eyes; soaring with the illumination and enlightenment of the Eagle, scurrying over the Earth with the soft innocence of the Mouse, thundering across the plains with the wisdom of the White Buffalo, lumbering strong and without fear through the forests with the strength of the Black Bear.

He heard the singing of many nations, saw the eyes of many peoples, touched their joy, felt their melancholy at the passing of the seasons, shared their euphoria at the approach of a new solstice–

Cha-chink, cha-chink!

The gang members slowly gathered around the outside of the Chief's circle as the old man turned, chanting:

"We dance in the Southern direction of summer's coming
We move in the green light of the Mouse…"

Then the old man opened his eyes and saw the young men, the boys, saw the knife held by the nervous initiate… and smiled.

He held up the medicine bag filled with coins and gestured toward the serrated blade.

"I'm in the middle of a ritual, in case you haven't noticed," he said.

"Crazy motherfucker," muttered one of the boys.

Chief Wetbrain laughed but there was no humor in it. He faced the boy with the knife. "I feel like I don't belong here, either, but I can't go back home because I don't belong there anymore. Not that they'd have me, and if they won't, then… who *will* take me?" He reached out and massaged one of his stumps. "Get drunk and pass out under one trailer, have it back over you and crush your legs–do this once, and people think you're incompetent."

"Just take the money," said another.

The nervous boy with the knife pointed the blade toward the Chief's throat, bent low, and took the medicine bag from the old man's grip. "Sorry," he whispered so the others wouldn't hear him.

Then the boys were gone–*cha-chink, cha-chink, cha-chink!*

Something of the Bear touched the Chief's question next, circling like a comet, coming closer:

We dance in the Northern direction of the sun's setting

We move in the dark light of the Bear...

Across the street, the boys divided the money among themselves and then dispersed.

All but one.

Cha-chink!

Something more then attached itself to the Chief's question.

His journey was almost finished, the Circle strong and unbroken, the ritual nearly complete.

"We dance in the Northern direction of Wisdom," whispered the Chief. *"We move in the white light of the Buffalo."*

There.

It was finished.

He could die now.

He held his saxophone tightly.

They were coming for him—Eagle, Mouse, Bear, and Buffalo—and he would go with them with joy in his heart.

(*They that are born are destined to die; and the dead to be brought to life again...*)

He played on, his music calling out until well after dusk, until the handsome-suited ones were no longer in sight. His breath was leaving him, and he paused, holding the instrument near his pale lips.

Beside him lay more coins, so shiny and new, tossed down by others who had passed by after the boys had robbed him.

He knew now that the boy with the knife would be returning, but Chief Wetbrain had no desire to leave this place and seek safety in man-made shelter. The Circle would make his death painless.

A soft spattering of rain touched him. The cool droplets filled him with peace and acceptance.

(*...and the living to be judged, to know, to make known, and to be made conscious that He is the Great Spirit, the*

Maker, the Creator, the Discerner, the Judge, the Witness, the Complainant...)

I am the center of the Circle, he thought.

I am We.

The Harvest is mine.

The time is upon me to—

—the spell was suddenly broken by a loud thunderclap.

And just as suddenly he was only a pathetic and crippled old drunken Indian, alone in the city at night and getting slowly soaked to the bone.

Far from the desert, far from his heritage, for the first time in his long and many years, Chief Wetbrain realized something that crushed toward his center, breaking through the Circle, pounding toward him like a stampede of spooked horses: Here, in this place where starlight could not reach him, there *had* been others like himself—lost ones, questioning ones—and he had touched all of them, in a way, by asking his question, but why did it all feel so *useless* now, here in the rain?

He looked at his saxophone, lifted it toward his lips, but then all strength and purpose left his body and he let the instrument drop onto his lap.

Not to touch the Earth, but to touch just One of this Earth, just once, just to know that someone would remember that he'd been here.

In the end I turn sentimentalist. Oh, goody.

Matotipila smiled down on him, *Tayami* wept, and *Wanagitacanku* made room in its heart for him as the Eagle, Mouse, Bear and Buffalo approached quickly.

"Who will take me?" he whispered to all of them. It was so cold, so wet and chilly and desert-night cold.

"I will take you," said the Eagle.

"As will I," replied the Mouse.

The Black Bear and White Buffalo agreed, as well, and began crossing into the center of the Circle, seen only by Chief Wetbrain's haunted eyes.

He clutched his saxophone to his chest, suddenly so very lonely... and afraid.

He closed his eyes and waited for the communion.

Silence.

Warmth, then; sudden, touching his face not like the wing of the Eagle, or the paw of the Mouse, or the claw of the Bear or hoof of the Buffalo, no; this felt like the touch of a hand–

He opened his eyes and looked into the face of the nervous Blade Boy.

"You hungry?" asked the boy.

Chief Wetbrain tried to nod his head. The boy produced a cheeseburger from a wet paper sack. "You eat. Damn well ought to eat this–you paid for it, after all." The boy smiled and picked up the saxophone.

"Where is your knife?" asked the Chief.

The boy patted his jacket pocket. "Got it right here. One of the rules is, whoever's got the blade is in charge. I almost forgot about that. Good thing I remembered, or them assholes would've wailed on you something serious."

"Ah..." Chief Wetbrain took another bite of the cheeseburger. It was delicious.

The boy admired the sax. "I used to play one of these things in a New Orleans club a few years back. I was pretty good, but no way I could make this baby sing like you can. Teach me?"

Chief Wetbrain smiled and nodded his head.

The boy stepped into the Circle and at once began looking around frantically. "Whoa, Chief, where in the hell did these animals come from?"

Smiling, the Eagle, Mouse, Bear, and Buffalo touched both of them, whispering friendship and long life.

"Who will take me?" asked Chief Wetbrain.

"I'll take you," said the young man. "I got plenty of room at my place." Then he blew into the saxophone, and Chief Wetbrain rejoiced at the sound, the sound of summer and illumination and wisdom and inner-vision… and friendship.

"Little crowded in here, don't you think, Chief?"

A moment, then Chief Wetbrain asked: "Is that better?"

"You know it."

The Chief watched the heavens for a moment and saw his answer soaring there, then kissed the night-wind and smiled as the Mouse turned back to him, deciding to stick around for a while.

MATTHEW IN THE MORNING

"We are scattered—stunned—the remnant of heart left alive with us, filled with brotherly hate."
—*Mary Chesnut's Civil War Journals,* May 16, 1865

HE WAS FOUND at three-forty in the morning, hanging from a tree less than one half-mile outside of the camp. He had used a set of horse's reigns to do the deed. So tight had the reins been pulled by his body's drop from the thick limb, so deep had they sunk into the flesh of his neck, that only the bones beneath the fragile skin had prevented his head from being separated from his body.

His name was Luther Wade, Private, Rifleman, 6th Mississippi.

He was found by the camp doctor, who had been unable to sleep, just as he'd been unable to sleep for the last three days. The doctor walked quietly back to camp and enlisted the assistance of a private on watch. They took a wagon and one of the more rested horses and went back to fetch Private Wade. His body was cut down as gingerly as was possible under the circumstances, then laid out in the buckboard and taken back to the field hospital where the doctor wiped his bleary eyes, shook his head at the pitiful sight, and said, "Damn war can't last much longer now. This boy might have been home in a few months." He didn't want to look on a sight like this. In the last five days he'd amputated seven legs, three arms, and numerous hands and fingers. None of them had gone particularly well because the conditions here were unspeakably filthy. His head was still filled with echoing screams of young men lying on the operating table, begging him to kill them. His boots were caked with blood. His hands, though washed, still felt like they were covered in the blood of brave young men taken too soon from their homes and forced to fight in a war where both sides were doomed no matter who won.

At least there was still some whiskey left for the coffee.

"What do you suppose made him do it, sir?" asked Tyler, the young private whose terrible duty it had been to assist the doctor in retrieving Private Wade's remains and transporting them back to camp. "Ain't we lost enough good men on the battlefield? What kind of a coward goes out in the night like he done and—"

The doctor waved his hand, silencing Tyler. "Be damned careful how you use a word like 'coward,' son. Every man has his breaking point. You got no idea what made him do this."

Tyler shrugged. "I didn't mean no offense, sir, it just seems to me that if a man can come away from what we seen at Cold Harbor, then he's just about seen the worst there is."

"Has he now?"

"That's just my opinion, sir."

The doctor gestured at the body. "Did you happen to know him?"

"Luther? Yessir, I did. I mean, we weren't best friends or nothing, but I knew him well enough to play some cards or have a pleasant enough conversation during watch. Ain't nothing he said nor did that would lead me to think he'd ever do a damn fool thing like this, nossir, not a thing at all."

"This late in the war, our beloved Confederacy is full of surprises. Right down to its smallest elements," said the doctor, pulling his pipe from his pocket and tamping down what little remained of the sad, bitter tobacco he'd taken from the body of a prisoner who'd died on his table late last night. The Union soldier had known he was going to die from the severity of his wounds, and so had asked the doctor to write a note for his parents. The doctor had obliged the soldier, patiently sitting next to the table while the young man–who could not have been any older than fifteen–dictated a short letter with broken words and incomplete sentences. To show his gratitude for the doctor's help, he offered the pouch of tobacco that was in his pocket. "My father swears this is the damned finest tobacco there is, yessir," he'd said, then died without telling the doctor his last name.

The doctor still had the letter in his pocket. He would carry it with him, he suspected, until the good General Robert E. Lee came to his senses and mustered the courage it took to admit defeat and sent a messenger to Grant requesting terms of surrender.

The doctor looked at Luther Wade's body. "What's that?"

"Sir?' asked Tyler.

"There's something inside his coat, behind his back–see it there, son?"

"Yessir."

They lifted Wade's body, only half turning him over before the object was revealed.

Wade had pinned an envelope to the back of his uniform. It was addressed, simply, this way: **To Whoever Finds Me.**

The doctor removed the envelope from Wade's uniform and then wiped off as much of the blood as was still wet enough to be wiped away. Inside, Luther Wade had wrapped the letter in a small piece of torn blanket, perhaps suspecting that rain–or his own blood–might stain the envelope and seep through to the pages within.

The first page had only a few lines on them, giving the names of his parents and asking that the reader please be kind enough to see that the following pages be posted to his parents' address, which was written in a strong , steady, legible hand.

The doctor leaned back against the buckboard, tucked the letter under his arm, and managed to get his pipe going at last. The tobacco tasted like dried manure but he was going to smoke all of it.

The Union soldier had offered it like it was the most precious thing he possessed; it didn't seem right to simply toss it away because its flavor wasn't to his liking. Might as well have pissed on the poor kid's body, if that were the case.

The doctor puffed away on his pipe, thinking.

"You gonna read the letter, sir?" asked Tyler.

"Yes, Private, I am. And since you were the one who found him, I guess that means you've got something of a right to read it as well, considering the way he addressed the envelope."

"I don't see as how that'd be proper, sir."

The doctor stared at Tyler. "I am not one who believes that killing yourself is necessarily a coward's way out. It is my belief that a body'd have to be in a lot of pain in order to think a death the likes of *this* was preferable to breathing in the air of one more morning. So I am going to read this letter, and then you will read it, and we will at least be able to speak truthfully about Private Wade's reasons for taking his own life when others start in with their half-assed guessing. He might have killed himself, but Luther Wade was a soldier who fought for our beloved Confederacy, and that alone dictates a certain amount of respectfulness at his death, it requires we do what we can to maintain some of his dignity, for there is no man more dignified on this Earth than one of our Confederate boys in his uniform, be he alive or dead, be that death in battle or by his own hand." He offered the letter to Tyler. "Would you care to be the first to read it, Private?"

Tyler looked down at his feet and coughed. "Afraid I don't read too good, sir."

The doctor nodded. "Then cover him up and come on over to my tent. I'll make some coffee for us and then I will read this letter aloud. Somehow I think it important that his last thoughts be shared with someone."

"Yessir."

"And Private?"

"Sir?"

"Since no one saw us cut down his body nor bring it into camp, I'll ask you to not speak of this for the time being."

"Yessir. Still seems a damned fool thing to do, hanging yourself."

"We're all hanging ourselves, son, from the moment we're born; just takes the rope fifty or sixty years to snap tight, that's all."

To My Dearest Mother and Father:

By now you have undoubtedly heard about the circumstances of my death, and for that I offer my deepest apologies. It was never my intention to disgrace my uniform or the good name of our family, but circumstances have made it necessary that I do not die a hero's death in battle or return home alive and whole.

I must also assume that the papers back home have by now told the sad tale of the battle at Cold Harbor. Though we are not privy to the papers out here, I can tell you this much: No one who wasn't there could begin to capture in words the horror of the slaughter that we took part in. I harbor no great love for the Union Army nor its soldiers, but I must confess to you here that, toward the end of their last charge, it began to turn my stomach, how easy it was to kill them. That dreadful storm of lead and iron seemed more like a volcanic blast than a battle. It did not matter that the Union Army were armed with their new repeating rifles. Our boys had dug in well, creating massive entrenchments in which we were well protected in the earthworks and suffered little from the federal fire. But still, General Grant insisted on a second charge from his soldiers.

It took almost a full day for them to prepare for their second charge, which came a little after four-thirty in the morning. Thousands of Union soldiers crawled out of their entrenchments and marched toward us. It was like shooting cans off a fence. I cannot speak for what happened farther down the line, but where I was, no Union solider was able to get closer than twenty feet of our earthworks before being cut down–and often cut in half–by our fire. It was deafening, a boiling cauldron from the incessant pattering of shot which raised the dirt in geysers and spitting sands. The men fell and fell and fell. Blood ran thick as mud all around us. It was over in half an hour. The stunned attackers recoiled and sought the protective cover of their trenches, having left thousands upon thousands of their comrades lying on the field. Their dying screams are in my ears still, even as I write this from the relative safety of the field hospital camp.

Oh, my dear parents, I have seen the carnage in front of Marye's Hill at Fredricksburg, and on the old railroad cut which Jackson's men held at the Second Manassas, but I have seen nothing to exceed this. It was not war; it was murder.

Something took place during the battle which I need to confess, but first I must ask you to think back, if you can, to when my beloved brother Matthew and I were children. I promised you, Mother, that I would watch over Matthew during this damn war, and watch over him I did. He was never far from my side. I want you to know this, to know that I tried to be a good and loyal son and brother, one who did everything in his power to keep his word.

I remember, when we children, the joy I would experience when I awakened to see Matthew in the morning. It never mattered to me that he was so slow-witted and deliberate of speech; a purer and more gentle soul I have never encountered–nor, I suspect, has anyone. Not this side of the angels.

Do you remember how he would always rise before any of us? How he would quietly dress himself and start the coals in the stove so it would be all warmed up when you rose, Mother? Then he would take that big old tin can of his–his "treasure chest," he called it, remember? And he would go outside and look for treasures to place within.

Lord, how I can remember those days when, trapped inside by the rain and unable to go out and play with the other children, Matthew would entertain us with a show of his treasures. "Here is a button from a king's satin shirt. Here is a feather from an angel's wing. Here is a cup once drunk from by our Lord Jesus." ow I loved those moments.

Over the last several months, Matthew had taken to singing a song during the long marches to and from our battles. He sang it so much that many of the men learned the words and have been singing it ever since. It goes: Come raise me in your arms, dear brother, And let me see that glorious sun, For I am weary, faint, and dying, How could that battle lost or won; Do you ever think of mother

In that home far in the land? Watching, praying for her children, If I could see that home again!

The men would often sing that line over and over: "If I could see that home again!"

A fragile dream, with blood soaking through your boots, but at least a dream that was still kept alive.

I am sorry for the rambling nature of this. The trip from the battlefield to this new camp is still fresh in my mind. Allow me to tell you something of this journey, which for me will soon reach its end.

I held onto the tailgate of a wagon filled with the wounded, letting it pull me along because my boots had begun to fill with bloody mud. Rain fell in slanted, steely pencilings. There was a constant murmur, the groans of the wounded as the long slow agonized column wound between weeping trees and wet brown fields. I could hear their teeth grinding and even the faint scrabbling of their fingernails against the planks of the springless wagon bed. It was the same road we had followed into battle, only now we were going in the opposite direction and there was no reappearing sun nor crackle of Union gunfire to cause the troops to hasten their steps.

Our faces were grey, the color of ashes. Some had powder burns red on their cheeks and foreheads and running back in singed patches in their hair. Mouths were rimmed with grime from biting cartridges, mostly a long smear down one corner, and hands were blackened with burnt powder off the ramrods. We'd aged three lifetimes when Grant ordered that second, suicidal charge. The captain was calling for us to rally, rally here, rally there, but there wasn't much rally left in any of us, not after that damned battle. There wasn't much left in me, anyhow. I was so empty and cold and tired it was all I could do to hang onto the back of that damned wagon and let pull me to where the flag marked the field hospital and the encampment beyond it. I was worried too about not having my rifle, but if having it meant that I had to look down at the bearded man in whose chest I'd buried it deep and pull it out of him, then it could damn well stay where I'd left it. Then I happened to look down and Lord if there wasn't one just like it lying in the mud near my feet. I picked it up, stooping and nursing my bad arm, and nearly lost my hold on the wagon. My arm was still seeping from the bullet I'd taken during the last charge.

Jaded horses and mules refused to pull; demoralized and badly-shaken drivers, with straining eyes and perspiring bodies plied their whips vigorously to no effect; difficult places in the road were choked with blazing wagons set aflame to save their contents from falling into the hands of the enemy.

Hundreds of men dropped from exhaustion. Even more threw away their arms. The demoralization at last began to spread even to the officers, who did nothing to stop the straggling. Many of them seemed to shut their eyes to the hourly reduction of their command, and rode in advance of their brigades in dogged indifference. It was among the saddest sights I have ever seen. But still there was, if one looked closely enough in certain eyes, something left of the old spirit which had made the Army of our beloved Confederacy famous throughout the world, and inscribed its banners with the most dignified and glorious names of the war.

Still I could hear the echo of tired, broken men singing: "If I could see that home again!"

Regiment by regiment the columns lurched forward as the rain grew heavier, rifles sloppily dressed at right shoulder shift and the men—as well as the too many boys—stumbling like drunkards or shuffling along like a simpleton weighed down with the shame of it all. Soon the wheels of the wagons and artillery had churned the road into shin-deep mud. There were halts and countless delays, times when the men had to trot to keep up, and other times, more frequently, when they simply stood in the rain, waiting for the man ahead of them to stumble into motion while the mud and filth grew wetter and thicker and pulled at their cold feet. The muskets grew heavy. Haversack straps began cutting into our shoulders, drawing blood. The road was littered with discarded equipment, empty boots, sabers and Bowie knives, overcoats, Bibles, playing cards. All that day as we moved along the column we came upon regiment after regiment halted by the road, the men leaning on their rifles or sitting on pieces of debris from the battle that had found their way to this spot.

As I looked at all the bitter remnants left behind, I could easily imagine Matthew in the morning, armed with his treasure chest, gathering these items and saying, "Here is a playing card from a magician's deck, here is a page from a Bible once read by a preacher with a voice of gold, here is a strap from the reins of Traveler, the finest horse in this war."

I can feel him in the morning, still. His gentleness, his wonder, his affection and playfulness. Never has a man had a more loving brother than I had in Matthew. And when I think of the way the other children used to tease and mock him I no longer feel anger; I feel pity–and not for Matthew, for them. In their haste to make him an object of ridicule, they denied themselves the honor of knowing the purest soul they would ever have met. The laughter he could have given to them, the mysteries of this world he could have unveiled to them. They are all the poorer. As we all are now.

And not only in the morning, but now I find that I can see Matthew in the stars at night.

I find, most especially on a night like this, that the thought gives me comfort and courage. I see and feel the Matthew we all knew, he of the slow wits and deliberate speech and tin can of treasures.

Remember him that way; I think he would have wanted you to.

I once asked him why he made up such stories to accompany every new "treasure" he found. I remember he said to me, "We don't know no different, now, do we? How do we know that this feather did not come from a angel's wing? Or this button from the shirt of a king? It's all down here, Luther, buried low in the ground. Mysteries for us to find and wonder about. Someday, maybe someone will find a button from my shirt buried low in the ground, and maybe they will hold it and clean it until it shines and say, This is a button worn by a brave soldier, and as long as I carry it with me, his spirit will protect me from harm."

I know, Father, how you always despaired that Matthew never learned to properly read or write, even when the two of us signed up he was unable to write his entire name and I had to do most of it for him. But I tell you this, dear Father, I tell you this as the son who was always a good student and quick to learn and of whom you were always so proud: I might have been well-educated as far as book-learning went, but I would gladly give all that knowledge back to have been able to see the world for just one day the way my dear brother Matthew saw it. His was a wisdom born not of books and learning, but of wonder and a joy for the details of life that few of us ever know–or if we do know it, it is only as children, and too soon crushed under the weight of adulthood.

And adulthood come fast to a boy on the battlefields of war.

War changes a boy into a man very quickly; and even more quickly does it change even the man.

I ask now, Mother and Father, that you lay aside this letter for a moment and ready yourselves for what I have next to tell you.

Matthew is dead. He died by my own hand. The bearded man I spoke of earlier, the one in whom I left my rifle buried in his chest–that was Matthew. I killed him during the final moments of the second charge at Cold Harbor. I did this with full intention in my heart of ending his life. And though I beg your forgiveness, I cannot say that I am sorry for having killed him.

The Matthew that we knew and loved, the Matthew of the morning treasures, was dead long before I attacked him in the smoke and blood and under the scream of cannonfire.

I began to notice the change in him a few months ago, after a brief but terrible encounter with a Union regiment that left many of our fellow Confederate boys dead. It was the first time Matthew had killed a man. He began to shake as he looked down upon the body of a boy no older than fifteen, then he began to weep; quietly at first, then with greater violence. I held him close and comforted him, not caring a damn about the looks some of our fellow soldiers gave us. I told him that it was all right, he had to do it, but my words did little to soothe the pain of his soul.

"It was so fast," he cried. "He was standing before me just a moment ago and now he's dead and I killed him and he'll never see his family again and his mother, she'll be sad for the rest of her life."

The Matthew you knew and loved began to die that moment.

Over the next days, weeks, and months, I saw Matthew's acceptance of death and violence grow from the frightened acceptance of a child to the cold-hearted disregard of a bitter, battle-weary soldier. The light in his eyes dimmed, then died altogether.

He became one of our regiment's fiercest fighters during battle.

He became something of a monster, and I was powerless to stop it. If I could have, I would have stood in the middle of the blood-soaked ground and beseeched God Almighty to stop this war for just a few hours so that I might be able to bring back the Matthew we knew. But God has recently stopped listening to the prayers of the Confederacy. Maybe He never listened at all.

There was one instance, seven nights ago, when a ghost of the old Matthew showed itself to me, and for a moment I thought perhaps he could be saved.

I found him with an injured rabbit cradled in his arms. He was stroking its head gently and singing a soft song in its ear. I remembered then, how he had found that robin when we were children, the one with the broken wing, and how he had nursed it back to health.

I reminded him of that and he smiled at me. For a moment, he was the brother I had always known and loved.

Then he grabbed the rabbit's ears and twisted its head and snapped its neck. "Everything ends up getting buried down low in the dirt," he said. "Death is terrible, and it is the end of all we try to do, so why not help it along?"

I cannot hope to describe to you the coldness in his voice and the emptiness in his eyes.

I knew then that I had failed him.

I knew then that the Matthew I loved was dead.

I knew then that I had to kill this heartless creature who stood before me.

Mother and Father, you would not have wanted him back, not the way he was, not this thing he had become. I know that you must have great disappointment–even hatred–in your hearts for me at the moment, but you know that I have never lied to you.

Our Matthew was already dead.

It was only a matter of choosing the right moment.

The second charge of Grant's men had begun their broke retreat. Smoke lay heavy on the field. Several of our men then climbed from the earthworks and continued firing on the retreating soldiers.

Matthew was among the first to leave the earthworks.

I found him a few dozen feet away, using the butt of his rifle to break open the skulls of Union boys who, though wounded and lying in their own blood, were still not dead.

Matthew was screaming, words I dare not repeat here. Worst of all was the laughter that lay underneath his cries. He continued to beat and kick and stab and kill any wounded man he could find.

All the while his screams mixed with his laughter and landed hard on my ears.

It was the sound of something nailed down and in torment. It was the sound of war's madness at its height of power.

I readied my weapon and charged at him, burying the blade of my rifle deep into his center, driving it with such force that I saw the blade finally come out his back.

He slid down the barrel of my rifle toward me, the gaping wound in his chest making a horrible wet sound, like a starving man slurping a bowl of soup.

I hefted my rifle and lifted his feet from the ground. For a moment the light of a nearby fire illuminated his face, and I saw his eyes.

In them was gratitude.

He had known all along, somehow, that what he had become was unfit to return to the world of families and shops and hard candy and music in the square and littler boys who gather their treasures in the morning.

"Forgive me," I whispered to him.

He smiled, and sang to me: "I remember you, my brother, Sent to me that fatal dart; Brothers fighting against brothers, Well, 'tis well that thus they part."

I let go of my rifle and embraced him as well as I could as he sank to the ground, pulled down by the bloody mud. I stroked his cheek and kissed his brow and told him that we would always love him.

If he understood me, he said nothing. I can only hope that heaven is merciful and allowed him to know; I can only hope that God is understanding and welcomed Matthew into Heaven with open arms, understanding that war had forever ruined the wonder that was my brother.

That is all.

It is a little before two in the morning as I write this. I cannot live with the sins my soul has acquired during this war. I cannot live knowing that I failed my brother, that I was busy killing other men while a monster crept in and took his place. My only comfort is knowing that Matthew was able to reclaim his old self at the very end.

Take me out to the battlefield, let me hear the shells flying by. Let me hear the sound of the cannons, and the cries of the brave men dying. Let me go to this place where I can feel the pain and the coldness and the loneliness that there must be for men such as myself, those who tried, those who failed, those who stood by and did nothing.

Let me take with me all my shame. Let it be buried low with me. Let my body never be found until its flesh is dust. Let the years scatter the pieces of my memory so that someday, perhaps, another child such as Matthew will come upon a trinket that once was mine, and he will wipe away the dirt until that trinket shines, and he will hold it up into the sunlight of a peaceful day and blink against its brightness, and say to himself, "This is part of a medal from an honorable man's chest. I will put here, with the feather from an angel's wing and the button from the silken shirt of a king."

Maybe they will feel me in the morning, or see me in the stars at night.

I know Matthew will be there.

Good-bye, Mother and Father. I have always loved and respected you both deeply. I shall miss you. I hope someday you will find it in your hearts to forgive you weaker son for what he has done.

May God bless and protect you through all the lonely places that you walk.

With Love, Your Son,
Luther

The doctor stared at the last page in silence for several moments, then placed it atop the others on his table. He shuffled through the pages until he found the very first one, which bore the name and address of Private Luther Wade's parents. This page he set apart from the rest.

"Dear Lord," whispered Private Tyler.

"Indeed," replied the doctor.

He then poured them another cup of coffee, adding to it a generous portion of the remaining whiskey.

Outside, the sun was breaking through the night's gloom. A bird sang sweetly in the distance.

Soldiers coughed and grumbled as they awakened and began preparations to move out.

"That song Private Wade spoke of," said the doctor. "Do you know it, Tyler?"

"Only that part about wishing to see home again."

The doctor nodded, fired up the last bit of tobacco in his pipe–somehow, it didn't taste as bitter now–and puffed away for a moment.

"I know that song well," he said finally to Tyler. The last verse, in particular, I have always found haunting. It goes, 'Brother, take from me a warning, Keep that secret you have won, For it would kill our aged old mother, If she knew what you have done."

He then sat very still, staring at Tyler.

After a few moments of silence, Tyler took a deep breath and met the doctor's gaze. "Oh, Lordy, sir, you don't mean–"

"It's *exactly* what I mean," said the doctor firmly, and he picked up the envelope and the remaining pages of Private Wade's letter and tore them all in half, then half again. He rose from his seat and walked outside his tent and tossed the pieces into the nearest fire, then stood and watched until they were burned to black.

When he re-entered his tent, he found Tyler standing over his table, reading the only remaining page from the letter.

"Why did you do that, sir?"

"Because this goddamned stinking war has already caused enough good, decent parents too much grief, that's why. How do you think his mother and father would be able to go on if they knew the truth? Isn't it bad enough that they'll have to live through seeing their beloved Confederacy fall–and we both know it *will*, Tyler–all the while knowing they've lost both their sons? Are you so weak that your conscience cannot abide keeping this a secret so as to spare two grieving parents a burden of pain that no human being could possibly endure? *I am not that weak, Tyler.* For weeks now all I've seen is the pain and agony and pointlessness of death and violence and I've had my *fill*, do you understand me, Private? I could not take away any of these fine soldier's pain and suffering, I couldn't take it away from their families, I was impotent in the face of war, useless and ineffectual." He snatched away the page with the Wades' address on it. "Well I can spare these two people a *little* of the pain, and that is *precisely* what I am going to do. But you have to help me, Tyler. Are you willing to do that?"

"It don't seem right, sir, I mean–"

"None of this is right, Tyler. It's up to us, as those who will survive this slaughter, to take the necessary steps to *make* it right. I cannot order you to help me, Tyler, I can only ask, and I do so now: as one battle-weary man to another, will you keep the contents of Luther Wade's letter a secret? Will you help me spare his parents that final measure of grief that might very will kill both of them?"

Tyler swallowed once. Very hard. Then nodded his head. "Yessir. And I am a man of my word."

The doctor placed a hand on Tyler's shoulder. "Thank God for that, Tyler. Thank God."

The doctor sat down at his table and found a fresh envelope and piece of stationary, then copied the Wades' address onto the new envelope.

"Sir?" asked Tyler.

"Yes?"

"Private Wade's body."

"Yes?"

"The way it is, I mean…how can you explain something like that?"

The doctor paused for a moment, thinking.

"It happened like this, Tyler: this morning Luther Wade asked me to look at a horse that was harnessed to one of the wagons—one of the damaged wagons. As I was examining the horse, Luther Wade was attempting to fix the undercarriage of the wagon. The horse spooked and bucked, pulling the wagons down from the rocks upon which it rested. Luther Wade's neck was caught under the weight of a wheel, nearly severing his head. That is how I will write it in my report and that is how you will tell it."

"Yessir." Then: "Doctor?"

"Yes, Tyler?"

"I'd like to say it's been an honor to spend this evening in the company of a man as fine as yourself."

The doctor smiled. "I'm just a glorified butcher these days, but I thank you for the sentiment, Private. Tell your commanding officer I wish to speak with him before you leave. I want to make sure he knows that you have been of great service to me."

"Thank you, sir.

"Thank *you*, Tyler. Now go. Look down low in the ground for buried treasure."

Tyler smiled, saluted, and left the tent.

The doctor stared at the blank page before him, then, after closing his eyes and humming a bit of a certain song to himself, set pen to page and wrote:

Dear Mr. and Mrs. Wade:

It is my sad duty to inform you of the deaths of your two sons, Luther and Matthew, at the recent battle of Cold Harbor. Both of your sons were good and decent men and fine soldiers, and both died bravely in defense of our beloved Confederacy...

He paused, then, and listened.

And, perhaps, somewhere deep in his soul where a weary man holds tight to the remaining dreams of childhood, he felt near him the presence of a young boy slow of wit, deliberate of speech, and pure of spirit.

"Here is a letter about heroes," he whispered. "Here is a pen once used by Shakespeare. Here is a page from a book stolen from a secret kingdom where magic never dies."

Publishing History

"Man With a Canvas Bag" originally appeared *Dark Delicacies II: Haunted*

"Cocteau Prayers" originally appeared in *Things Left Behind*

"Yellow Sleeves" appears here for the first time

"Mail-Order Annie" originally appeared in *Cat Crimes Through Time*

"… He Didn't Even Leave a Note …" originally appeared in *A Little Orange Book of Odd Stories*

"The Queen of Talley's Corner" originally appeared in *Five Strokes to Midnight*

"Danaid Night" originally appeared in *A Little Orange Book of Odd Stories*

"Aisle of Plenty" originally appeared in *Graveyard People: The Collected Cedar Hill Stories, Vol. 1*

"The Obscenity of Gloves" originally appeared in *A Little Orange Book of Odd Stories*

"Need" originally appeared in *Corpse Blossoms*

"Sometimes, First Thing in the Morning or Very Late at Night" originally appeared in *A Little Orange Book of Odd Stories*

"At the 'Pay Here, Please' Table" appears here for the first time

"In the Lowlands" originally appeared in *Murder Most Feline*

"Mermaid in Denim Lonely" originally appeared in *A Little Orange Book of Odd Stories*

"Triskaidekaphobia" appears here in this form for the first time; previous version first appeared in *A Sea of Alone*

"I Never Spent the Money" originally appeared in *Things Left Behind*

"When It Is Decided That the War is Over" appears here for the first time

"Esmeralda; No Fanfare, Please" originally appeared in *Things Left Behind*

"Duty" originally appeared in *Vivisections*

"She So Loved Her Garden" originally appeared in *Things Left Behind*

"Rose of Sharon" originally appeared in *Careless Whispers*

"The Ordered, the Necessary, the Unavoidable" originally appeared in *Things Left Behind*

"Long Red and the Needle Patrol" originally appeared in *A Little Orange Book of Odd Stories*

"Saviour" originally appeared in *Cemetery Dance Magazine*

"In the Direction of Summer's Coming" originally appeared in *Graveyard People: The Collected Cedar Hill Stories, Vol. 1*

"Matthew in the Morning" originally appeared in *Murder Most Confederate*

About the Author

GARY A. BRAUNBECK is a prolific author who writes mysteries, thrillers, science fiction, fantasy, horror, and mainstream literature. He is the author of 19 books; his fiction has been translated into Japanese, French, Italian, Russian and German. Nearly 200 of his short stories have appeared in various publications. Some of his most popular stories are mysteries that have appeared in the Cat Crimes anthology series.

He was born in Newark, Ohio; this city that serves as the model for the fictitious Cedar Hill in many of his stories. The Cedar Hill stories are collected in *Graveyard People* and *Home Before Dark*.

His fiction has received several awards, including the Bram Stoker Award for Superior Achievement in Short Fiction in 2003 for "Duty" and in 2005 for "We Now Pause for Station Identification"; his collection *Destinations Unknown* won a Stoker in 2006. His novella "Kiss of the Mudman" received the International Horror Guild Award for Long Fiction in 2005.

As an editor, Gary completed the latest installment of the Masques anthology series created by Jerry Williamson, *Masques V*, after Jerry became too ill to continue.

He also served a term as president of the Horror Writers Association. He is married to Lucy Snyder, a science fiction/fantasy writer, and they reside together in Columbus, Ohio.

Gary is an adjunct professor at Seton Hill University, Pennsylvania, where he teaches in an innovative Master's degree program in Writing Popular Fiction.

His nonfiction writing book *Fear in a Handful of Dust: Horror as a Way of Life* has been used as a text by several college writing classes. Gary has taught writing seminars and workshops around the country on topics such as short story writing, characterization, and dialogue.